AS IT IS
IN
HEAVEN

*Also by Niall Williams
in Large Print:*

Four Letters of Love

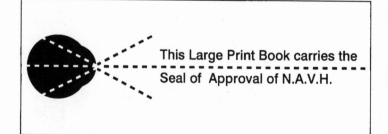

This Large Print Book carries the
Seal of Approval of N.A.V.H.

AS IT IS
IN
HEAVEN

NIALL WILLIAMS

Thorndike Press • Thorndike, Maine

Published in 2000 by arrangement with Warner Books, Inc.

Thorndike Large Print ® Basic Series.

The tree indicium is a trademark of Thorndike Press.

The text of this Large Print edition is unabridged. Other aspects of the book may vary from the original edition.

Set in 16 pt. Plantin by Juanita Macdonald.

Printed in the United States on permanent paper.

Library of Congress Cataloging-in-Publication Data

Williams, Niall, 1958-
    As it is in heaven / Niall Williams.
      p. cm.
    ISBN 0-7862-2282-4 (lg. print : hc : alk. paper)
    1. Teachers — Ireland — Fiction. 2. Women musicians
— Ireland — Fiction. 3. Man-woman relationships —
Ireland — Fiction. 4. Ireland — Fiction. 5. Venice (Italy)
— Fiction. 6. Large type books. I. Title.
PR6073.I43273 A9 2000
823′.914—dc21   99-053710

28.95

12-17-99

Gale Group

For Chris, who made the garden,
and for Deirdre and Joseph,
who play the music in it

"... on earth as it is in Heaven."
> — Our Father

"... ma gia volgeva il mio disio e'l velle
si come rota ch'igualmente e mossa,

l'amor che move: i sole e l'altre stelle."

"... as a wheel turns smoothly, free from jars,
my will and my desire were turned by love,

The love that moves the sun and the other
   stars."
> — Dante, *Paradiso*

I

1

There are only three great puzzles in the world, the puzzle of love, the puzzle of death, and, between each of these and part of both of them, the puzzle of God.

God is the greatest puzzle of all.

When a car drives off the road and crashes into your life, you feel the puzzle of God. You feel the sharpness of its edges fall on top of you and know the immensity of the puzzle from the force of the life being crushed out of you. You want to lift the pieces and throw them away into the darkness. You feel the chill of loss, the drafty air, as if the walls of your soul have been knocked down in the night and you wake to realize that you are living in a vast exposed emptiness.

When the man driving the car turns out to be a drunken priest who receives only minor injuries, you wonder if God was ever there at all, or if the puzzle itself was your own invention to excuse the existence of the

9

random and the brutal where they criss-crossed our days.

Philip Griffin wondered. He wondered what crime his ten-year-old daughter could have committed, what grievous error she had made that had drawn the priest's car upon her that afternoon. What fault could his wife, Anne, have been guilty of as she drove into Ranelagh to collect rosin for her daughter's half-sized cello? In the weeks and months following the accident Philip Griffin asked the questions and could arrive at only one answer: there was none. The fault was his own, the judgement had fallen not on them but upon him. For it was the survivor who suffered. In the weeks following the funeral of his wife and daughter he had scoured the burnt bottom of his soul for the myriad failings of his love — the days he had said nothing, had returned from work with some bitterness and left the children doing their homework, telling them to leave him alone when they came with copies, raising his newspaper like a draw-bridge and retreating inside the loveless world of facts and news, until a knock came on the room door and he walked out to tea; the evenings he did not tell them he loved them but told them only to go to bed and be quiet or he'd be cross. He searched out each

10

of his failings and then concluded that they were so numerous it was perfectly clear why God had smote his life with suffering. Understanding that was the only way he was able to continue living, for in his eyes his living with the hurt was a kind of cleansing. Mary and Anne were in heaven awaiting him, and he would be there to join them one day, when he had done whatever he could for his remaining child, Stephen; when life had at last purged his sins and cancer would arrive.

There was peace in that. The puzzle of God was not so bad after all, and Philip could endure suffering, knowing that at least when it was over it would mean he was forgiven.

In twenty years that day had not come. His son, Stephen, had become a schoolteacher and moved away from Dublin to the west. The fracture that had fallen between them the day of the crash, when they had each retreated into great guilty rooms of silence, had grown steadily wider, and the father had felt each year the weakening of his ability to reach his son. Stephen was a lone figure; he was tall and silent and intense, and had vanished from his father into the world of history books before he had finished his teens. Now he arrived one weekend a month to sit opposite his father in the sitting room and correct copies and read the newspaper while Puccini played on the small stereo and the light died in the street outside.

"Hello."

It was a late-autumn afternoon. The chestnut leaves had fallen in the garden and blackened the grass, which Philip Griffin did not rake. A small man, he sat in the front window with the Venetian blinds open and watched the road for the coming of his son's car. When it entered the driveway, he had looked away and gazed at the air as if watching the music. He heard Stephen turn his key in the door, but he did not get up. He sat with his hands on his knees and waited with the terrible immobility of those who have lost the means of talking to their children.

"Hello," Stephen said again.

The music was playing. His father raised his right hand three inches off his knee as a greeting, but said nothing more. He was listening to the singing like a man looking at a faraway place. There were words in the air, but Philip Griffin did not need to say them, he did not need to say: "When your mother was alive, she liked this one," for Stephen already knew it. He knew the terrible sweetness of the melancholy in that music and how it soothed his father to be there within it. He said nothing and sat down.

On the small tape recorder beside his chair Philip Griffin turned up the volume and let the music fill the space between them. They had not seen each other for three weeks, but sat in their armchairs, surrounded by Puccini, as if the spell of the music would bear no interruption and the memory of the slim and tall figure of Anne Griffin was walking in the room. The sorrowfulness of the aria was cool and delicious; it was beyond their capability of telling, and while it played, father and son lingered in its brief and beautiful grief, each thinking of different women.

The heavy golden curtains of the room were tied back from the window; they had not been closed in many years, and their gathered folds held within them the ageing dust of the man who sat there every day. Philip Griffin had his face turned to the open Venetian blind, and bands of orange light fell across it as the streetlights came on. He was sixty-eight years old. He had never been handsome, but had once been lively. Now his hair grew like curling grey wires over his ears and in his ears, while the crown of his head was so bare it looked vulnerable

13

and expectant of blows. As he sat he held his hands in his lap and sometimes looked down at them and turned them over, as if searching for traces of the cancer he imagined must be growing inside him. He was a tired man who had grown to dislike company. The place in his spirit where he was broken had grown so familiar to him, and he had so long ago abandoned the notion of any fingering or magic that could repair it, that his living had assumed a frayed quality, waiting for the last thread to give.

The music played, he held his hands. When three arias had ended, he reached down and clicked off the machine. "Well," he said, and looked through the darkness of the room to see with astonishment the changed face of his son.

2

You can know a lot about a man when you are measuring him for trousers. You can know his own sense of expectation about the world and whether he feels himself fitting into it or not. Sometimes he has grown beyond himself, and the extra inches that may be the loss of youth are hidden by the quick thumb on the tape measure. Sometimes the inches are the inches of pleasure and the man allows them like the proof of his own expansion, the feasting and fortune he has known. He can be told he is larger now, for he feels the responsibilities of his age and is not yet aware of his own diminishment. The tape measure tells a thousand stories. As a tailor in Clery's, Philip Griffin had made a legion of men fit better into the world and, looking at his son in the armchair, knew the slackness of his trouser belt, the looseness of his collar were the tell-tale signs of love or death. God could not kill the whole family before him, he figured, and so he knew it was the former.

"Put on the light," he said.

Stephen stood up. When he clicked the switch, his father was startled even more by the look of him. Stephen had emerged from adolescence with an angular air of oddity; his body was thin and long and crooked, and his head was enormous. He was almost twice the length of his father. But as he stood there in the room the thinness of him seemed stretched by the pressure of his feelings. His clothes did not fit him; you could put three fingers inside the belt of his trousers, his father thought, your whole hand inside his shirt. The tailor had seen this shrinking often before, he had measured men who trembled silently in the dressing room, feeling the wasting of themselves beneath the power of a passion, but it belonged to springtime. It was a Maytime rapture, an annual fact of men in their clothes like the brief season of happiness in summer when satisfied love made every man larger in his chest by an inch. No, this was different; Stephen was alarmingly thin, and even before he had turned his face fully towards his father, Philip Griffin had begun to formulate who the woman might be.

"I'll make tea," Stephen said.

"If you want."

"Do you?"

"If you're making it." Stephen turned to leave the room. "I don't need the light," said his father, and sat back into the darkness when the switch clicked. Alone, he quickly glanced outside at the old car Stephen had driven up from the west and saw that one side of it had been recently dented.

"My God," he said aloud to his wife, and then reminded himself not to talk to her while Stephen was in the house. He sat and listened. He heard the loping of his long son moving about the kitchen down the hallway. It was an empty place, made all the more so by how full it had once been with the presence of a woman and two children; on its clean counters and polished tabletop were the memories of the ten thousand meals of childhood, the smallest of tarts and jam, the hiss of the iron and sizzle of fry. They were not entirely vanished into the walls, and Philip Griffin knew that as Stephen made the tea and stood by the counter the sense of loss would still be potent. He should have sold the house after Anne and Mary died. He should have moved out and left the place; for no matter how glowing were all the moments of the past, the first years of marriage, the happiness of Stephen's birth, then two years later, his sister Mary, the tumble and laughter, the evenings at the

Dublin Grand Opera Society, the Christmases, none of it mattered or survived that afternoon he had been called from the tailoring in Clery's to come to the hospital and identify his wife and daughter after the car crash.

He should have sold the house then, but didn't. He couldn't, the grief was too great. He breathed the death in the living room air, the sorrow that lingered in the stairs, until it got inside him. He never knew that a small man could carry so much grief and was amazed that the years did not diminish it but amplified it, until the day three years ago when he had woken up and realized with a huge sigh of peace that at last he was dying.

Now, as he sat in the darkness listening to Stephen in the kitchen, he knew memories grew sharper with time. For the measure of his pain in losing Anne Nolan was the measure of his love; perhaps if he had loved her less he might have endured the world better afterwards; perhaps it was never intended that we give ourselves so much to one person that the vanishing of their face makes us feel the world is only a shadow. So, as he sat there in his armchair looking towards the street, he prayed that his son would feel the emptiness of the kitchen like a pain, and somehow realize he must not love too deeply.

"Here's the tea. Do you want the light?"

"Not unless you do."

"All right."

Stephen left the light off and came in carefully with the tray.

They sat with their tea. In the time since he had realized he was dying, Philip had not mentioned it to his son. He hoped the illness would sweep through him swiftly. He imagined waking one morning moments before his death and then surrendering in a long gasp; his good suit was ready in the closet with one of the silk ties from Harry O'Connell up in Brown Thomas. He would be no burden on Stephen and didn't want his son worrying about him. The boy had had enough. No, any day now it would arrive; for a man who had already put up with as much as he had, there would be no painful deterioration. He was certain of it. One day he would be alive, sitting in his chair, the next he would be dead.

He sipped his tea and looked at his son. He even looks like a history teacher, Philip decided. There's something dishevelled about history, goes well in a tweed jacket, or even a corduroy. But not those jumpers he wears, not on a man over thirty. No, a man should wear a jacket.

"How is school going?" he asked. It was what he always asked, and always received the same answer.

"It's fine."

And there was comfort in that, too, like throwing a ball back and forth to each other, the familiarity and simplicity of its rhythm making everything seem in its place in the world.

There is no way he can tell me, thought Philip. No way he can begin to say, I have fallen in love. And that this is already different from anything else, that already he knows that there is a greater magnitude of feeling in his heart than he had possibly imagined before. There is no way he can tell me, even as I cannot tell him I am dying.

"That's nice tea," said Philip, and looked down at his hands. He waited some time and said, "Will we get to evening Mass?"

They left the house and pulled the door shut and went into Dublin. Philip drove the car and Stephen sat beside him. The night had fallen. There were no stars or moon. While they drove, Stephen said nothing. His knees were crooked up in front of him. His breath steamed the window excessively; the warmth of his thoughts about the woman he had met rose against the glass until at last his father asked him to open the window. When he did, Gabriella Castoldi flew out on the night air 160 miles from where she was in the city of Galway. Stephen rolled up the window, but it was quickly fogged with her again, the car air smelling increasingly of white lilies and clouding the view ahead so utterly that neither of the two men could bring themselves to mention it but instead drove on, peering outward through the fogged windscreen of hopeless love.

The journey was fifteen minutes. Philip parked the car in NO PARKING before the gate of an office building. He saw the sign but paid it no attention, getting out of the car with his hat on his head and telling Stephen not to bother to lock it: when the plot of your life is written, there is no need to worry about trivialities. The two men stepped onto the path; they smelled the lilies escaping with them and noticed an elderly woman waiting for the 46 bus raise her nose and catch the scent as it passed down the street. But they said nothing about it. Silence was the family code.

Philip touched the brim of his hat slightly. He stepped into the street without looking.

But nothing was coming; it never was. That was the monotony of being spared:

God was always there before him. The Dublin evening pressed like a damp cloth across the backs of their necks, and the two men hurried across to the door of the Church of the Blessed Sacrament. When they opened it, Mass began. Philip Griffin took off his hat. He knelt into the pew farthest from the altar, closed his eyes, and told his wife there might be a delay, but he hoped he would be there before too long.

3

That evening they played chess in the dark. Not that it was entirely dark, but the only light came from the low table lamp in the hallway and cast elongated shadows across the board, making the pieces larger and giving the impression to anyone passing outside that the men were playing with giants. Over the years of Stephen's visits it had become routine to play after Mass. The language of chess was much like the secret language of men's clothes, only it took longer to discover. Now Philip knew that there existed in the movement of the pieces a communication infinitely more true than anything he and Stephen might have said to each other.

So, as one game followed the next, the movement of the chess pieces was the ancient vocabulary through which Stephen began to tell his father that he was daring to believe in love. All his moves signalled it; his knights flew into the midst of the board, his bishops ventured crisscross along diagonals that bespoke the innocence of a beginner or the blind invulnerability of dreams. Stephen moved his queen constantly, taking the piece in his fingers and holding it a moment suspended above the game before once again releasing it to the danger of the board.

Stephen lost the first game, and then the second; by the time they had begun the third, his father had already understood the turbulence of his son's heart and wondered at how he was managing to play at all. They had played together for years. Once Philip had been the Master; he had first learned the game as a boy with the Christian Brothers in Westland Row. Later, he played against the newspaper, opening a pocket set in the tailoring room and playing against the puzzle between stitches, looking at the solution only before he pulled on his jacket and walked across the emptied ground-floor lobby to go home. He had taught his son when Stephen was fifteen, and beaten him consistently until a June evening five years later, when the matchless audacity of Stephen's moves told his father that he had finished rearing him. From then on, the fluctuations of his form reflected his spirit so keenly that within five moves of beginning a game, Philip Griffin could already tell the depth of Stephen's grief, anger, or frustration.

So it was. They did not speak, they played chess in the dark. They played without a clock, making the moves the way other men beat a ball with a racket or a club, releasing the demons that lay in the low places of their spirits, and seeing arise in the ever more complex patterns of the board the perfect reflection of their lives.

"We'll play again?"

Stephen had lost for the fourth time and was already resetting the pieces when he asked his father. It was past midnight. Three times the tape of Puccini's *La Bohème* had replayed itself, and Philip Griffin had lowered his head until his chin was propped just above the board on the knuckles of his joined hands. He cannot play himself out of it, he thought. No number of games will free him from thinking of her. He looked down at the white king's knight, which had already begun the new game by jumping forward. What could he tell Stephen? How could he instruct him in caution, in restricting the wild movements of his pieces that so clearly told the story of his heart? He could not. He looked at the backs of his hands and felt the papery skin at the top of his cheeks. He felt an enormous tiredness opening itself like a great cloak within him. He wanted to go to bed, but he played again, and again after that. Time ran away; no cars moved down the empty suburban road outside. Dublin was asleep beneath its streetlights, the autumn night foggy with dreams, while son and father played on. They did not look up from the board, nor did Philip remark when the scent of the lilies arose and filled the room. He breathed their perfume and kept his gaze fixed on the queen, recalling how Anne, too, had smelled of those flowers, and realizing there and then that life repeats itself over and over, and that, though the game might change, its patterns were the same, his son's loving was his own, and it would be morning before Stephen exhausted himself telling of it and fell across the chessboard asleep.

4

While Stephen slept, his father watched him. The king's knight's pawn was in his son's hand, but his body had slumped backward into the armchair. Whatever move he had intended to make was frozen in his hand and the game lay suspended, its communication broken, like a missing page in an old love letter.

Philip Griffin watched him. He had watched him for thirty years, watched him more carefully than any father watched his son. He loved Stephen as a wall loves a garden. He knew his son's life was lacking in excitement or joy, but believed that it needed to be fiercely protected from the treachery of dreams.

He watched over his son. The visions that rode Stephen in sleep gave his face the look of fearful anticipation; his eyebrows were knotted, the lids of his eyes shut tight. His father did not think to move him. He had waited almost half an hour for Stephen to make a move, not looking at him in the half-light, keeping his eyes fixed on the board and continuing to read the fable of his son's loving. In that half an hour he had realized that the love was not returned at all yet, and that the desperation of the position that Stephen kept creating in each game was the plain metaphor of his heart. When at last he dared to look up, Philip thought at first that time had stopped. He thought it was he who had died and that it was his spirit looking down at the stilled picture of the world as he was leaving it. Nothing was moving, there was no sound in the room nor in the street outside, and he had to lower his hands slowly to touch the armrests of the chair to be sure that he was not floating away.

It would have been a peaceful death; but almost at once a new pain arrived swiftly. It lanced him like a kitchen knife: he was not going to die just yet, he was not going to be allowed to sit out his days and wait for the moment when he would topple sideways from his chair onto the carpet and meet his wife and daughter again. No, he was to live to see this: to see the unrequited love of his son burn the boy's soul until there was nothing left of him, too. Philip was sure of it. That the relationship might unfold happily, that it might be reciprocated and the feelings amplified, was a foolish impossibility to him. Even to think that was a way of thinking he had long ago abandoned, and he remembered it now only as the skin remembers its scars.

In the sudden spring that arrived three years after his wife and daughter had died, Philip had opened the door one morning to feel the warmth of the air come like a caress across his face and to hear the birdsong, rapturous in the awakening limbs of the old chestnut tree. Spring was throbbing in the air, he saw it but somehow could not accept the pleasure of it. It was as if the grief had already enwrapped his life and he had settled into it like a comfort. It was easier to live like that. But that morning, as he travelled to work, he kept noticing the small tilting trees that grew in grass verges next to the path; they had leafed overnight, it seemed. He looked at them as if seeing them for the first time and wondered if it was three years since the last spring. That afternoon he had slipped away from the shop and left a pair of trousers in the hands of young Dempsey while he went to the doctor. Walking across Dublin in the remarkable blue of that afternoon, catching something of the quickened heartbeat, the gaiety that moved tangibly through the crowds on Grafton Street, he had no idea exactly what he was going for. He sat in the high-ceilinged waiting room of Dr. Tim Magrath's surgery on Fitzwilliam Street; the window was raised on its pull cords and the city stayed with him. When at last he was called in, he took the big doctor's handshake and held on to it. Philip had tailored Tim Magrath's clothes for eighteen years, and although he had spoken to the doctor often and about every possible subject while measuring him in Clery's, he had never consulted him and they had never met anywhere else. That afternoon, when Tim Magrath saw him there, he had imagined at first that Philip Griffin had come to make a delivery, that he had forgotten some trousers or a jacket and the tailor had been good enough to bring them over. It was only when he felt the hand of the other man holding on to him and noticed that he had brought nothing with him that he realized there was something else. Philip sat down on the leather couch. He left his hat on and looked directly at the doctor's grey eyes.

"I can't feel any joy," he said.

Tim Magrath said nothing. He felt the eyes of the patient staring at him for an answer, but was so surprised that he had to get up and look at the street outside. He watched the cars passing for a moment.

30

"My wife died. My daughter died with her."

The doctor felt a shiver of guilt run down his spine; he had heard of the crash, of course, but had missed the funeral, and then let the facts of it slip away beyond acknowledgement.

"It was three years ago," Philip said, "and it's just, I can't feel any joy. In anything. Maybe I'm not supposed to. But I just thought I'd mention it to somebody. I wonder, will I? . . . I just can't seem to." He was not distressed, he spoke about it as if telling a mildly unusual facet of his diet.

Tim McGrath did not know what to say; he looked out the window. (He did not yet know the prescription for loss, and would not even understand the ailment until four years later, when he would return from golf at the Grange on a Saturday afternoon and find his wife, Maire, dead on the bed upstairs. Then the loss would descend upon him and he would walk out across the manicured summer lawns of his front garden and feel nothing. Then he would recall the tailor and realize with a blow that made him sit down on the grass that in fact he knew nothing about healing.)

But he did not know yet that the incredible world could vanish from the living as

31

easily as from the dead. He looked out the window and watched the traffic in a practised way that he knew looked as if he were thinking. Finally Dr. Magrath turned around to face his patient. "Are you sleeping at night?" he asked.

And that was it. When Philip walked back across the city to the shop, he had a bottle of sleeping tablets in his jacket pocket. He had never taken them, and gradually allowed the promise of spring to die away into the wet summer of that year, taking with it the faint prompting at the corners of his mind that perhaps there was a way back to joy. By the autumn, the relentless and immutable progress of sorrow had continued like an intimacy in Philip Griffin's heart. He anticipated affliction and imagined that by doing so his life was more bearable.

No, happiness did not run in the Griffin family, it fled away; for them there was no relief to balance tragedy. In quiet moments after Stephen had moved to the west, Philip had begun to hope that his son's life would simply escape into ordinariness, that nothing remarkable would happen. But now, sitting opposite him at the chessboard in the dark, he realized that was not the case. And worse, that he was to live to see it.

He looked at the chessboard and memorized the position. He would lay it out again after Stephen had driven away and study it for clues. He knew the woman Stephen was in love with was unsuitable, but was not sure yet why. Perhaps she was married or did not care for him at all.

It was a little time before Philip stood up and moved past the sleeping figure. He moved out into the hallway and in the hot press found a blanket. When he came back and laid it over his son, the young man seemed to him to have grown younger. He was smaller, too. And for the four hours that remained until morning Philip decided to sit there in the armchair opposite him.

They had had so much time together since the day, that day; years of living in the same house that had taught them the fine skills of walking in empty rooms and being aware of the ghosts. They had lived around each other as much as with each other. But the invisible bond that held them together was the searing memory of those first moments after the accident when they had seen each other for the first time and stood in mute but tearless rage as they felt the burning pain of love and the perishing of hope. The funeral had been automatic; it was as if two other people and not Philip and Stephen were there. But afterwards, in the unnaturally stilled days when father and son came from their rooms in the house only when they knew they would not encounter each other, when they stole down the stairs laden with the guilt of having survived, the bond between them had grown. It grew without their speaking of it. It grew while they lay in their beds in the dark, sleepless and angry, asking God over and over why it was they who had lived. Why not kill me? And as week after week passed and they still lived on, the man and his son washing the dishes at the counter, hanging out the clothes on the line where the ghost of the mother was already standing, Philip and Stephen carried the burden of their survival in exactly the same manner. They did not speak of it but took the puzzle of their days everywhere with them, growing an identical jagged wrinkle across the middle of their foreheads and talking fitfully in the brief periods of their night sleep.

Now, fifteen years later, Philip Griffin saw that his son had not entirely escaped the habits of those years. For at once, instants after the blanket had been put across him in the armchair, Stephen began talking in his sleep. His words were unintelligible at first, and even though his father got from his chair and knelt down beside him like a priest, he could make nothing of them. He touched the sweat on his son's forehead, where it glistened in the low light. He was startled at how cold it was. It was as chill as seawater. He was thinking to get another blanket, or wake Stephen and move him to the bed, when he finally realized that the words his son was speaking were Italian.

5

Stephen Griffin had first seen Gabriella Castoldi playing violin in a concert in the thick-curtained upstairs room of the Old Ground Hotel in Ennis in County Clare. He had not intended to be there and marvelled often afterwards how one moment leads to the next, until the pattern of our lives seems inevitable. He worked as a history teacher in a grey school by the sea at Spanish Point twenty miles away and lived in a house with no curtains, where the Atlantic sprayed his windows and whispered like a mystery in every room. He had lived there for three years since taking the job. The day he came for the interview he drove west until he met the coastline and knew at once not that he wanted the position but that he wanted to be there in the west, for that sense of arrival in reaching the edge of the country. He had searched for the house for the same reason, finding a place that was small and damp but, unlike so many of the other old cottages, turned outward to the sea. Its front-room window looked out over a small slope of burnt grass that fell away in a sharp cliff into the alarming pounding of the tide. When he sat in the front room and looked westward into the slow movement of the swollen waters, he did not know it but he was the mirror of his father sitting in Dublin.

"History is disappearing," the principal, Mrs. Waters, told him at the interview. "Nobody wants to do history anymore. It's a terrible shame." The students preferred computers, she said with a tone of derision. "History is long and difficult, Mr. Griffin; there's a lot of reading in it," said Mrs. Waters. "That's the reason. They don't like reading. They're too lazy. Your classes will be small. But maybe you'll be able to change all that." It was a little threat. Mrs. Waters was a big woman with a small mouth; she seemed to know that the smallness of her mouth betrayed some lack of feeling and had overpainted her lips, which she pursed constantly to reassure herself. She sat across the table from Stephen and wondered would he do. It wasn't everybody who could stick it out, the west was bleak in the winter, and between the broken Atlantic skies and the rough sea, few souls not born to it endured. So Mrs. Waters imagined, sitting in the neatness of her principal's office and priding herself on the rigid indestructibility of her own person.

"You think you might like it here?" she asked Stephen.

"I can't tell you," he said.

"I'm sorry?"

"The future has no history. We can't know anything of tomorrow, can we?"

Mrs. Waters stared at him; it was an outlandish remark, and she had to pause a moment to decide if she was being insulted.

"I think I will, that's why I'm here. But I don't know." Stephen looked directly at her. "I'd like the chance to work here, I know that."

It was not exactly what Mrs. Waters wanted to hear. But she nodded and pursed her lips.

"You'd teach all classes?"

"Yes."

"We believe in discipline here. We have school rules."

Stephen said nothing, he simply looked back at her, and Eileen Waters could not tell if he was agreeing or not. She was a good judge of men; she often said so. She had judged her husband, Eamon, at forty-three and married at last, congratulating herself on not surrendering to any number of brutish fellows and finding in the assistant librarian in Ennis the quietest man in Clare. He had not disappointed her. She was a good judge. But with Stephen Griffin she was lost. It was a feeling to which she was not accustomed, and to escape the discomfort, she decided on him. He was the best of the three applicants by far, she told herself. That he was the only man and the other two women candidates had both seemed powerful, competent figures who might have challenged her was beside the point. No, this fellow is the best. It was only when Eileen Waters stood up to congratulate Stephen on getting the job that the thought occurred to her that he might be a dreadful teacher. It was only a passing impression, and she drove it, like everything else, resolutely out of her mind by shaking Stephen's hand forcefully and telling him three times how wonderful it was all going to be.

In the years before he arrived at the concert in Ennis that Friday evening, time had stopped for Stephen Griffin. He had found the house and moved into it, taken the job at the school, and fit his life into the routine of both of them, paring down his days until they had arrived at a still and unbroken sameness.
Then time stopped altogether.

He was the teacher who lived in the house. He was a quiet and shy man. He didn't go to the pubs at night, nor join the little golf club on the dunes at Spanish Point. The Clancys, who lived in the small cottage down the road, hardly saw him; the word in Marrinan's shop was that he was writing a book and wanted to be left alone. And so he was. He taught his classes, he lived in the house by the sea and visited his father in Dublin once every month. He felt himself grow old.

Then one day he was asked to buy a ticket for Michael Mooney's concert.

6

He was called Moses Mooney. He had a great fluff of white beard and walked down the streets of Miltown Malbay with his head held backward to let it flow. He had two coats and wore them both in winter, one on top of the other, so the fullness of his figure as he came towards you seemed a statement of intent. His eyes were blue gimlets. He had sailed the seas of the world for many years, and three times died and lived again according to his own tales. Each encounter with God had left him with the remarkable blueness of his eyes made brighter and the rosiness of his cheeks proof of the health-enhancing properties of resurrection. He was an extraordinary man. Moses Mooney had grown up in a house of music, the notes were in his ears when he was born, for his father, Thomas, was rumoured to have fiddle calluses on his fingers when he arrived in the world and his mother was the singer Angela Duff, who had made men weep in the kitchen when she sang "Spancil Hill."

He had grown up with the music and then left for England and the sea. It was on the third of his meetings with God, when he was fifty-two years old, that Moses Mooney realized what he was to do with his life and returned from the shores of Brazil to Miltown Malbay with the project of building an opera house by the sea.

At first, of course, it was not an opera house. He told the people who would listen to him in bemused amazement in Clancy's bar that it was a concert hall. That the sides would be removeable to see the sea, and that in summertime they would lift off to let the roaring of the ocean meet the playing of the music in the fabulous symphony of Man and God. He was perfectly clear about it. Everything about him seemed convincing, and for as long as his vision remained the wildest and least probable of all dreams, the people indulged his fantasy and bought him drinks. Moses Mooney was a figure around the town, that was all. He did not tell anyone yet that the building was to be an opera house, nor that the music he had heard in God's company was not like any other and that only later when he had arrived back on the shores of Brazil and heard on an old radio the singing of Maria Callas did he recognize that that was the music of God.

How he intended to build the opera house was not at first clear to him either. All he knew was that he had to come home to Clare, that his travelling days were over, and that this project was what he had to pursue until the day that he died. When he arrived back at his home cottage, the roof had fallen in. There were two cats living in the parlour in a clump of old thatch, and when Moses stood in the doorway, they came to him with such gentleness and affection that he told his neighbour he would name them after his parents. It took him three months to get the house partially repaired. He had money saved from his sailoring, and before he had declared his full intentions, he used what he had left to buy an acre of ground next to the golf course at Spanish Point.

And there it remained. The west Clare opera house. Grass grew within the barbed-wire boundaries of the field, while all about it were the fairways and greens of the golfers. Every day Moses would walk across the field and imagine the dimensions of the building shaping around him; from the whispering of the sea winds he dreamed the singing of the future, the magnificent music that was as yet unheard by everyone but himself.

Other than this vision, Moses Mooney

showed few signs of oddity in his behaviour. He was a churchgoing man and kept himself comfortably once he had repaired the cottage. He was the owner of a thousand tales and could tell them with such conviction that two priests, three bankers, and one insurance man were among his regular company in the late-evening sessions in Clancy's. He had gone out into the world and brought more than his share of it back with him, and when he told of unknown tribes in Chile, the bizarre habits of the male cockatoo, or the weird majesty of a communal dream shared by each of eighty sailors one night after a storm off the Cape of Good Hope, no one walked away. He finished a story and sat back, palming his great beard gently, and then sipping his stout as if chastened by the things he had lived to see.

It was two years after he had bought the field that the idea of the concerts came to him. When he first dreamed the opera house into the space where the tufts of grass blew in the wind, he did not think of how the money would be raised. It was only afterwards, when the emptiness of the field began to spread in his mind like an ache, that he wondered if there was not a serious flaw in God's vision, or if perhaps he had resurfaced too soon in the southern Atlantic before getting the entire message. With the childlike innocence of the visionary, he had supposed that once he announced his intentions the money would be forthcoming. When it wasn't and nobody stopped him on the street with the offer of finances, he decided that information was the problem, and stayed awake all the following night making three bright posters with red and yellow crayons, announcing the number of the bank account he had opened and telling the good people that he was going to donate his field and all his personal savings to the cause of building a place for music of the sea. He hung the posters the following day before dawn. The town was asleep and only a brisk salty wind passed along the street. Thomas and Angela, the two cats, had followed him from the house and stood together beneath the lamppost while he pressed home the thumbtacks. When he had done all three, he walked down the empty town with a pure and clear pride glistening inside himself; he was as clean-souled as after Communion, and turned to look back at the announcements with such a blaze of joy that they might have told of the coming of Christ Himself. Moses Mooney walked home and went to bed. He slept with the two cats at his feet and dreamed the town was waking up and seeing the notices, an infection of delight enveloping the people at the whimsical originality, the daring and wonder of the plan, and the queues spreading from Bank Place down to Clancy's.

When he awoke he was like a new man, and had the flushed rapture of those who know they are about to see their dreams realized. He imagined the money adding up, he totted the imaginary figures and was able to elaborate the plans for the opera house, extending the balcony and adding a small restaurant, where chamber music could be played in the summertime. He laughed at the miracle of it all, the simplicity of how things happen in the world, of how his seagoing days and nights, the endless blue journey towards the limit of all horizons, had arrived at this, the meaning of his life. He did not go out that day. Nor the next. He let the dreams bank up like snow. It was three days later when he at last allowed himself to go out, to walk down to the town and find out what had happened. He arrived at the bank just before closing and asked to check the balance in the account.

It was exactly the same amount he had started with.

He had to lean on the counter to keep

from falling. The teller did not look at him, but kept her eyes fixed on the blue light of the terminal screen. Moses heard the water gurgling in his ears like laughter and kept staring at the figures on the docket until he could no longer hear or see anything. The vanity of hope and the mockery of all enterprise flooded through the sluice gates of his brain, bringing with them the hopeless realization that he was utterly alone and carrying away in a single instant any possibility of help. He gripped the counter he could no longer see, he felt his throat tighten and gag him, and then he fell to the floor with a soft thump.

It was seven days and fourteen tests later before Dr. Maguane could confirm for certain that Moses Mooney was blind. The procedures had been complicated by the patient's inability to tell whether he could see or not; he sat before charts without a word and kept his blue eyes fixed so perfectly on the letters that at first the doctor was certain he could see them. He sometimes called out the letters with such accuracy that Maguane himself had to walk up next to the board and peer at the smallest of them to be sure that Moses was right. The whole business was complicated even further by the blind man's declaration that he could see them perfectly clearly in his mind. The examinations of his eyes were not conclusive either, and it was only when Dr. Maguane saw the patient reaching for his fallen stick that he agreed to give the diagnosis and shatter the town with splinters of shared guilt.

When Moses Mooney was brought home to the cats on the first afternoon of his declared blindness, the balance in the opera house account rose by £600. The following week there were £400 more, and although it was still far short of the impossible goal, it was enough to send Moira Fitzgibbon of the Community Development Association to visit Moses Mooney by the fireside in his house and tell him the good news of how the people were responding.

What nobody knew was that although Moses Mooney had lost his sight, he had gained omniscience and knew already. On the vast seas of his blindness he sailed now, guided by no stars and not daring to dream. He sat in his house, with few visitors, and retreated to the warm exotic landscapes of his imagination. The world had no place for vision, he told God.

And yet something had lingered on. For, one year after Moses Mooney had awoken in his blindness, Moira Fitzgibbon had contacted the Italian embassy. She had heard of a touring Venetian ensemble sponsored by the embassy and phoned to ask them if they could play a concert in Miltown Malbay for the opera house fund. The woman from the embassy had never heard of Miltown Malbay, she sounded the name like Milano and told Moira to wait. When she came back on the line she said, Send a letter, we'll see.

At any moment the plot might have turned in another direction, the lines left to dangle, disconnected, and the meaning lost. But Moira Fitzgibbon wrote the letter, and when the Italians wrote back, saying that they would not come to Miltown Malbay but would donate one half of the takings from the planned concert in Ennis, there was a sense of rightness about it, like the smallest part of an elaborate puzzle, the sense of things fitting and bringing the unlikeliest of moments together.

Two days later Stephen Griffin was asked in the staff room to buy a ticket.

7

Vittorio Mazza did not want to play in Ennis. He did not want to play in Ireland at all. The day after he arrived in Dublin with the other members of the ensemble, he woke in his hotel and saw with alarm the peculiar greyness of the light. He imagined the cause was the net curtains and drew them aside, only to discover with grim astonishment that the grey was the colour of the sky. A steady October rain was falling, the Dublin traffic was blocked in apparent perpetuity, and the people who moved on the city path below wore the downcast and mottled expression of desolation. Vittorio gasped with the awfulness of it, blinked his eyes, and opened them only to understand that he had arrived in the haunting landscape of his worst dream and that Dublin seemed to be the place that for sixteen years he had been calling Purgatory.

He lay on his bed and ordered room service. When it did not arrive, he was confirmed in his fears that the city was a kind of prison. The misery of the place was leaking in on him, the massiveness of the melancholia so potent that at first he thought he would not be able to stand, never mind play. He was the lead violin; he was Vittorio Mazza, he was fifty-eight years old and had been playing the violin for half a century. He had played in twenty-two cities in the world, and although he had never achieved any personal fame, he was known as a quality musician, and it was he who had been sought by the impresario Maltini when the Interpreti Veneziani was being founded.

Now he lay on the bed in his white shirt and wept. The dream of Purgatory had first tormented his sleep sixteen years earlier. It was May, his mother was ill, and Vittorio Mazza was in love with Maria Pecce, the beautiful wife of the baker Angelo. Due to the obsessive jealousy of the baker, who imagined no woman as beautiful as Maria could be faithful to the likes of him, the meetings of Maria and Vittorio were arranged with great difficulty and at odd hours of the day and night. Maria was known to everyone because of her extraordinary good looks and raven-black hair and had to slip from the bakery in a variety of scarves and coats, even during the furnace heat of that Maytime. When she came to

Vittorio, she was often naked beneath her coat, and as he pressed her to himself, the vapours of fresh dough entangled with the scent of the rose petals that she scattered on her innumerable baths. He could not believe that she loved him, but ignored as best he could the muted voice in the back of his brain that it was really the music that had brought her into his bed. She had heard him play Rossini in the Gala at Easter, and the moment had fired her with such reawakened passion for the rapturous and infinitely tender quality of life that she could barely sit out the concert and wait until the violinist was in her arms. The passion between them was instant, and remarkable, for they didn't tire of each other's body but made a kind of hungry loving, as if trying to devour one another's limbs and mouth and arrive at the essential stuff of the soul.

Vittorio knew the affair was doomed, but was helpless to escape. He knew he should tell Maria that he could not meet with her on the morning after his mother had taken another turn in her illness. He should have left Venice and driven to Verona. But when Maria came to his door, the look in her eyes erased his words, and his gratitude for the comfort of her breasts washed over everything else. Later, she lay like a dark cat on the pulled-back sheets of his bed and he played Schubert on the violin over her, not yet knowing that his mother had died.

When he found out, it snapped him like a Communion wafer. He met the anger of his sister's eyes at the bedside of the corpse and knew at once there was a judgement upon him. He did not sleep for three nights; he lay in the bed like a ship moored in mid-sea and waited for the horizon of the dawn. He waited through three nights and then came downstairs in his mother's house one morning to hear on the radio how the baker Pecce had killed his wife with a knife.

Since that night, Vittorio Mazza had lived sixteen years in the solitude of his guilt. He played music, but found little joy in it. At night he fell headlong into the same dream, over and over again. A grim place and a grey sky. Greyness everywhere. The feeling of wet concrete touching his face and the sense of his descending endlessly downward through-out the night, journeying down a slippery and rat-grey pathway where cold rain was falling.

It was, he knew, the condition of Purgatory that he carried around with him. It was the place his soul had fallen into, and much as he wished that sleep would one time bring him the warm and fabulous caress of

53

Maria Pecce, in sixteen years he had not found it. He suffered the torments of his nights and woke exhausted into the light of the morning, like a swimmer surfacing from a great depth. The sunlight revived him, and he could move through the day briefly postponing his despair. But that morning, in Dublin, Vittorio Mazza awoke and looked out and felt the familiarity of misery smite him with the frightening awareness that the condition of his sin had deepened. This was worse than anything he had known previously. For the city, on that fourteenth consecutive rainy day in October, had taken on the air of a mortally ill patient, and under the persistence of the drizzling sky every man and woman seemed to Vittorio to wear the dulled expression of a longtime heartache. The grief of his own condition seemed to have leaked out into the city in the night, and made everyone and everything the cousins of affliction. Even the buses that shouldered with infinite slowness through the traffic past the hotel suggested the impossibility of hope and progress here, their engines thrumming a despondent music and the passengers, with their faces to the streaming windows, looking out on a journey that would last forever.

Vittorio lay back on his bed and pressed

the palms of his hands against his eyes. He wanted to cry out, but rolled himself over until his face was pressed against the pillow. Why had he come here? He should have turned down the offer; how could he bear this desolate grey place? He raised his head and looked for the wine bottle he had bought the previous evening. He knew that it was empty, for he had emptied a bottle of wine every night before lying down for the last fifteen years, but he still searched the room for it, as if to confirm that it was morning and the umbrageous light was not the vivid dark of his dreams.

Vittorio Mazza lay on the bed in his Dublin hotel for an hour in an ooze of cold sweat. Then he rose and dressed himself quickly, his trembling fingers fumbling with the buttons of his white shirt. He did not trust himself to shave, for he was in too great a hurry. He had not unpacked and had only to put in his toiletries and draw on his thick black coat and silk scarf. Then he was ready. He wrote a short note to tell the others he had fled: *"Sono tornato in Italia — lontano da questo Purgatorio,"* and then slipped out the door with his violin case in his hand. If he hurried, he told himself, and shut his eyes in the taxi, he could be back in Venice by sunset.

It took two days before the consul from the embassy could discover for certain that Vittorio was gone. The first of the evening concerts had to be cancelled, and the ticket holders were turned away into the pouring night rain with the promise that the concert would be rearranged. They were not told that the lead violinist had fled their country in the appalling vision that it was the place of the damned. They took the news without protest, like a people used to disappointment, and walked off into the rainy darkness without umbrellas.

There was no funding for a replacement, and at a meeting in the gilt-mirrored room of senior consul Costanza, where the walls were painted in Naples yellow and the carpet was the blue of the Maytime Mediterranean, a decision on the fate of the ensemble had to be made. There was a file laid out on the polished mahogany table, containing within it the letter of Moira Fitzgibbon of Miltown Malbay. Then Isabella Curta, who was a junior secretary, told the consul that there was a violinist from Venice living in Kerry. Her name, she said, was Gabriella Castoldi.

8

Like Vittorio Mazza, Gabriella Castoldi had arrived in Ireland in the rain. It was the infamous hard rain that fell throughout the month of October three years earlier, when she had come on holiday in the small red Fiat of the poet Pollini. They had driven from Tuscany through the Brenner Pass and taken two weeks to cross France and arrive at last in the downpour of Rosslare harbour. They peered out at Ireland through the windscreen wipers and looked in wide amazement at the battered backs of warehouses and sheds. Pollini was twenty-eight and looked like a man who had fire for breakfast. His hair was blond, and the slow combustion of the poetry-making within him gave his face an expression of ferocity and desire. Only the backward motion of his head as he flicked his hair betrayed his arrogance, and as he steered the car slowly into the middle of Rosslare, he told Gabriella for the fourteenth time on their journey that he was not lost.

It was Pollini who had told her about Ireland. He had told her it was a wild and magical country, although he had never been there. He lay alongside her in the narrow bed in Eppi and, against the tacit waning of their passion, urged her to leave Italy and visit Ireland. He had discovered the richly fabled country through its poetry and read aloud in Italian the translated cadences of Yeats. He knew their loving needed rescuing and thought that they could move quicker than the failing of desire.

Gabriella was a teacher of the violin and five years older than the poet. She had two feckless brothers and no sisters. She had outlived both her parents, developing in the process of her days a severe measure of the world, against which everything fell short. She had an expectancy of grief and wore it in the soft pale circles beneath her eyes. No man had diminished that sorrowfulness in her thirty-three years, and it was not until she met Alessandro Pollini that she first imagined it might be possible to find someone who shared the innocence of her view that the world could be perfect. The poet loved her fiercely; she felt his glances were like silk scarves drawn slowly across her body, and it was not until six months into their relationship that she began to fear that it was her unhappiness that drew him. It was true, however. Pollini loved her for her vulnerability and had given himself to her in the vain belief that he could make her whole. He attended concerts she played in Venice and Verona, and sat mesmerized by the cold passion she brought to the music; she believed in rigour and rectitude, and while she bowed the notes of Vivaldi, her eyebrows met in a narrow frown of concentration that the poet loved. She played perfectly and yet, when the concerts were over, lacerated herself with the harshest of self-criticism, appalled at the slightest flaw and the injustice she had done the composer. Pollini was entranced by her. Or so he thought, not realizing that it was the intensity of his own reaction he loved, the quickened thrumming of his own heartbeat as he strode through the streets to the concerts. As a poet of twenty-five, he had been acclaimed widely for his first collection, *Spontaneo*. The praise had been so unexpected and so lavish that he had woken one morning believing he possessed a soul that was infinitely more sensitive and attuned to the sweetness of the world than anyone else's. He got out of bed and carried his soul like a golden chalice. Then he met Gabriella Castoldi and was amazed at how moved he felt by the bruised and tender quality of her eyes, and offered her the chalice, thinking he would witness the miracle of her transformation under the power of such a love as his.

But it had not happened. He had courted her with freesias and poetry, and watched himself languishing in the tossed sheets, as if enacting a scene. When at last she had come to his bed, he had visions of roses bursting from the walls and wings growing from the backs of men. He imagined the air itself would take on the perfume of permanent springtime, and he kissed her with a passion that was beyond anything he had known. However, when, two weeks later, he watched her play one of the concerti of Mozart in the Palazzo Musica in Venice, he was struck like a blow with the knowledge that he had not yet loved her into happiness.

Now they drove into Ireland. They drove west along the southern coast in the great disappointment of that outrageous rain. (They did not know that the downpour was already on the point of ending, and that within four days the Gulf Stream would bring a freakish Indian summer that would last into November and make children and old men feel the winter was already over.) It was not only the grey skies that dismayed

Pollini, for he had lived through grim Venetian winters; this was something more, a desolate quality he sensed in the grim houses along the roadside, as if they huddled there in the misery of all weathers, barely enduring. When he turned on the radio, he heard the news of a corrupted minister in Dublin, and that a woman had been strangled to death on a farm in County Meath. He wanted an imagined loveliness, a rapture that would make vanish the failings of their passion. He wanted fairyland, not this, and sped the car towards the coastline of Cork, taking the wrong way twice and stopping at a butcher shop where a dog gnawed a bone to ask what the number of the road was. Nobody knew. They told him it was the road to Mallow. He was flushed with embarrassment and sat back in the red car in a collapsed silence. His method in the world was straightforward; you proceed straightforward, you go after what you want, and when you meet an obstacle you ignore it, you go straight through it. Belief is everything. The world will surrender all its treasures if you bang down its doors. So he had raced the car forward in the failing light of late October and carried Gabriella Castoldi in a gesture that since time immemorial has been made against the waning of love: the flight to a new place. Pollini drove with impotent rage and passed through many small towns and villages, not noticing that he was moving constantly inland and away from the extraordinary beauty of the coastline, and only stopping again in the ten o'clock darkness when Gabriella suggested they should stay the night where they were, in a damp guesthouse in Mallow.

The following morning Alessandro Pollini awoke with a head cold. The pressure within him had begun to leak outward, and although the rain had already lifted and the day moved through a dozen different weathers, he knew that love was subsiding in his heart and that he had not the strength to stop it. While he laid back his head and closed his eyes in the passenger seat, Gabriella drove them towards Killarney and the mountains. He slept and woke all day, and by early evening, when they had arrived at a place that overlooked the dazzling crystal of the lakes, he had not the strength to go out for a walk. He went to bed and felt the love draining from him. He stayed in bed the following day, afraid to get up and speak to Gabriella, lest she notice the alarming and unstoppable emptying of love from his eyes. For three days afterwards, Pollini urged it back; he announced love to himself and flashed his looks at the mirror before going down to breakfast. But at last, on the bridge outside the triangular town of Kenmare, the relationship ended. Gabriella told him to go home.

It was a moment that would haunt him for the rest of his life. When she had told him that he no longer loved her, he had denied it. It was impossible to fall out of love like that; it was the place, it was the rain and the mountains, there was something oppressive about the country, about being there on that wet island in the beginning of autumn. It was a place of death. Love was doomed here. He did love her, more than anything. He took Gabriella's hands in his and bent to kiss them, but she held his face instead and turned it to her. She told him she loved him still, but that it was over, and at that moment he shook uncontrollably and his tears flowed on the bridge beside her, knowing that it was true. Gabriella held him in her arms but did not weep. Then she made the decision that was to change inexorably the rest of her life and make the memory of that moment burn like a Roman candle in Alessandro Pollini's mind fifteen years later, when he would return to Ireland to search for her memory: she told him to go back to Italy and leave her there.

She had decided to stay in Ireland.

(It was cowardice, the poet admitted later, when he was in old age and had three times married women younger than himself. It was cowardice that had made him not try to convince Gabriella to come back with him. It was the fear of considering too closely that new discovery, the unbearable reality of the emptiness of his own heart. He would have had to travel back across France in the small car, sitting beside the beautiful woman, with the dead child of their loving propped between them. Worse, he would have known it was he who had killed it.)

Pollini left Ireland the next day to return to Italy, and Gabriella Castoldi remained in Kenmare. It was not something she had planned to do, and she did not for the moment have any idea what would come next in her life. She wrapped a long coat about her and went walking about the town. It was a quiet place in the autumn, with the mountains rising on three sides and the Kenmare River running swiftly towards the unseen Atlantic. Mists lingered in the mountaintops, and on a windless afternoon descended to the town, enveloping it as in a fairy tale. The day after the poet left, Gabriella walked around the triangle of the streets of the town. She looked in the windows and bought herself two apples in the small greengrocer's near the bank. The shop belonged to Nelly Grant, a fresh-faced woman of sixty who looked like forty, wore green fingerless gloves, and believed in the healing powers of fruit. She herself had come to Kenmare from England twenty years earlier, and viewed lone visitors in the autumn with a knowing look, understanding in an instant how easily the mountains and the mist seduced them into never leaving. Nelly Grant knew when she saw Gabriella that the town was enticing her. She had seen the man leaving in the red Fiat and imagined she could detect in Gabriella the ashen look of the end of an affair.

"These please."

"Two apples? Anything else, dear?" Nelly paused, she let her eyes look over to the far stall, where she had a basket of ruby grapefruit, whose bitterness she knew was the perfect antidote to heartache.

Gabriella did not get the message, and the shopkeeper did not press it. For although she had come to believe completely in the restorative powers of the proper fruits and nuts, and had even converted a great number of the local population to the sweet figs of Portugal and the bottled olives of Morocco, she sensed that Gabriella was not yet ready for the suggestion, and simply slipped a free clementine into the paper bag with the apples.

It was mid-afternoon when Gabriella left the shop and walked out of the town. She already knew the roads and took the rising curve in the direction of Killarney, walking to meet the descending mist and the mesmerized mute faces of the sheep, grazing the grass edges for eternity. Cars slowly passed her. The light was thin and pale, there was a washed translucence in the air, and the feeling of it touching her face was like the tears of someone else. The views into the valley as the road rose were colour-washed with fallen cloud. There was a hush like a blanket, and Gabriella imagined she was walking in the secret landscape of dreams. It was a timeless place. There were no houses, no sounds but the running of small streams, streaking the rock and grass of the mountainsides and gleaming like elvers. Water crossed the road and fell over the edge down into new streams that arrived at last in the lakes below. She walked on. She walked as if the walking itself carried her nowhere and the action of her footsteps was merely a gesture, like treading water, to keep herself alive.

The afternoon in autumn so quickly married the evening that the light that lingered one moment was curtained with darkness the next, and before Gabriella at last stopped on the road from Kenmare, she was moving in a damp, impenetrable blue, with only the scattered lights in the valley below visible. She stopped and stood, eight miles from Kenmare, in the October darkness. She had eaten the apples, and her hand in her right pocket held the clementine. Her hair and face were wet, her heart ached for the lost loving of the poet, and she imagined him in a narrow berth belowdecks on the ferry crossing the English Channel and vanishing from her life. She wanted to cry out and fall down, but instantly attacked herself for being so weak, and instead ate the clementine and walked back towards the town.

The following morning she walked even farther out of Kenmare. She took two apples and two clementines, and when she was twelve miles from the town she strode off the curving roadway and made her way upwards through the old trees and the dying rhododendron until the mud had painted the bottom of her dress and her hair was flecked with pieces of fallen leaf. When she was exhausted, she stopped and sat upon the trunk of a fallen ash tree, looking about

her in the cool shade of the slanting mountain trees, dizzy with the sense of the world
below her. She sucked on the green air, and
sat in the undergrowth of the Kerry mountains. She did not move in that motionless
place and imagined how long she could remain like that, and how long it would be before the birds might forget she was living
and land on her limbs like a tree. She held
her breath and put her hands outward, as if
expecting gifts. She held them outward so
long her fingertips ached, and then her
wrists weakened as though they were inca-
pable of holding up any longer the burden
of living.

Then she turned and saw a deer six feet
away from her.

She did not move, and the deer didn't either. His head was at an angle and his nose
lifted into the new and strange sweetness of
the air. He had found her scent a mile away
across the mountain and tracked it to here,
and now did not know what to do. Gabriella
allowed herself to do nothing but smile.
Briefly there was no sound, then the stillness of their being there was filled with the
thousand minute noises of the turning
world, the haw of the deer's breathing, the
ephemeral vapour of its presence on the
mountainside uncertain as a vision, and the

sound of its flanks heaving. The deer moved its right foreleg and the ground crackled tinnily with the stuff of ancient twigs and pine needles beneath the deep mulch of a hundred years. The deer lowered its neck and nosed the ground where Gabriella had walked. She saw its great muscle flex beneath the brown hide and knew the strength of the animal. She imagined the animal's massive turn and bound and flight away through the mountain forest, the crash of alarm its charge would signal as it climbed farther and farther from the green stillness of that moment that was like a deer's dream of paradise. If she moved, it would take flight and run until it arrived at last high in the mountain to drink the clear running water of safety.

But Gabriella did not move. She was enchanted. She closed her eyes a moment and felt the coolness of her eyelids and saw the green shadows dancing beneath them. She pursed her lips to taste the moisture of the mountain forest and knew for sure that she was not dreaming. When she opened her eyes, she saw the deer eating the coiled peel of the clementine. It was a moment which she would long remember. She would remember it as the mysterious beginning of healing, the untranslatable language of God speaking in nature and stopping the world in a green moment.

The deer lifted its head and looked at her. Somewhere a bird flew and the last leaves of a high tree quivered with its presence. The mist drifted like a veil across the little opening where Gabrielle was sitting. The deer looked away, and then back again, as if deciding that the strange figure of the woman might be companionable, and doubting for the briefest instant its own instinct of fear. Then, slowly, moving on the point of haste but not in haste, tempting the vision to transform and frighten it, but knowing that it would not, the deer walked away. It was three minutes before it vanished and Gabriella stood up.

"Grazie," she said, and began the slow wet journey back down the mountain.

The following day Nelly Grant knew that Gabriella did not need the ruby grapefruit and offered her instead the fortification of bananas. Bananas ensure us against the suddenness of violent emotions, she told the Italian woman, and put two in her bag with a conspiratorial smile. Gabriella was carrying her violin case, and when Nelly asked her was she going to play, Gabriella said, "I need a lot of practising."

That afternoon she played Vivaldi in the small clearing among the trees where she had met the deer. She did not expect him to return, and he did not — at least not so that she could see him — but she played nonetheless, making the notes move through the changeless frozen time of that beautiful place where only the air and the trees listened. It soothed Gabriella to play. She played for an hour; she played with a flowing motion in her bow and heard the music reach a point so near to perfection that even she could not find the smallest flaw. Above the treetops the broken pieces of the pale sky glistened like glass. No clouds were moving. The air was scented with pine, and the stillness of that secret place shimmered with the music.

When Gabriella had stopped playing and returned down the mountainside, she had decided she was going to stay and live in Kenmare. She did not yet know how or for how long, but as she walked along the black road back to the town and felt the rain coming in her face, she knew the decision was irreversible.

It was three days before she got a job in the vegetable shop of Nelly Grant. By the time the summer arrived and her skill on the violin had been discovered, she was invited to play three evenings a week before the great fireplace in the mustard-coloured lounge of The Falls Hotel. It was there that Isabella Curta, junior secretary of the Italian embassy, had discovered her, and been so moved by her playing that she had written down the name Gabriella Castoldi, and was able to recall it two years later when Vittorio Mazza fled back to Italy.

9

On the first Friday of November, Stephen Griffin did not know that his life was about to change. He had long given up the vanity of supposing that life was something you could plan, or that wishes and desires could be achieved. For years he had lived in a kind of ghostly nowhere, a place of continuing days and nights whose only feature was its own unremarkableness. He expected nothing, and opened his eyes each morning in the back bedroom of the small house by the sea, uncertain as to whether he was among the living or the dead.

This was nothing new. He had a facility for living with ghosts. As he grew up in the house of his father, he had grown used to encountering his mother and his sister in the shadowy corners of the past. It did not frighten him, and he soon understood that the treasured moments of his family's loving remained undiminished and unvanquished despite the passing of time. Indeed, it was the sweetest of sorrows, and when he was alone in the house as a young man and startled himself with the sudden vividness of a certain moment — his sister, Mary, coming down the stairs with the doll Philomena — he discovered that the grief was assuaged by the understanding that for some things time does not pass, it recycles.

Life in that house in Dublin had taught him to cherish the company of the invisible. When he went to university and began to study history, it was the now familiar presence of the disappeared that attracted him. He sat in the glass-fronted room of the library and lost himself with the ghosts of the previous three hundred years. He kept his head down and his eyes moving on the pages, but his mind took flight, and soon even his body was elsewhere, a fact noticed only by old Murtagh, the ancient librarian assistant, who himself had long ago vanished into the books of Thomas Hardy. The power of language was a conjuring magic, it magicked doors in castles and courtyards, and through them Stephen entered. He was the student humped over in the library, reading the books until the night porter came round clearing the tables and sending him home. When he rose and walked out into the glitter frost and million stars of the

Dublin night, he was walking with others in a different place. He had abstracted himself from the world so thoroughly that by the age of twenty-one, when he was in his final year, he hardly needed the book to be open for him to slip into the past.

He was a quiet fellow. He did not go to the dances on Friday nights, nor heed his father's urging to go down and sit with the others in the students' bar. So solitary was his life that Philip Griffin grew fearful that his son had been overprotected since the trauma of the tragedy and would never emerge in the plain daylight of the world. He sat downstairs and worried, while Stephen lay in the bedroom overhead with a book propped on his chest. It did not bother Stephen that no other student was like him. He passed the summer exams, and within two years had read every university book of merit on the subject of European history at the turn of the century. His face grew pale as paper; his eyes had the peering expression of the myopic, and his lips thinned and grew light-coloured, as if they had never tasted fruit.

He lived in books, and by the time he was ready to graduate with honours from the history department of University College, Dublin, his complexion was delicate and radiated the grey light of imminent illness. In May of his final year he stood in the doorway of his tutor's room, and Dr. Margaret McCormack realized that he was almost lost to life. She had seen students almost devoured by the study of history before, but it had always been temporary. Usually they reached a point — often in April — when the sudden sweetness of the sensual world swept over them. Their books became weighty and dry in the perfumed air that spun and dazzled and was blown about with almond blossom.

But for Stephen Griffin it was not like that. For three years he had sat in the lecture halls and quietly taken his notes in longhand. He handed in his papers on time and worked through the brightening days of spring, barely lifting his head when the brilliance of the May sunshine made his pages too white for reading. None but his father had told him to stop, and even Philip Griffin surrendered, imagining that his son knew better than he what was needed for a university degree.

So, in the last weeks of his final year, Stephen stood in the doorway of his tutor's room and told her he was hoping to be accepted for the master's degree, and then the doctorate. Dr. McCormack looked at him and then looked away. The sunlight flooded into the room through the window behind her, she could feel its warmth pressing on her back.

"Doctorate?" she said. "I see."

"Yes," he said, hanging there in the doorway, his eyes gazing downward, as if he had just confessed a crime.

Dr. McCormack had to hold her breath. She had been teaching for twenty years in the second-floor room which was the reward for her own schoolday acuity at history, a permanent office. And she despised it. But she was fit for nothing else; she knew it, and knew that each day she moved further along the dull inevitability that had been her life since she came to college to study history. There in the sunlight she looked at the pale man with the white face and thin black hair. He was transparent. There was about him such a pitiful shrinking from life that it caused a lever to release in Margaret McCormack and the truth of her own lifetime of withdrawal, timidity, and ungrasped opportunity to be unloaded with a crash upon her.

"The doctorate, yes," she said, and touched the stilled flowers in subdued yellow that decorated her dress. The sun was two warm hands on her back. She felt her own dust falling in the air.

"I'm hoping you'll give me a recommendation," said Stephen.

That's not what you're asking, thought Margaret McCormack. You're asking for an escape, you're asking to be allowed to slip in here to one of these box rooms where you can gather books on the shelves and turn the pages of students' essays until they tap on your shoulder and say next year is your retirement.

Margaret did not answer him at once. She felt a varicose vein on the inside of her left leg begin to throb, and turned from him and sat down.

"Thank you for telling me," she said and, looking down at the coffee mug that held her pens, added, "I'll certainly give it my consideration."

In fact, she had already decided. By the time Stephen was walking down the green carpeted corridor to the library once more, Margaret McCormack had made up her mind that Stephen Griffin was to be saved from her own fate, and that the rejection he would feel when the letter came telling him he had not been accepted into the program would in fact be the coded message of her own mercy ushering him forward into the world. He was worse than she, she thought;

he was a book. And only twenty-two years old. She sat at her desk after he left and felt a sense of mission. It's everything he wants, but only because he cannot imagine facing the terrible realities of the world. He does not really want it, she thought, it is fear. She touched the small drops of perspiration that had arrived on her top lip. She knew what it was like to have no gift for small talk and feel the alarming sense of being the only person unable to relax into a fragment of conversation or idle a moment with a colleague on the stairs. She had recognized herself so acutely in Stephen Griffin that she could not bear it.

She picked up her pen and wrote a letter to the head of the department outlining why she could not recommend Stephen Griffin for the master's program at this time. She finished the letter as the sun was moving from her window. Then she put her head on the desk and softly cried.

By midsummer of that year, when Stephen had been turned down for the master's program, he received an offer of a place for the Diploma in Education course. He was so astonished by the rejection that he did not think clearly of the possibilities of his life but enrolled with the narrowed vision of those who have lost confidence in their future. One year later, he emerged from university a teacher. It was not a career he seemed suited for; at first he read from the textbook and lost the class, and it was only when he stopped reading and looked down at the pupils that he suddenly realized he was building a wall between them and himself. He stopped reading in class after that and began a new, risky tactic: talking the history out, telling it, unwinding the moments as if they were the first slender threads of a long, deeply entwined rope that led, impossibly, all the way back to that very moment in the classroom, the very instants of their breathing there in the school. And somehow it worked. Somehow the seriousness of him, the undiminished intensity of his focus, won over the classes, and the brightest followed him while the weakest looked away in dreams.

10

Stephen Griffin had bought the ticket for the
concert when Moira Fitzgibbon had brought
them into the staff room at breaktime. Every
teacher had taken two, and although he had
no intention of going himself, never mind the
impossibility of bringing anyone, he had
taken a pair of tickets and put them in the
pages of *Ireland since the Famine.* Half the staff
were not intending to go either, and some of
the men unknowingly mirrored the behaviour of the boys outside by teasing each other
about who would be interested in classical
music. They threw the word "culture" at
each other like dried dung. Their laughter
proved their distance from it. It was a thing
for the women. But they bought the tickets
anyway, to give them to their wives or put
them on the windowsill, for Moira Fitzgibbon had a forbidding sense of mission as
she stood among them. She was not slow to
remind them of the sorry fate of Moses
Mooney or to make them feel an uneasy guilt

at how many of them had singularly failed to teach her anything and how the failure of her Leaving Certificate examinations in six subjects was the single most unmentioned achievement of the school in the past fifteen years.

Stephen did not intend to go to the concert, not because he disapproved or wanted to distance himself from the notion of such music in a place like west Clare, but because there would be people there. Then Moira Fitzgibbon pressed the tickets into his hand. She was a small woman of thirty-three who had, since leaving the school, become a leading member of the Community Development Association; she knew her mind, but not books, she told the other members on the night of the first meeting, asking for all business to be read aloud and excusing herself by explaining without embarrassment that the education system had taught her nothing and she was taking night classes in reading.

Stephen finished school and went home at four o'clock. The wind was blowing and the forecast was for worse. The darkness was already falling into the sea. He sat in the front room and turned on the radio. It was four hours before the concert and he had no intention of attending. With the music on the radio and the muffled company of the dark sea outside, the room was an island in November and he was soon asleep. It was the way he finished every schoolday in winter, drowsing in the corner armchair into a forgetfulness, like slipping through the back door of the world. His dreams were not fretful or anxious but a changing tapestry of recollection and mild invention, which was in fact the history of his heart. His head lay tilted to one side, and his white face looked painted in the deepening shadows. If he had died then, there in the armchair, the world would have moved on without him with little pause or regret, like a winter army leaving the long-suffering wounded to fall behind in the snow. He was a casualty of circumstances, and as he sat slumped in the chair, with the music playing and the sea breaking in the wind outside, he had no idea that rescue was at hand.

Stephen dreamed he was a child on the stairs. He was standing on the small landing where the stairs turned, and his mother was downstairs in the kitchen cooking. It was only when he looked down that he realized he had legs, for he seemed frozen and was unable to move even when Anne Griffin called out his name and his sister, Mary, came running past him with her doll

Philomena. He heard his name being called again, and then saw the long, slim figure that was his mother appear at the bottom of the stairs and say to him, "Stephen, are you coming down?" And still he could not move. The wallpaper with its printed flowers in yellow and gold seemed to give way beneath his hand as he reached for something to grasp, and then there was music playing. It sounded like a cello, like the simple cello music Mary made that swam around the house and was soft and easy, and still he could not move his legs, even when his mother said again, "Stephen, are you coming down?" And he wanted to, wanted with all the desperation only dreams can hold, as he saw his mother walk away into the kitchen and heard the music grow louder and louder still, swaying the stairs, the hallway, the house itself, until he had to turn his head and let out a cry and open his eyes to see the darkness of the room about him.

He lowered his head into his hands and felt the filmy sweat of his dream.

Then he heard the music.

It was coming from the radio. It was a Mozart quartet. Whether Stephen had heard a fragment of the music as he was sleeping or whether he had dreamt it, the strange synchronicity of its playing to the tune and tempo of his dreaming was a manifestation of something. He sat up in his armchair and felt strangely that the music was for him. Whatever makes the world move moved the world then for Stephen Griffin. Whatever causes the drear of ordinariness to shake and be dazzled with brilliance, until the illumination changes forever the shape of the thousand moments that follow, it dazzled then. Though Stephen did not quite know it. He listened to the piece until it was over and then heard the announcer on the Clare station say it was the Interpreti Veneziani, who were playing that evening in the Old Ground Hotel in Ennis.

One hour later he was driving past the night fields of Inagh in the ten-year-old yellow Ford that was the only car he had ever owned. He drove with a kind of jerky, quick-slow motion, pressing on the accelerator and letting his foot off again at each bend, until the car slowed and he pumped it again. It was a style of driving that sickened any passenger but had become so habitual to Stephen that he hardly seemed to notice the way his foot pressed the pedal as if it belonged to a piano. Foot on, foot off, the car seemed to row forward like a yellow gondola, pressing and easing against some invisible current that was flowing ceaselessly against him in the darkness.

He drove on with music playing in his head. His face was a white moon pressed forward over the steering wheel. Wind buffeted the car. Bits of hedgerow and black plastic flew through the beams of the headlights. The wipers smeared the spits of rain each time they passed and made the car blind and seeing in turns. The night was breaking up, and Stephen had to grip the wheel hard to keep the car in the centre of the narrow road. He drove until he saw something coming against him; it too motored down the centre of the road, which fell away at a slope into the running murk of the ditch on both sides. When the two cars were close enough to threaten crashing, they veered over and with a mad gaiety swished past each other before retaking the centre once more. Sometimes the drivers managed frantic salutes as they flew past, desperately trying to keep from knocking off the wing mirrors.

The journey was dark. The road wound wildly across bogs that stretched away into the fallen night and soaked in the rain like parts of a vast sea creature. Soon the rain that was blowing across the front of the car was blowing directly at it. And still Stephen pumped the car forward, lurching it towards the destiny he did not know was as simple and momentous as falling in love. He was in a state. His thin lips were dry, but his face was wet. He kept thinking of the music, the music playing like that, and the dreaming and the music becoming one. The car radio had never worked and neither had the fan; so he imagined the music playing, and to its even tempo rubbed at the windscreen with his sleeve. Not that he could see. He was travelling a wet blackness that might have been circling upon itself like a tail, but still he pressed on.

He was unlike himself with the fierceness of his intent. But with the mysterious illogic by which one instant of life becomes charged with passion, he would not surrender or turn back in the rain for anything.

On the passenger seat beside him he had the tickets for the concert. He glanced over at them and in that moment made the car veer sharply to the left. The wheel hit the top of the ditch and he thumped his head against the fabric of the ceiling a half dozen times before he was able to bring the car skidding back into the slick centre of the road.

And across the other side, to crash nosedown into a ditch.

God.

11

Sitting up in his bed and grinning as the fierce teeth of the Atlantic bit off the slates above him and flung them a hundred yards into the fields, Moses Mooney told the cats not to worry. Thomas and Angela were curled in the warm place where his knees bent in the blankets, and he stroked them blindly as he spoke. The black cat called Angela purred and turned her head in against him. The important thing, he told them, was to realize that the future was indestructible. That no force could arrest it, and that it proceeded with the same relentless and undiminished energy as the sea itself.

"You can't drown if you are born to die in your bed," he said with a giddy glee, raising the great tangle of his beard to let out the laughter like birds. "Nothing stops the future. Oh no," he said, "indeed no."

The rain quickened like a pulse beating against the window. The night thrashed about with the growing storm, taking the salt from the sea, until even in the thickly curtained bedrooms and kitchens of Miltown Malbay the air tasted of bitterness and disappointment. It was such a night. The stars had withdrawn behind the many layers of the gusting clouds, and there was no moon. Only wind and rain. Moses Mooney nodded his head and patted the cats to reassure them as the window in his bathroom flew open and he felt the breath of the sea coming in about him. "Ha ha, smell that," he said, and raised the eyebrows of his blind eyes to catch what he knew was the scent of a storm in Brazil moments after he thought he had drowned for the third time. Here it is, he thought. Here is the shaking up of the world.

"Go on. Go on," he said.

Then the lights went out.

Moses Mooney knew it, though he could not see it. He heard them going off in the town and thought that the darkness of all his neighbours was a symbolic blindness and a token of God's sympathy for him. They were all to share his vision, he realized, and lay back against the pillows, which were wet now like tears. It's black for miles around, he told the cats with mixed comfort and awe, catching a glimpse at the same instant of that elsewhere which he alone saw, where

Stephen Griffin had crashed the yellow car into the black bog water of the ditch on the road outside Inagh. And in that dreamlike and vivid moment of clairvoyance, Moses Mooney saw the collapsed figure of Stephen Griffin, and he clapped his hands together in the bed, relishing the wild improbability of all plots before reaching out and patting the cats in the darkness.

12

Moira Fitzgibbon was late. She had already been to the Old Ground Hotel twice that day to make arrangements and meet the quartet when they arrived from Limerick. She had learned a few phrases in Italian in honour of the visit and listened to the music of Scarlatti and Vivaldi for two weeks. When she stood in the lobby of the hotel to meet the musicians, she felt her head spinning. They shook her hand and stood, smiling with the strange complicity of those brought together over music. Any fear or dread Moira had felt passed like a grey bird and left her feeling she herself had wings. When the musicians went to their rooms, she drove back to Miltown Malbay to cook dinner for Tom and her two children, but afterwards watched through the back window above the sink as clouds advanced in across the Atlantic. She washed the dishes and prayed. She prayed first that the storm would not come; then, when the first black bullets started falling, prayed that it would not be a real storm, that it would pass over.

By the time she had collected Aoife Taafe, the babysitter, and set the two girls in their pyjamas in the sitting room and said good night to Tom, who was heading down to the pub, Moira Fitzgibbon was half an hour behind herself. A week earlier, planning the evening, she was already back in Ennis by now and Tom was minding the children and it was not raining. Now she hurried out of the house into the gale, and when she sat into the car she let out a cry at the ferocity of the world outside and the mad bouffant of her hairstyle. Then, as her car was moving out into the street, the lights in Miltown Malbay went out. She knew her children would be crying and Aoife running for the candles, but Moira Fitzgibbon drove away anyway, drove out of the darkened town with the tight fervour of a pilgrim, and rocked herself slightly forward, as if her own momentum might aid the car or the wind carry it onward like a sailboat.

A mile outside Miltown Malbay the darkness was thickly fallen. The fields were the fields of childhood nightmares, whose cows and sheep blew off the edge of the world in hurricane and tornado. Wisps of barbed wire had come undone from the fenceposts and whipped across the road in the wind. Plastic bags, drink cans, stuff blew from no-where and danced. Then the rain thickened and beat faster than the wipers. Why? Why is it like this? Moira Fitzgibbon asked. On the one night, the one night. Who would go out on a night like this? There'd be nobody there. God, Why?

There was no answer from the heavens, but there were red smears on the wind-screen, and when the wipers cleared the rain she saw the red backlights of the crashed car in the ditch ahead of her.

13

Stephen did not realize rescue was at hand. He was at the bridge of his life without knowing it and sat stunned in the rainy night, unable to move. His head hurt, but not badly, yet he could not free himself from the fierce grip of the dream of dying. He imagined he was his mother and his sister. He was in the car they drove that afternoon so many years ago, and this was the crash, the suspended moment when their lives had stopped and dreams perished. This was the instant the world had become immobile and deaf and mute, and the darkness had fallen in like earth on a coffin. He imagined with terrible clarity the anguish of it, the sheer and merciless shattering as the other car came crashing in on them, the jerking backward of his mother and Mary, and the cries; if there was time for cries. Stephen imagined it as he sat there in the crashed car, and he could not move. He felt the steering wheel, but it seemed unreal, and the pallor of his hands upon it was the lone white thing in the darkness.

I cannot move, he thought. I cannot move from here.

And if the car had blown up and burned there on the side of the road, Stephen Griffin would have burned with it and not regretted it, surrendering to the ceaseless prompting of his life that grief triumphs on earth and that all our plots unravel in the end.

But then Moira Fitzgibbon arrived. When she pulled open the car door, the rain lashing down on her head made freakish streaks of her hairdo and the taste of her makeup washed into her mouth. She spat and called out, but Stephen did not move. He was like a deep-water swimmer uncertain whether to kick for the surface and kept his eyes looking at the long-gone world where the spirits of his mother and sister were so close it made him ache.

"Mr. Griffin, is that you? Do you hear me? Mr. Griffin?"

There were mudspatters on Moira's stockings, the heel of her left shoe was loosened, and the navy-blue outfit she had bought for the evening of Venetian music was soaked against her back. She had no idea why the sky had fallen in or why hers had to be the car to first come upon the crash, knowing that she could not drive past it although everything in her had wanted to. She understood nothing yet, but cursed God and cursed the weather and cursed Tom and the west of Ireland and the god-forsaken roads like this that were full of holes and went on for miles and made this man crash in front of her.

"Feck it. Feck it. Oh God, forgive me, feck it. Mr. Griffin! Mr. Griffin!"

She cried out his name, as if he could help her understand. She looked out the back window to see if help might be coming, but saw only the emptiness of the dark fields un-relieved by light or hope in the harsh, star-less wind. She said Stephen's name loudly again, and then, as she reached in to shake him by the shoulder, her knee touched something on the passenger seat, and she discovered a fragment of meaning and held up close to her face in the darkness the tickets for the concert.

14

Gabriella Castoldi, Paolo Mistra, Piero and Maria Motte were already sitting at the front of the concert room in the Old Ground Hotel by the time Stephen Griffin arrived there with Moira Fitzgibbon. He was still in a daze and passed up the red carpeted stairs of the hotel unsure in which world he was walking. When he had felt the woman's hand on his shoulder in the car, he had imagined at first it was the buffeting of the storm. Then she smacked his face and turned him towards her. He remembered her: the woman from the staff room, the woman they said afterwards was the dimmest pupil the school had ever had. He remembered her. Moira shook him from himself. They had gotten out of his car together and were blown along the road to hers. When they sat into it, Moira turned the heat full on and they drove towards Ennis in a gusting tropical balminess that dried their clothes and hair stiffly and made the rain-run places of Moira's makeup look like the tracks of ancient tears. She was taking him to the hospital, she told him, even though she would be late for the concert.

"I want to go to the concert," he said. He said it very calmly, without looking at her. He was stooped forward towards the windscreen, with his black hair fallen over his right eye. "I want to go to the concert."

(Later, when he was sitting at the fire in the house by the sea, listening to another storm blowing in across the invisible horizon of the nighttime, Stephen would wonder back to that moment and smile at the strange and unknowable conspiracies of the world, how the notion of the concert had become a resolve and how the night had almost blown him off its edge before the woman pulled over. He would read it for its meaning, and glimpse in that evening the shape of the world, a puzzle so intricate that not even the millionth part of the outer edge of its frayed pieces is discernible until so much later. Then it would make sense to him, and he would understand that the journey to the concert was the beginning of the most important journey of his life, and that the moment he insisted on going to the concert, he was acting out of a blind foreknowledge that told him it was the right thing to do, supposing that rightness was something that existed for every moment of every life and that the possibilities of humankind were so myriad and tortuous that knowing the right thing to do and then choosing it were the longest odds in man's history. But just then in the car Stephen had chosen; and later, to that moment, like an old explorer fingering the route he had taken across the unknown, he would trace all his happiness.)

They drove past the hospital to the hotel. Moira talked. She told him about Moses Mooney; she told him she wasn't sure why or how she had become involved in the concert; Stephen had probably heard of her in the school, she said, she was too stupid for them to teach her anything, so it was the last thing she expected to be doing, running a concert of Italian music in Ennis; she had two children for goodness' sake, and Tom is back in Miltown Malbay now, sitting on a high stool and telling jokes about how his missus is off having a bit of culture. "Agri or horti, that's his joke," she said. "That's what he says, because I'm thick. He thinks that's a great joke. They get you to do it because they don't want to do anything themselves, Tom says. Why are you running it? he says.

"And I can't answer him. Especially when you see a night like this and you think you're mad. You're just mad, Moira. There'll be nobody there and you'll be walking in like this in a state with your eighteen-pound hairdo looking like a wet monkey's backside, and four Italian musicians looking at you wondering why in the name of . . . I'm talking too much, I'm sorry, Mr. Griffin, I always talk too much when I'm nervous."

"Stephen."

"Stephen. Sorry, Stephen. Would you open that? See is there lipstick in it?"

The carpark was full. Moira bumped the car onto the footpath outside and then apologized to Stephen for forgetting he had just had an accident. When they got out of the car the rain was not falling. The ivy on the front of the old hotel was lit with hidden lamps, puddles glistened with reflection, and the slick black of the tarmac might have been the low waters of a canal in Venice. Or so Moira imagined. She raised her head as Stephen lowered his, and they strode forward with the brief invulnerability of the rescued.

At the front door they heard the buzz of people and the strains of the strings playing. For an instant, they imagined the same thing: that their watches had stopped and time had moved on without them, the concert was about to end. But by the time they had reached the doorway at the top of the red stairs, it was clear that the musicians were only warming up their instruments, and Moira Fitzgibbon blinked tears of gratitude, seeing the throng of people waiting in the rows of high-backed dining chairs and realizing that there was something fine and good and true in their being there, and that the bringing of the music and the people together that was the dreaming of old Mooney was worth the price of her hairdo, the ruining of her new suit, and the enduring of fatigue, hardship, and mockery.

In the delay, Councillor O'Rourke had seen his opportunity and taken Moira's position at the front of the room. He was a skeletal man with a sharp nose and the largest Adam's apple in Clare. He was a man who believed in men, as long as he was leading them, and derided Moira Fitzgibbon for her bluntness and well-meaning, and for not being at home. He held his nose high and smiled with narrow squints of his eyes, turning the immaculate whiteness of his soap-scented hands and letting only the rise and fall of his gorge betray how he disliked the company of his constituents. He was about to announce the opening of the evening's concert when the figure of Moira Fitzgibbon appeared. He lifted a white hand

and let the dismay suck and plunge in his throat. Bloody woman!

"Moira." O'Rourke mouthed her name without sounding it and smiled thinly as she came through the room. Stephen Griffin sat in a chair towards the back, and Moira Fitzgibbon walked away from him, minding the loosened heel in her left shoe and taking the nods and greetings of the audience, who, she realized with a flood of warmth and thanksgiving, were the people of Miltown Malbay, dressed in their best and looking at her like a friend. When she reached the podium at the front of the room, Councillor O'Rourke stepped aside slightly and hovered. Moira turned to the musicians. "I'm so sorry," she said, "there was a man crashed off the road." She motioned towards Stephen with her head; it was the smallest movement, but the musicians looked down into the audience all the same. They were already feeling the extraordinary electricity of that room, the heated expectancy that fanned upwards towards them. It was as if they were bringing music for the first time to a country long deaf and only recently healed, as if the notes they were about to play were the ancient medicine of youth and happiness. The Italians sensed it in the air like the presence of white birds; Paolo

Mistra fingered his cello and felt the sweat running across his left wrist and down inside the cuff of his white shirt; Piero Matte moved his neck to the right before placing his violin and found the cords of his muscles were tightened like a boxer's. Gabriella Castoldi looked down; she too was astonished, the simplicity of these people sitting there, the generosity of spirit, a man who crashed off the road and still came to hear the music? Tonight, if ever, please, God, she thought, may I do the music justice.

15

Life is not simple, nor love inevitable. Stephen sat with his hands on his knees and his head stooped over. The black thinning mop of his hair fell forward, and when he looked down he saw the thick mud on his shoes from when he had stepped out into the ditch. He moved them back beneath the seat as if they were evidence against him, obscure proof that he was a misfit. It was a common feeling for him. He didn't quite fit and, knowing this, took it with an embarrassed acceptance, as if it were an unsuitable birthday gift that could not be returned. So he sat there waiting for the concert and kept his head low between his shoulders.

Then the music began.

It began with pace and rhythm. It swept into the air like a bird with four wings, as the four musicians bowed their strings and released the notes that had been gathering within them all evening. The music flew through the room and filled it with a kind of sweet breathing that rose and fell in the breasts of the audience. They were mesmerized at once. The musicians played beyond themselves, and within instants of beginning they knew it was a concert they were to remember years later. They dared brief glances at each other; Paolo Mistra looked up from the cello into the face of Gabriella Castoldi and saw the light gleaming from it. They were playing Scarlatti's Quartet in C minor, and by the time they had reached the allegro the warm air of the long room seemed to be dancing in white shapes above them. The room grew warmer each minute. (Kiaran Breen startled himself by standing up in the middle of the audience to look towards the window and see if it was not in fact morning and the sun was coming up.) In the middle of the third piece the audience started taking off their coats. Briefly they jostled in their seats and then lay the coats across their laps, so that from the front of the room their bright blouses and blue and white shirts looked like spring in Italy. The music transported them. Every man and woman was already in some Italy of the mind, and the storm of the November night blew outside with all the fruitlessness and ineffect of a government warning. When they had finished playing the Vivaldi, the people swept to their feet and let their coats fall to the floor. They applauded loudly and with such frantic joy that Piero Motte felt tears spring up in his eyes. With the applause ringing in the high chandeliers above them, the musicians looked at each other in bewilderment. The room was balmy with delight. And when the people sat again for the slow and romantic melancholy of the Puccini, they were pillowed on a deep and heartfelt gladness. Eamon Waters took the plump and warm fingers of his Eileen's right hand and held them in his lap. Smelling the deepening scent of her perfume rising in the heat of the room, Jack Nolan at fifty-seven kissed Margaret Mungovan on the side of her neck and only barely kept himself from telling her he was ready to marry again. (It did not matter, for she knew it already, and when the music began once more, she allowed her head to lean against his shoulder and let him know in the silent language of perfume that she wanted his arms around her.)

In the back row, Stephen Griffin held his face in his hands and stared at the woman playing the violin. He, too, had been taken from himself by the music; the music offered an invisible opening to another place, and through it, like a secret river, flowed the

frustrations, sorrows, and ceaseless longings of everyone there. For each of them, it
became the music of themselves.

By the time the Puccini was being played,
Stephen found himself looking at no one
but the slender figure of Gabriella Castoldi.
Even when she was playing the quick fluttered notes of the Vivaldi allegro her expression remained one of frowning intensity.
The bow flew back and forth across the
strings like a sweet yet almost unendurable
torture. Stephen looked at the woman
whose name he did not yet know and his
heart raced. The air in the room wavered
with warmth. Men and women closed their
eyes and, in the minor pause between notes,
swallowed hard the emotions that rose
within them.

Then, suddenly, it was over.

The last note was played and the music
stopped. There was a pause, a long beat in
which that Venice of the mind lingered in
the hot humid room of the Old Ground
Hotel. There was a held moment of
nothing, of silence, as if no one who sat
there wished to embark on the home
journey, to emerge once more in the November rain. Nobody moved. (Later, Piero
Motte would swear that when he looked
down at them, every single man and woman

had wet faces and suntans. He would tell his aged father in the *pasticceria* in Burano that in the old music they had revealed a new invention that night, a kind of heart travel, he would say, that took them all, *tutti,* to the place of Vivaldi — which is not Venice but Vivaldi himself. They did not applaud, he would tell his father. They could not.)

And how long passed before the first hands clapped could not be measured in time. It was a slow awakening, full of reluctance and dawning amazement, like sleepers rising from the most sensuous dream. Men raised their hands to clap and felt the dampness under their armpits and across the shirts on their backs. They stood and noticed they were in their stockings, and had slipped off their shoes earlier, in the mistaken certainty that they were sitting by the waterside. The women clapped their hands beneath their chins and felt their own air fanning them back from dizziness. Councillor O'Rourke, who had slipped out at the beginning of the concert to attend to mobile-phone calls, now stepped back in the door on the wave of applause. He smiled, raised his head to show his throat, and held up his hands to applaud so that Moira Fitzgibbon could see him clearly.

The possibility of an encore vanished in

the wave of people spilling forward towards the small stage. Stephen did not move; he stood applauding and lost sight of the musicians as the crowd swelled about them. He angled his head to see the woman better, but she had stepped off the podium and was lost to him amidst the jostle of the Miltown Malbay people. His mouth was dry, his eyes burned. In his chest his lungs seemed to have collapsed. He could not breathe. He felt as if he had been struck in the throat. There was a moment when he thought he would fall down; then he looked up and blinked at the chandeliers and was able to move quickly from the room.

Once he made the doorway, he could move faster, and took the red carpeted stairs three at a time, hurrying down into the lobby like a man escaping a fire.

The cool dark dampness of the evening after rain was like a blanket thrown over him. Now he could breathe. He walked out of the grounds of the hotel and past the pulling-away cars and the dazzling lights of the homeward bound. But he did not want to go home, he wanted to walk, to keep moving until he could travel all the way back into the feeling of the concert. He walked around the shut shops of Ennis and heard the music of Venice in his mind. Stephen

Griffin walked, mute, beneath the moonless sky. It was two o'clock in the morning and he was six miles out on the Inagh road. He had been walking for four hours and not once lost sight of the face of Gabriella Castoldi.

16

Stephen did not go home that night. He walked as far as his car and sat inside it, certain at first that the sensation he felt when he got in was that of sinking. Rain had softened the world; the scar where the car had ploughed into the ground was opened like wet lips. Stephen closed his eyes and expected slow decline into the sucking soft mouth of the bog. Soundlessly, the lemon car eased to the right; he felt the gradual collapse and tender sighing like fire sizzling into water. Then it stopped and the car sat there.

It was still sitting there at eight o'clock the following morning, when Patrick Mulvihill passed in his tractor, supposing it to be the abandoned remains of some young lad's drunken evening, until he saw the figure of the teacher sitting behind the steering wheel.

It took Mulvihill six minutes to tow the car from the bog. It was Stephen's second rescue.

"There is no such thing as stillness," he said to Mulvihill, when the car had been pulled onto the road and the farmer had come back to unhitch the rope. He was a short man in a thick coat, his grey face was a balled newspaper. His facial expressions were so crumpled it was impossible to separate them more than: Wrinkled, or Very Wrinkled. He gave Stephen Very Wrinkled, and amidst the lost, closed-in folds of his red face his green eyes glinted.

"She's all right," he said, smacking the bonnet of the yellow car and ignoring the driver. "You took her too fast round that bend on the greasy road. Made terrible rain last night."

"I've been sitting here all night wondering what to do," Stephen said.

"The rain's gone, but the road's still greasy."

"How do you know what to do? God, I don't. I didn't think that . . . I never expected. It's not what you . . . well, maybe for some. But I'm not that kind of man. I just . . ."

"You don't notice it in a tractor, with the heaviness."

"I want to see her again," Stephen said.

"But in a light car like that. She could slide right off easy enough."

112

"I have to. I have to see her again."

Mulvihill paused; he made crinkled lips and raised his face to where the light was breaking on the far side of Ennis.

"That's exactly right," he said, and reached down to untie the tow rope. "That's exactly right," he repeated, and then walked back to his tractor.

"Goodbye now," Mulvihill said over his shoulder, climbing into the cab and throwing in the rope beside him, puttering off down the road towards the dawn, disproving once again his brother's belief that he needed a hearing aid, proud of his conversational skills, and certain that the younger man had no idea he was deaf as a stone.

17

Stephen's life had already begun to change. It was too soon yet for him to know outright, he was a cautious man and too long accustomed to his own unremarkable history to suppose his life could catch fire. He did not yet sense that the fluctuation in his heart rate, the fuzziness of his hearing, and the sweetness of tart apples were the early signs of love. He was disturbed, he was upset; he admitted that much, and knew too that it was because of the woman with the violin. But just as one day he had accepted that no sleep was deep enough or dream powerful enough to bridge him to the next world and meet the lost half of his family, so too Stephen Griffin had long accepted that he was to be alone. Imagining love is real makes life hard, and so he had instead moved it beyond the history of his future, leaving it rolled up and put away like a scroll of fairy tales in the farthest corner of his heart. Now, on the morning after the concert, it was not love he was thinking of. He was not thinking he had to see Gabriella Castoldi again so that she might see his face or speak to him, find an attraction in the timidity and melancholy of his character, that she might fall in love with him; it never entered his mind. Instead, he thought that the desire that was running along the arteries of his arms, that was tingling in his fingers and making them beat softly on the top of the steering wheel, was only the desire to hear her play the music again.

He drove into Ennis. The shops were not yet open, and the narrow streets had a desolate air of aftermath. The chip-bag and beer-can litter of tawdry romance was strewn along the gutters of wet footpaths. Dogs roamed and sniffed the dead butts of love talk and other promises and pissed the walls and moved on.

Stephen parked the car by the River Fergus, hurried across Parnell Street and down through the empty market to the Old Ground Hotel. The wet air woke his face and gave him a polished rawness like a fruit thinly skinned. He walked in the front door and past the reception, bounding up the stairs, as if some mission was balanced on the point of failure and his smallest of worlds could only be saved by arriving on the first floor.

The doors to the concert room were closed, and when he held on to the cold metal of the handle, he was astonished by the heat of himself. He stepped into the room; it had not yet been tidied, and the chairs, pushed back in lines slightly askew, spoke more of the leaving than of the concert. Stephen moved to his own seat and sat down. He put his hands under his chin and stared up at the empty space where the Italians had played. He closed his eyes and sought the image and the sound of them; he sat there in the low susurrus of the muffled morning traffic, the distant clink of china and cutlery downstairs, the squeak in the chambermaid's trolley moving down the hall, the tramping of the hundred schoolchildren and the shopkeepers and their customers, the steady unstoppable noise of the small town with lorries and vans and buses and cars, and in that galaxy of sounds he listened for the music of yesterday.

What it was about the music he couldn't say. He didn't know the simplest of all mathematics, that the potency of the relation was in direct proportion to the needs of his own heart, that man plus woman equals both nothing and everything, that the factors of love are hope and chance, and that the million variables between two people depend more on the second than on the first.

He sat in the room, but was unable to re-engage the spirit of the evening. He tried to hum himself into it, and was sitting there humming, a tall man who had not slept all night, his hands clutching his knees, his shoes muddy, the bottom of his trouser legs dark with water stains, and his eyes closed, when Margaret Meade stopped hoovering the top stair of the red carpet and looked in the door. She was forty-seven years of age, had fallen in love twenty-two times, four-teen with men she had never spoken to, and recognized at once the signs of a serious fall.

"Hello, love," she said.

Messages are everywhere, if only we can read them. Margaret was a woman who knew the whole history of hope in love; she knew the front and back pages of each volume in the library of lovesickness. She knew the music Stephen hummed was more than music and that the rocking in the chair was his way of tunnelling back into the mo-ment when he had seen the woman; it was his way of being close to her. She knew how the heart fooled itself, how the forced muting of the loudest emotions travelled through the body itself and found expres-sion in pimples, bumps, lumps, diarrhoea, cramps, vomiting, sweats hot and cold, dry mouth, toothache, rashes of every kind, itchiness, general flakiness, and fourteen varieties of trapped wind. (Once, she had loved a married plumber from Tulla so intensely that, knowing she could not tell him outright, her stomach swelled to nine-month pregnancy, and to carry the hugeness of her attraction she had to wear maternity clothes for two months; notwithstanding, she continued dismantling the central heating pipes by night so that he would return daily and she could watch the place she loved on his backside where the low sling of his jeans didn't meet his shirt. And all for love.) Margaret Meade could have told Stephen so much, but he was not yet ready to listen, and the message and the moment passed. She stood inside the door and watched him rocking and humming in the chair. There was a kind of beauty in it, the hopeless and desperate figure he cut at half past nine on a Friday morning; she was moved by it and glad she had worn the darker stockings that made her legs look younger than her face. She drew herself up ever so slightly and touched her hair before calling to him again.

"Love?" she said, and then smiled.

Stephen jumped up from the chair. He licked at the awful dryness of his lips, then quickly took from his left-hand pocket his ticket to the concert.

"There it is," he said, looking at the ticket like some rarity he had mislaid, and keeping his eyes firmly on it as he paced across the concert room and out the door past Margaret Meade.

She watched him go. "Oh, love," she said softly, and then picked up the hose of the hoover and dragged it into the room, whose dust she knew was richer now for the feelings that lingered there.

Stephen left the hotel no better than when he had arrived. He walked down the curve of O'Connell Street still holding on to the ticket. He loped along as if he was going somewhere. He was thirty yards up the street when he noticed Nolan's music shop, and he went inside and bought the only Vivaldi disc there, a cheap version of *The Four Seasons*.

Then he had something. He had something tangible of the evening and felt an easement of the pressure of desire, knowing that once the music was playing, once he could sit and listen to it, Gabriella Castoldi would be with him again.

But she was already. She was there waiting when he arrived at the small house by the sea. She was there in the roundabout road

119

he took, avoiding Miltown Malbay and the school and coming in secret to his own house; she was there in the very fact of him feeling that he should take the phone off the hook and not answer the door; she was there in the trembling of his hands as he put on the disc and pressed Play, as he sat in the seat that looked westward into the sighing sea and heard the first notes with the volume turned up loud enough to make the music system tremble. She was there. She was not playing the music, but was the music. And Stephen Griffin set it to Repeat even before "Summer" was midway through, even as the downrush of the strings made wildflower meadows of the air and the life of every leaf and blossom gathered, pulsed, exploded with free riotous expression, until the room itself was mid-season July and the fullness of the music scented everything and made beat the dry and dust-filled corners of the world in which he had been living. He had never heard music quite as he heard it then. He did not know the sharpness of his own senses or the tenderness that poured through his ears. He watched the sea and listened to Vivaldi, moving his head backward and forward to the rhythms of the strings, until at last, in the ninth "Spring," his eyes were closed and he was standing up, his whole body conducting the energy and passion of the music into the deep places of his heart, where only now he was beginning to admit that he had fallen in love. He was too afraid to think it. He was too certain that the moment the walls about him were breached he would not be able to bear the incipient grief and loss he associated with love. He was certain, too, she could not love him. But the music played on, insistently beating on the vulnerable hidden-away part of the soul that longs for the sweetness of another person like the sweetness of God. He wanted to see her; God, he wanted to see her again, and with the despair of that unfilled desire and *The Four Seasons* like a wild clock advancing Time so swiftly that years of the heart passed, he brought his hands to his forehead, cried out, and sank into the armchair by the window.

18

When Moira Fitzgibbon arrived outside the
house, she heard the music playing and knew
that she was right to have come. Once, she
would have surrendered to the protocol of re-
spectability and would not have called on a
single man; but with each new day she
emerged more as herself and felt a growing
confidence in the intelligence of her heart.
She had been right about the concert, the
people had come, and that morning there
was radiance and astonishment on the streets
of Miltown Malbay. Word of the concert had
arrived almost ahead of its audience, and by
the time the lights had come back on with the
return of the first car, the town already knew.
Those who had not gone to the concert accepted the news of its success with silent
dismay; but during the night they washed
their consciences in a deep salty sleep as
sudden showers blew in off the sea and swept
through the damp bedrooms like a scouring
God. The wind ran through the town and

gathered all spite and bitterness, so that in the morning all awoke full of unanimous praise for Moira Fitzgibbon. The begrudgers had disappeared, transformed into the good citizens of earnest support who made it their business to mention in Hynes's, Galvin's, and other shops that they had so enjoyed the music. Moira had been right. She brought the profits from the concert to the bank to lodge them in Moses Mooney's account and there met Eileen Waters. When the principal congratulated her, Moira felt a surge of weakness and water in her eyes, but shook her own sentimentality free with the knowledge that a day earlier the same woman would have crossed the road rather than meet her.

"Well, when you believe in something," Moira said.

"Yes. Oh, that's right," said Eileen Waters. "Absolutely right."

"You don't like to just give up on it." Moira let the phrase linger a moment and, there in the bank, collected another of the small victories that were becoming common for her. Was it her imagination that made the November street seem brighter, livelier, that morning? was there dazzlement falling? was there an all but imperceptible lift in the air that made men seem to move more lightly from their tractors or salute across the erratic hotchpotch of parked cars in Bank Place with a broader sweep of their arms? Were the twin babies of the Kellys ever laughing like that before? Moira wondered, sauntering along the footpath. Was it always like this, and she had failed to notice? As if enlightenment was a condition of Miltown Malbay that noontime, harmony seemed everywhere. People had their best day. They were illumined with an inexplicable sense of things being right in the world. Their own ordinariness seemed majestic, and in all the coming and going of their everyday shopping and conversation, from the market to the post office, from Galvin's to Hynes's, they were like the townspeople in paintings of towns and villages of long ago, when time was slower and everything more innocent.

And it was the concert. Somehow it was, Moira Fitzgibbon told the dashboard of her car, and drove to Stephen Griffin's house, where she had seen the yellow car earlier and knew that he could not be working.

She heard Vivaldi playing when she opened her car door and stood, allowing her heart to understand the situation before moving up to knock. She knocked four times to no answer and looked up at the clear sky without discouragement, as if it were the next white page of the story only just coming to her; then she walked around the back and let herself in.

"Autumn" was playing, that slow collapse of notes that made the air itself seem to fall as Moira stepped inside the back kitchen. Once she arrived in it she knew she had trespassed some intimacy, that the simplest sights and smells of the domestic disorder were private revelations, and that the stack of unwashed dishes in the sink, the opened cartons of sour milk left by the windowsill, the grey smudge that was an ancient sponge, the dusty cobwebs like netting across the corner of the ceiling, these were each as vulnerable and naked expressions of the heart as rough, raw, first-draft poems. She knew more about Stephen Griffin with each step, and held herself briefly in the kitchen until the myriad impressions had flown into the farthest corner of her mind. Then she called his name.

"Mr. Griffin? Oh, Mr. Griffin?"

He did not answer, and Moira walked slowly from the kitchen to the door of the sitting room. Everything about that minor journey — the condition of the carpet, the faded greyish quality of the wallpaper, cool as old skin when she touched it, and the swell of melancholy in that movement of the music that was tangible in its pain and dying

— made her afraid. When she put her hand on the door and moved it ever so slowly open, she was inseparable from her own visions of television women detectives arriving on the scene of murder.

She eased open the door and put her head around it first. Then she saw him: Stephen Griffin, poleaxed, lying back in the armchair with his head turned to one side. His right hand conducted in a slow waving. His eyes were closed; he did not sense her beside him, and even when she said his name again with some alarm, nothing happened. Then Moira pulled out the plug of the music system.

"Mr. Griffin?"

Stephen opened his eyes. He did not want to.

"Mr. Griffin, are you all right?" She was standing over him. She did not ask him if he was injured or ill or if he wanted to get up; she did not suppose that he had been drinking, nor that a sudden seizure had knocked him back into the chair. Moira Fitzgibbon was more intelligent than that. The knowledge had gathered in her before she had to think of it.

"I said I'd call in because of tonight," she said. "I have a complimentary ticket for the concert in Galway."

19

Stephen took the ticket. Of course he did. He took the ticket as if it were a hand reaching down to him and drove the yellow car to Galway that night to hear Gabriella Castoldi play Vivaldi in the Town Hall. By the time he had arrived in his seat, his inner organs had each contracted into tight balls of anticipation and he carried them like a bag of stones inside the tight sweated cotton of his shirt. But when the musicians came onto the stage and Gabriella lifted her bow to the first note, the stones dissolved and everything was forgotten. He could breathe. There was a scent of lilies in the air, and as the concert continued, this time he did not take his eyes from the slender woman with the sorrowful face. He looked at her throughout. There was something about her face, he thought, something there in the places beneath her eyes, in the washed and drawn pallor of her skin, the smallness of her mouth, which was turned so minutely downward, the furrow in her brow as she frowned over the instrument and gazed down along the strings as if looking for evidence of the impossible. She is as fragile as the violin, he thought, and thought of the mesmerism of her sadness and how it merged into the notes. He loved how she played and loved the sorrow, too, seeing some part of himself reflected in her, the way lovers do.

Since Stephen Griffin had abandoned the idea of romantic love, he was not even aware of it emerging like translucence on his face, sweetening his tongue, and giving him the strange radiance of saints. He was not aware that Paolo Mistra and Maria Motte, across their cello and violin, could notice it, or that Gabriella herself recognized him as the man who had crashed his car and was now placed like a yellow light in the fourth row. Stephen did not think of these things. He was aware only of wanting the concert to continue indefinitely, of feeling the uneasy combination of peace and longing battling in the lower regions of his stomach.

When the interval arrived he realized his clothes were wet, but not that the man and woman sitting next to him had been soaked also, nor that the scent of lilies was emanating not from the stage or the perfumed ladies of Galway town but from between the fingers of his two clasped hands. He wondered if he should get up, if a walk around the foyer might dry him off, but when he moved his feet forward and saw the extent of the stains behind the knees of his trousers, he sat still while everyone else moved. He was so intensely in his own world that the ceiling might have fallen on him and white angels descended and he would not have moved but waited for the concert to resume.

The second half passed dreamlike as the first. When it ended the audience stood to applaud, and fanned the scent stageward. Standing quickly Stephen felt his head become a stone; its weight nearly toppled him, he lost the balance of himself as though the world he stood in was suddenly tilted now. He looked down, he opened his mouth to suck in the air, he reached for the back of the seat in front of him and then raised his head to look at her before she left. And for the briefest moment, a semiquaver, the slightest note in the music of what happens, he saw Gabriella Castoldi see him standing there.

Then she looked away.

20

And nothing more.

No words, no greeting, no meeting after the concert. A shambles of desire collapsing steadily in upon itself.

And some form of all this Philip Griffin read in his son's position on the chessboard that long night while Stephen slept with the queen in his fingers.

"God, Anne," he said, "it's worse than I thought." He lowered his head, and his bald pate caught the streetlight and flashed like an orange moon falling to rest on Stephen's arm. The size of his son compared with him made Philip's desire to cradle him in his arms first awkward and then impossible. He could not even reach around the girth of him in the armchair, and comforted himself with the small gesture of taking Stephen's free hand. The other one was still holding the chess piece, and the father knew enough not to disturb it, for it might easily be the branch his son clung to, keeping him from drowning altogether in the other world of dreams. He knelt there on the carpet and took his son's hand. Pools of a clear black sadness kept filling inside him, for he imagined it was hopeless, because everything about Stephen was, and that hopelessness was Philip's own. He could not look at his son without feeling that the difficulties his son faced in the world were the failings of himself, that every pain and hardship Stephen endured were caused by some lacking in Philip, and that the true measure of the progress of manhood is the ruthless exposure to all fathers of the indefensible vulnerability of their children.

He could see the future the way one sees accidents half-moments before they happen. He could see his son's heart breaking, and wanted to cry out against it. But he did not. Instead, he knelt and kept his head down against Stephen's hand, feeling the heat of desire still burning away in the skin, the raging inside him as he alternated between struggle and surrender, rolling his head, moaning, humming fragments of music and waving the chess queen like a slow-motion baton to the orchestra of dreams.

"What'll I do, Anne?" Philip whispered, for she was standing not far away from him.

"What'll I do?"

He did not raise his head to look at his wife; he did not need to. She was more vivid than seeing could make her, and her advice was more audible for being silent.

It was not yet dawn. But the slow high hum of the milk van outside signalled the beginning of morning. Once, the clinking of bottles being delivered had woken Philip Griffin by Anne Nolan's side, and daily he had kissed her the kiss of good morning while she slept on and he sat and slowly stood to look out the upstairs window at Tom Boylan and his son slipping in and out of the gardens with empties and refills. It was not the kiss of the passionate or raptured, it declared no intent further than the ordinariness of loving her, and most often she did not respond to it in her sleep. It had become to Philip Griffin the milk-bottle kiss, the beginning of a new day, a motion reflex of his heart so natural that years later, when the milk bottles had been replaced by clinkless cartons and Boylan's son only sometimes took his father on the rounds, Philip Griffin still kissed his wife with the delivery of the morning.

He heard the footsteps in the leaves beneath the chestnut tree in the garden and thought, young Boylan slips over the wall of

MacMahon's next door. He can do eight houses that way while the father gets to drive the float at walking pace past the sleeping houses. The footsteps moved quickly up across the grass, and the single carton was left by the door, then the figure of Eddie Boylan moved across the opened blinds towards Lynch's. Only when he had gone, and with him the fleeting memory of the morning kiss, did Philip Griffin try to stand up, only to find that his knees had locked.

"Shaggit."

He couldn't move. He pressed down on the armrest beside Stephen, but wasn't strong enough to raise himself; he was trying for the third time, cursing his knees and the absurdity of age, when the queen fell from his son's fingers and Stephen woke up. It was a moment before the startling reality of Stephen's dreams disappeared and he saw the old man kneeling beside him.

"I was getting something. You dropped it," said the father. "Shaggit, I can't get up. Feckin knees."

There was a pause, Stephen didn't move. He rubbed his eyes, he felt the dryness of his lips and saw the chessboard in the half-light by his father's head. Then, as Philip Griffin raised the queen in his left hand as an explanation, Stephen supposed he had only closed his eyes for a millisecond, that the chess game was still continuing, and that the extraordinary journeys on the hump-backed hills of his dreams where he had been looking for his voice had been an illusion so condensed that in fact no time had passed. He stood up and bent down. Philip Griffin clasped onto him. His son's hand was damp with ardour, and as Philip was pulled to his feet, his heart sank further with the certainty that he was to live to oversee more failure and grief.

"God Almighty," he said, when Stephen had straightened him. He still held the queen in his right hand, but once he was standing he handed it to his son like an embarrassment he was glad to be rid of, and then announced he was going outside to get the milk for the breakfast.

While Stephen replaced the queen in the vulnerable position in the centre of the board, Philip opened the front door and stood outside on the step. He looked down at the carton on the mat and reminded himself to remind Boylan to put it on the windowsill instead so he wouldn't have to bend for it. He looked at the deep blue of the sky that was not yet lit with morning and felt the chill of the winter ahead on the small hairs at the back of his neck. He had imagined this would be his last winter, the cancer would finally overtake him, and he would not be sad. Or so he had thought. But now, standing there on the threshold of the house of his life and feeling the thin crisp quality of the air — the polished and brittle stillness of that Dublin morning that he knew would harden daily now until it became the brutal relentlessness of iron — Philip Griffin knew that he must try to live on for Stephen's sake.

"God, Anne," he had whispered when she had told him. He reached his hand to touch the red brick of the house to steady himself. Oh God. He heard her tell him again, more softly this time, as if she did not understand that the very gentleness of her spirit made him want to be with her all the more. She was the most tender woman, and while he stood with her on the doorstep he knew that more suffering was required before he could join her for eternity in heaven. No, he couldn't die and be with her yet. He stood there and looked down at the milk carton; he felt the V of cold where his cardigan exposed his chest, and he measured in a single look the distance between standing and lying down.

The first cars passed along the road towards the city, and the soft whoosh of their passing emphasized the absence of possibilities; once, he could have gotten in his car and driven into Clery's, stitching anger, loss, and mysteries into the hems of trousers and knowing that briefly they were resolved as he fit another man into the world. Now there was no escaping, but as he stood on his doorstep and felt the morning, Philip Griffin told his wife that she was right and that, in the strange physics of love, the weight on his heart would be lighter for carrying Stephen.

He bent and picked up the milk carton. He went into the kitchen and called Stephen in to join him. He boiled the kettle and made tea in the half-dark of the dawn, picking cups from the sink and rinsing them lightly while Stephen stood between dreams and waking, waiting by the table. Then, as the light was coming up across the back garden, both men sat down in their positions like pieces in a chess game, saying nothing, but dwelling in a gentle quietness that was as comfortable as old blankets and gathering themselves for the long game of Love and Death that lay ahead.

II

1

That morning Stephen left at ten o'clock and drove the yellow car from his father's house in Dublin to return to the west once more. He did not tell his father any more than he had already revealed in the chess game, but as he drove out the Templeogue Road, having waved goodbye, he had the strange sensation of having shared secrecies.

The moment his son had left, Philip had hurried upstairs and taken out his green Harris tweed, white shirt, and thick brown trousers. When he put on the trousers, he was pleased to discover that the material did not cling or bunch about the knees but fell cleanly to his feet. The line of the trousers was critical to a man's well-being. How often he had seen customers in Clery's with sagging and baggy trousers, miscut and misshapen, drawn by machines for men that did not exist and worn with a grey pathos, as if declaring how the wearer knew that nothing in the world ever measured up. When the knee pressed the trouser leg the line was lost, a man walked as if he were pushing a wheelbarrow, and shortly life provided him one. If the seat was tight, so too was the life, and soon no button or zip would restrain the pressure. It was a simple philosophy, the metaphysics of tailoring, and Philip Griffin applied to his own clothes everything that thirty years in Clery's had taught him about humanity. In his bedroom was a full-length mirror, not for the pleasure of his vanity, but because it was only when he was looking at himself in his clothes that he could appreciate the condition of his own health. So when he saw the line of the trousers in the mirror he was relieved; he was still the same distance from the ground as a year previously. None of the raised hemming that was the first sign of certain death was needed, and he began to think that the intrusion of the cancer might not be as far progressed as he had imagined. Then he put on the white shirt. It was cotton. Cotton is a cloth full of forgiveness, and even as Philip buttoned it over the small upturned bowl of his stomach he could feel the innocence in the material. When he had it closed under his chin he was in the morning of his own First Communion and was his father's hands doing the buttons under his seven-year-old chin. It smelled clean as grace; the buttons were just so, neither slipping back through the holes like those of inveterate gamblers nor resisting going through, like the shirts of bridegrooms. He ran his hands down the sides of his torso and delighted briefly in the smooth and simple elegance of a white shirt. Then he chose a tie; only three in a hundred men knew how to knot a tie. He had proven the figure once with young Dempsey, counting the inept nooses that choked the greater portion of their customers and suggesting it was among the critical wisdoms a father could pass to his son: how to knot a tie. He passed his hand across his face doing his, as if it were a blessing, and then took his jacket from the wardrobe. A tweed; you have to be a certain age to wear tweed, to have the woven strands of your own life reflected in the griefs, hardships, and pleasures of the cloth, and not lost within them like an overcoat. The green Harris was a jacket Philip Griffin had worn for fifteen years; the moment he put his arm through the sleeve he could feel its cool lining like a second skin. The comfort he felt in the jacket was a testimony to his own life, the weight of it, the roughness of the cloth that had diminished now to a rubbed softness; he wore it like evidence of himself, and once

141

he had put it on looked in the mirror to see if he still looked the same.

He did.

"The cancer hasn't shrunk you yet," he told himself.

He took the keys to his car and went downstairs. The urgency of what he must do struck him once more as he confirmed the direness of Stephen's heart by a glance at the chessboard in the sitting room. In the daylight it was more alarming than ever, and a moment later he was driving quickly into the city in the car that held like a stubborn memory the scent of white lilies. He drove as quickly as he could in the impossible knot of the morning traffic. The sky was pasty and mottled, holding away the light above the gathered clouds like a resentment, and preparing the lunchtime rain. Dublin barely moved in the early morning; rather, from the ringed estates of new houses that had taken away the mountains, cars hurtled a quarter of a mile and then slowed abruptly into the swollen and choked arteries of the city, where they inched like thick oil towards the heart. Philip Griffin drove a half metre behind the backside of a bus. He had not been in traffic since he had retired and felt with a small fall of his heart how the city had grown without him. We are smaller and more insignificant than we ever imagine, he told his wife. But then the scent of the lilies reached him again and he felt only the significance and urgency of his own role in the plot of his son's loving. He rolled down the window and waved his arm at the young driver in the car next to him.

"Emergency!" he cried out, and pulled the car into the outer lane.

It was half an hour later when he arrived in the waiting room of Dr. Tim Magrath. He had no appointment, but told the receptionist he needed to know how long he had to live and would wait to find out. He opened the button of his jacket and sat down. He took his fresh handkerchief and dabbed the top of his head. His head was damp and his lips were dry, but otherwise he showed no signs of a fatal illness, and for a moment considered the remote possibility that in fact he was not carrying a cancer after all. From the morning he had diagnosed himself he had never sought any medical confirmation; he had been more certain of his condition than any test could prove. The cancer was his companion, and on wet mornings in early summer he could sometimes feel it invade a new region of his bowel, moving like a dark liquid or a shadow in the undetected privacies of his organs. He read its evidence in a dozen different ways: in the slowness of his movements when he sat on the toilet, in the taste of chewed chalk that prevailed on his palate when he ate beef, in the interminable bouts of his gas, the sudden exhaustion in mid-afternoon, and the pain that was like passing marbles when he urinated. And of very many, these were only a few. Until the moment he sat in the doctor's waiting room he had not considered for one minute that he could be wrong. But now, briefly, within the inviolable comfort of the Harris tweed, and desperate for a stay of death to help his son, Philip wished heartily that he was. Or at least he wished that death was not so close, that the latest rumblings and squelchings he heard below his stomach in the early morning were not the telltale signs of the further progress of the disease. If I can live for another while, he thought. If I can live long enough to see Stephen through the far side of this. He swallowed the sadness that rose in his throat at the thought of his son, but it kept coming, and he had to tilt his head back and pretend to admire the ceiling.

An hour passed. Philip studied the backs of his hands, where he knew all manner of signs were made visible, and that the freckles and sunspots of early vitality became there the bumps and splotches, scaliness, discoloration, and moles in which every organ speaks. The more time passed, the more ill he felt himself becoming. It was too warm in the bright room; there was a cramping sensation in his left thigh, the toes of his right foot were going numb. He was breathing shallowly. He asked for a glass of water, but was even more alarmed when he drank it and realized it tasted of bitter lemons.

When the last patient had left the waiting room, Philip Griffin stood up, felt his heart racing, and quietly began to say the Our Father. It was not something he was accustomed to doing, and he began it slowly and carefully, feeling with each phrase the discernible slowing of his heart rate and the evanescence of his panic. Our Father who art in Heaven, hallowed be Thy name, Thy kingdom come, Thy will be done, on earth as . . .

"Philip."

Tim Magrath was standing in the doorway.

The doctor looked like his own grandfather. Since his wife had died he had suffered what was once called nerves, and was in fact the collapse of his soul. The subsequent vacuum in his chest had reduced his shirt size by four inches, and his head of hair seemed dusted with the white talcum makeup of a theatrical ghost. His eyes floated in sunken bags of skin and were caught in fine nets of blood vessels that looked on the point of bursting. Tim Magrath held his hands while he stood. There was no discernible line to his lips, as if he had sucked them in and mutely gnawed on his grief until only the thin gap remained. When he spoke, his voice was a whispery remnant of a voice.

"Philip, how are you? Please come in."

Although the man had changed, the room had not. Philip sat in the same seat as before, looked across at the bare trees of the square, and then made an announcement.

"I'm not a man who believes in medicine," he said.

Tim Magrath sat down. He held his hands still and made the slightest quivering in the muscles of his mouth.

"I'm not here for miracles, Doctor," Philip Griffin added.

"Tim." It was less than a whisper.

"I'm not here for miracles, Tim. I've cancer. I've had it for years. It's moving into the final stages now and I want to know how much longer I have." He paused and looked across at the doctor, who had slid like a shadow into a seat by the wall. "It's not fear," he said, "it's not that I want to cancel it out, it's just a question of how long, do you get me? I need a delay in it. That's all."

"I'm sorry. I didn't know. How long have you been . . ." The whisper died, the lipless mouth dried the words into an ashen silence, and Tim Magrath raised the fingers of his right hand to see if he could find them.

"I was never checked. I know it myself. It's here." He patted his stomach and below. "And here. Spreading. A pain in the morning like I've swallowed knives. There's an aching round the back, and this, see." He stuck out the wedge of his tongue. "That's not right, is it?" He had closed his mouth again before the doctor had even risen to look.

Tim Magrath did not know what to say; he himself looked more like death than the majority of his patients. He could outnumber the ailments of any of them and had already moved into that company of men whose gatherings in the clubhouse were dominated by discourse of disease and the dropped dead. He had weekly funerals to go to, and eyed the mourners with the small comfort of knowing that at least some of them would be at his. Now he lowered the grey head of his hair and looked at the fine carpet on the floor. He felt the disconsolate, irredeemable sense of dread in his soul, the feeling he had experienced daily since the death of his wife that he was in fact an impostor, that he had dressed himself in a fine suit and sat with patients for thirty-six years in a room where he wrote prescriptions for drugs that merely masked and postponed the true pain of life. That medicine cannot stop illness or death but merely divert it was a truth he had denied daily. To fifty patients a week there was little Tim Magrath could say, and even as his doubts in the efficacy of medicines grew, he was unable to sit by the bedside and say there is no cure for this condition we live in, and instead felt the gratitude and hope of the sick swim over him when he said, Take three of these every morning noon and night.

But Philip Griffin was different: he didn't want curing, he wanted time, and in the moments while Tim Magrath stared at the carpet he gathered in himself the resolve to speak the truth and not offer the bald man the bottle of tablets. When he looked up the patient was looking directly at him.

"It's for my son," Philip said. "He's in love."

2

And so, like medieval knights bound on a ceaseless quest for an obscure and chivalrous honour, for the defence of an unattainable ideal with which they themselves had only the briefest acquaintance but whose threatened extinction provoked in each of them the deepest resolve, for the victory of Love over Death, Tim Magrath and Philip Griffin plotted into the afternoon how they would slow down the cancer. The first thing to find out was the size and age and speed of the enemy. Philip needed tests. The earliest available appointment with Carthy, the specialist, was two and a half months later, February 1.

"By then you could be dead," Tim told him.

"I could," Philip agreed.

They sat on the moment and felt the November light dying behind them. Cars were moving outside with the illusion of progress, but the clock was almost standing still. February seemed several years away, and the fear of the winter ahead crept in their skin like age. The weathers of wind and rain, of chill, frost, and hail, blew in imagination at the backs of the old men's necks as they sat wondering how they would outwit Time. The stilled air was grey between them, and they held their hands between their knees and their heads bowed while the icy weight of the word "winter" lodged on their spirits like a sentence.

Then Tim Magrath spoke.

"Fall down," he said. "Go on, fall down, cry out."

There was a half-second, a moment it took for the complicity to register, and then, as if his seat had suddenly been thickly oiled, Philip Griffin slid down onto the carpet at the doctor's feet. His first cry was smaller than a bird's.

"Louder," the doctor whispered over him. "Scream it out, and keep doing it until you are in a hospital bed."

Philip opened his mouth wide and screamed. He astonished himself with his own sound, and looked into the space in front of him as if he could see the twisted shape of agony. He looked at the doctor standing over him and saw the urgency in the other man's eyes, the need he had to make this medicine work and see the patient carried out of his surgery to hospital; he saw it and he screamed on, raising and lowering the cries as Tim Magrath rushed out to his receptionist and ordered an ambulance, turning on his side and crying out the long cry that drained him like a sewer of the gathered and broken debris of his life, crying for himself, for the miseries and disappointments of his own childhood, the terrible fearfulness of the world that grew inside him, the timidity he had carried until the moment he met Anne Nolan and she blew it from him like a cobweb, the loss, the inestimable loss that was born out of knowing that he had missed so many opportunities to express love while his wife and daughter were alive, the death of loveliness, and the wounded bafflement of his son, for all of it Philip Griffin screamed on the floor, until he was howling out of an emptiness and grief that constituted a pain more real than the pain of cancer.

He cried out and wept until the sorrow exhausted him and he was lying in a hospital bed with a white sheet tucked tightly like a bandage across his chest. He had been given something for pain, he was told, and lay there in the soft pillowy mountains and valleys of his half-consciousness, waiting to be investigated. When he saw the doctor coming, it was as if from a very long distance, and his white coat shone like the illumined raiment of an angel.

3

Stephen drove west with Vivaldi playing in his head and the face of Gabriella Castoldi lingering between him and the windscreen. He saw her more clearly than he saw the road, and only a small miracle brought him round the bend in Kinnegad. He did not know yet the dimensions of his own heart or that love developed like a geometric progression and could increase rapidly in the shortest of time, without seeing or hearing or touching the other person at all. Neither did he consider yet that his life was changed entirely now and that while the turbulence of emotions churned within him he could not return to the ordinary life of teaching. He imagined it was something which would subside. But still he saw her face. All across the country as he drove she was there before him. He saw the angle of her head as she turned to the violin, the sharpness of her elbow where it bent below the fingerboard, the taut contracted muscles of her shoulder when she bowed the sharp fierce notes of "Winter." Crossing Westmeath he touched that shoulder with his mind and was surprised only that it did not stop the music in his head.

And all the time the progression was tumbling on, doubling, trebling in intensity within him as the car moved westward.

The west was a vast and soft wetness as he entered it. It was midday. The towns he drove through arose on the road after miles of greenery, their small clusters of Mass-goers hastening along with newspapers over their heads against the drizzle, or standing in against the shop window and watching the strange car pass. There was a soft grey complacency everywhere, as if the people were resolute in being undisturbed and guarded a kind of holy faith in mute sufferance and the continuing ordinariness of their lives. They were towns scheduled for by-pass.

Stephen drove in a semi-trance. He did not turn on the radio but listened instead to the concert that was now inside him. He tried to think of history, of Italy in the time of Vivaldi, of the city-state of Venice and the boats in the lagoon, the long and troubled fable of the Doge, and the fragments he knew of Venetian wars, conspiracies, and betrayal. If he could think of the history, if he could turn the pages of time and find in himself the dust of the past, he could make it home; if he could refind the dry and ash-laden language of the dead, he could refind himself and escape the sweating in his palms on the steering wheel, the throbbing in the left side of his temple, and the ceaseless drying of his lips. He wet them a thousand times between Ballinasloe and Loughrea, and for all the dampness of the grey air outside, the wet face of the day that kept sticking to the windscreen and would not be wiped away, his lips dried in an instant and then stung as if kissed by nettles. He tried desperately to think of the history of Venice. What did he know of it? He shut tight his eyes to concentrate, and opened them to swerve the car back onto the road. Venice, Venice. He couldn't remember. He slowed the car to thirty and held the wheel with his left hand, licking his lips and fingering with his right hand a place above his right eye, as if looking for the switch that would return the past and free him from thinking of the woman. He was two miles outside Loughrea. The mist was thickening into rain, and the car slowed until it was barely quicker than walking pace. The rain fell in a hush. Stephen let out a small cry and the car stopped altogether in the middle of the road.

There was a tremendous green quietness. When he rolled down the window he could hear the rain falling in the old grass of November. No bird was singing. He opened the window for air, but found none. Then he opened the driver's door, lowering his head as if to vomit and seeing in the rainwater pattern of the tarred road the squiggled shape of his own journey to understanding. A life cannot go backward forever, and as he raised his head Stephen Griffin knew that he could not escape what had already happened.

"I can't remember, I can't remember the books," he said. He said it without excitement or panic, said it matter-of-factly, as if cataloguing a comical loss that had already happened. He waited and wet his lips again. "What's the name of the history book for fifth years'?"

A pause; then he answered: "I don't know, can't remember. Book for third years'?" he asked, and then began to laugh. He laughed until his shoulders were shaking.

The dimension of his defeat was enormous, as his father might have told him the previous evening studying the chess game. When something of great size moves into the heart, it dislodges all else, in just the same way that the forward movement of the queen reshapes the board. So, with the arrival of Gabriella Castoldi in his heart, Stephen Griffin had lost history, dates, facts and figures that he had built his life around and that now on the wet road to Gort slipped from his mind and vanished in the air. He knew nothing of history now.

It was an hour before he could drive on. Or at least so it seemed, for although no car came or went on the black wet ribbon of the tar, time might have stopped for love. When Stephen drove on into Gort and across into Clare, he carried in the cage of his chest the ease of accepting love, and felt it lightly there like a white bird of promise and hope. It was the most ordinary thing, after all. It was the fulcrum of life, and if the years he had spent studying history had shown him that the world turned not on love but on hatred and greed, then this was the new unwritten history of the marvellous, of which he himself could be the author. The bird fluttered around the car as he drove; he was in love. It was all right. Love exists, he thought, and drove with his head out the window of the car, banishing for the time being the multiple improbabilities of courtship or requital, shaking the lank black strands of his hair in the rain and shouting a single long wavering vocable of hope as he sped on homeward to the sea.

When he arrived, the bird was still flying inside him. He parked the car and walked immediately round the back of the house and down the slope of the black rocks to the small shore. It was late afternoon. The tide was withdrawing towards the failing light on the horizon, and gulls blew up like newspaper over the fields' edge. Stephen walked on the wet rocks, and for the first time in his life did not study his footsteps but moved with the sure inviolability of the lover, briefly certain that the world would not trip him. With the tide out he could walk all the way around the rocky edge and arrive on the long beach of Spanish Point. The sand when he stepped onto it was clean of footprints. The winter tide had erased the past, and Stephen Griffin, walking in a long coat, his face wet with rain and sea spray, was the first and only of a new tribe. He set off down the extravagant beach, where the roaring of the Atlantic was a ceaseless accompaniment and even the soft plashing of his shoes on the shallow pools raised no sound. The sea was majestic in its tumbling and crashing, the size, the energy of it. Stephen imagined he had never seen it before and walked with his head turned sideways, bursting out laughing at the riotous boisterousness as the white surf was combed and ebbed in the froth of fulfillment. Rain ran down his face. He drank the saltiness on his lips and skipped two steps, not quite dancing, but moving in a growing giddiness along the sand beneath the enormous sky.

"I'm in love," he said. But the wind took his voice away.

"I'm in love with that woman," he called out louder, feeling the terrible release of the words like a pain that was part of healing. "I'm in love with her!" he cried again, only then discovering that the emotion was such that it would gather constantly inside him and hurt like an ulcer until he cured it with confessions.

He had reached the far end of the beach when the rain stopped. Evening was drawing swiftly across the sky, and the sea-birds had vanished inland. In half an hour it would be darker than ink; already the line of the rocks was smudged into the sea and sky, and Stephen would have to walk home around by the road. But he did not. He felt the bird flying in his chest and the dazzlement of love making him lighter and brighter than nightfall. For the first time in his life he felt the radiance of a pure and visionary faith. He was bright with enlightenment. It felt like a reckless surge of invincibility. He opened his coat and took it off. Then he pushed off his shoes. Soon he was standing in his underpants in the dark on the beach at Spanish Point, with the wind blowing off the sea cold against his skin. He walked forward into the frozen waves.

4

When the young Dr. Hadja Bannerje sat on the edge of the bed and told Philip Griffin that he had advanced cancer in his left lung and that the disease had spread into his bone marrow, the tailor received the news with no surprise and simply leaned forward to ask how long.

"How long have I to live, Doctor?"

The Indian was unsure Philip had understood.

"It is widespread," he said. "It is growing all the time."

"How long? Tell me."

"We can't tell the time precisely. It is not exact." He paused; the patient was waiting for more. "There is no science, Mr. Griffin, for the passing of a spirit."

"It's for my son," Philip said. "He's in love."

Dr. Bannerje looked at the old man and saw the watery signs of illness in his eyes.

"We'll do more tests," he said. "You can

consider radiation, but in your case . . ."

"Will I have six months?"

"You must have terrible pain. There are many with less than your condition who are dead."

"Will I have six months?"

The young Indian did not answer at once. He was twenty-nine years old and had come to Dublin from Bombay. The second son, he was the one chosen to be the doctor, while his brother had taken over the small family shop. He had a stillness like white linen folded inside him. But when he heard in the man's tone the desperate beseeching for life, Hadja Bannerje felt the grief rumple him like an illness of the stomach and acknowledged in himself the awfulness of reaching this place at the end of medicine. This, he thought, is beyond the last page of all the books I have studied. This is a place further than prescription.

And yet it was familiar to him. His dark eyes turned to the thin curtain about the bed, and for a moment he was not seeing it. He was a twelve-year-old boy seeing his mother when she was dying in the small bed in the back room with the candles lit beside her. His father had moved out into the tiny bedroom of his sons and transformed what had once been the untidy room of his marriage into the ordered and serene place of the dying. The old man had carried lotus and jasmine from the market in his arms and filled bowls, jugs, and vases about the room so that the scent in the air was more heavy and beautiful than sorrow. He had told Hadja death was coming, and the young boy had sat by the bedside waiting for it daily. His mother had lost speech, but lay in the bed weeping and moaning continuously until the medication daily slipped her through the door of oblivion and settled a small peace. When she awoke, two hours before she was allowed the next injection of the morphine, she opened her eyes to see Hadja sitting there and began weeping at once. She could move her hands only in hopeless wavering gestures that fell away from what they reached. Within minutes of her waking, the pain would burn through her again, and she would cry and groan with it. He had thought she was trying to tell him something, and time and again leaned down to moisten her dry and flaked lips and place his ear next to her mouth. But the message never came, she could make no words. Day after day she lingered in that place between living and dying. His father threw out the flowers onto a growing heap in the back yard and brought new ones, sitting through the night in that room where the pain kept coming back and death did not arrive. He held her hand as he would a child's crossing the road, but no crossing happened, only the agony inside her and the cries they could not cure. She endured for five weeks and two days, and in that time Hadja, who had already been nominated a future doctor by his father and his teacher, sat beside her bed and understood in her eyes that the beseeching was not for death but for life. She could not let go despite the pain, and the waves of it that rode her body could not wash away that final resolve to cling. His father had thought there was something she wanted to say to them, and had assembled the two boys, an aunt, and two uncles by her bedside. The heat outside fell on Bombay like hell's blanket, and the little group stood around the dying woman waiting. Hadja's father held a copybook and pencil to note down the slightest sounds that might have been curled-up words. But there was only moaning and the human evidence of anguish. Sweat dripped off them, and the perfume of the flowers made their heads swim. She might be trying to say goodbye to us, his father had said. But Hadja knew it was not that, and when, after elaborate and suggestive goodbyes, the aunt and uncles had gone, he stayed by the bedside and watched his mother's milky eyes flash with the desperate longing for him to help her. She did not want to die, and threw her head backward and forward on the feather pillow, crying out in terror when she saw the spirits in the room waiting to take her.

Dr. Hadja Bannerje remembered his mother in the thin white curtain about the hospital bed, and then turned to Philip Griffin.

"We have no science to say how long," he said. "We die when we die, Mr. Griffin. We treat the body, not the spirit, but sometimes it is the spirit that is sick. No medicine for the body cures the spirit." He paused and looked at the tailor, who was leaning forward in the bed as if for some hope in the doctor's tone, which was soft as the word "India."

"This is not what Mr. Higgins, the oncologist, will say to you. It is my own foolishness perhaps, and you will forgive me for saying it. But there is nothing here for you. Mr. Higgins will say you will die when the disease shuts down the vital organs."

"Soon?" Philip wet his lips. "Tell me."

The Indian nodded. "Mr. Higgins will say so," he said.

Philip Griffin slipped back into the clutch

of the blankets. He felt suddenly more ill than he had ever felt in his life, and imagined he could see each of his vital organs struggling under the duress of the cancer. His heart seemed to be racing, his breath was shallow, as if all the air of the world were swiftly being sucked away from him.

Dr. Bannerje watched the news age the patient. "Is there somebody I can call for you?" he said.

"No. No, thank you."

"I will come back and talk to you again," said Hadja Bannerje, turning slowly to draw back the white curtain from around the bed and walk out of the ward, the weight of failure on his slim shoulders and the smell of smoke about him as he saw his father on the evening of his mother's death setting fire to the great mound of dead flowers in the back yard in Bombay, the glitter of the stars, and the ashes of love spiralling upward and then falling and alighting in his hair.

After the doctor had gone, Philip Griffin lay in the thin air left to him at the edge of the world. The illness was increasing so rapidly, he imagined, that he could be dead by evening. Already he felt the cotton of his pyjamas loosening from the wastage of his body and feared that when he stood to go to the bathroom he would have to grab a handful of the material at his waist. He looked across the ward at two other men who were sleeping like corpses in the deep dream of their medication. Oh God, he thought, he will be destroyed if I die now. I can't die now.

He turned to his side and wept into the pillow. He smelled the smell of hospitals, in which there was no season or life, and was stricken with a new terror that he might never leave the ward again. In the big window a thin rain was blurring the view of Dublin like an overwashed watercolour, and sharp short gusts of wind blew, weakening the resolve of the sick to get better and be outside. But not Philip Griffin: I have to stop it, just delay it. Oh, please, God. If I die on him now I'll have done nothing but bring him grief all his life.

Where no one could see him, and while he was turned on his side towards the gloom of the November afternoon, he raised his right hand slowly to his forehead and blessed himself. He did not know if he believed that God could help, for He had not helped Anne or Mary.

Still, he prayed. He said the Our Father five times. Then, in the beginning of the sixth, he stopped. The pain was sharp in his chest and he clutched himself.

"Shaggit!"

He waited a moment. In his mind he saw the cancer moving like a shadow into a new, still healthy corner of his organs. The room darkened. The sky outside fell like the sea in thickened grey waves, as if the world was spinning upside down and the air was flooded and the light was lost. It was like night in daytime.

I don't know if you are there, Philip Griffin said in a silent voice. I don't know if you can hear me. But please let me live for another while. For my son.

He paused and hugged himself against the pain. Then added: If you let me live, I will try and do . . .

He couldn't find the word.

I will try and do some . . . some act of goodness each day.

Philip Griffin waited, but nothing happened. The pain continued like a fierce storm that November afternoon, pain like rain, falling like a cold monsoon on the head of Dr. Hadja Bannerje in the car park of St. Vincent's, where he missed his mother and promised himself to return to his father in Bombay at the end of his final residency, pain falling out of the grey heavens in a deluge of despondency and loss, until at last

Nurse Grainne Mangan came into the ward and turned on all the lights, and Philip Griffin did not tell her to turn them off.

5

The icy grip of the Atlantic cracked Stephen like thin glass, and his cries flew as shards into the air. He was breathless as the dead and saw the night sky disappear into the foam of a wave passing over him. Underwater he was borne towards the shore, and at last stood up in the rolling tumble of the tide and screamed. He screamed as evidence of his own durability, trying to outcry the noise of the waves and to free his jaw from the frozen fingers of death. His hands shook wildly, and then, as the wind caught him, his knees did the same, convulsing him in tremors until he was a blurry out-of-focus figure on the sand and had to kneel down and put his hands out like a man trying to hold on to the spinning of the world.

It was an hour before he had dressed himself, drawing the clothes over his wet and sand-stuck body, and walking gingerly up from the sea onto the roadside like a new arrival on the planet. When he reached home he sat and played the Vivaldi disc, this time not resisting the image of the woman playing the violin, and wondering only how he was going to see her again.

The following morning Stephen went to school and made an appointment with Carol Blake, the secretary, to see the principal at the end of the day. At once Carol noticed a difference in him, and from the magazines in which she read widely was able to interpret all aspects of men's motives and behaviour.

"Something up with him all right," she told Eileen Waters later during their tea break.

"Really?"

"Oh yes," said Carol, dunking her biscuit. "I'd say he's in love."

"Mr. Griffin? I hardly think so. With whom, for goodness' sake?" asked Mrs. Waters, relishing the unexpected foray into the wildly improbable.

"Some man, I'd say."

This news hit Mrs. Waters like two fists in the generosity of her stomach.

"A man?" she said.

"You can tell," said Carol Blake. "I can tell, anyway."

"Oh God."

Eileen Waters leaned against her desk.

News reports of sexual scandal and abuse in schools mottled in her mind, and she was suddenly stricken with visions of infamy. She took to her office. She could not sit down, she paced about, she plucked up her ruler like rectitude, and was still in a state hours later, when Carol Blake knocked on the door and introduced the figure of Mr. Griffin. The principal turned on him like a gunship and saw at once the confirming evidence of her own fantasy.

"Thank you, Carol," she said. "Close the door."

From the delicate manner of Stephen's sitting it was apparent to Eileen Waters that Carol Blake was correct, and how she had not seen it before she did not know. In the moments before she spoke she chastened her own judgement severely and made a minute shaking of her head at how devious the world had become. Then she pursed her lips at the teacher and narrowed her green eyes to say:

"You have a problem, Mr. Griffin?"

"I want to take some personal time," he said. His fingers were touching the desk, and his eyes were moving to the window.

Mrs. Waters moved her ruler forward an inch with both hands, tapping the two ends of it with her forefingers for the small comfort of something solid in the world. She felt her anger reddening beneath her makeup.

"I realize it's inconvenient."

"Yes, it is," she spat out.

"I'm sorry."

Righteousness lodged like a boiled sweet in her throat, and she coughed it forward, letting go of the ruler on the desk and seeing her right hand fly up before her.

"We are teachers. We are moral leaders in the community, Mr. Griffin. We have to think of the consequences of our actions. We can't simply behave the way everyone else does. I hope that's not what you think, because that's not what I want, that's not what I expect." She paused and reloaded, drawing air through her nostrils, and was delivering what she hoped was the full broadside of her gaze when Stephen said:

"It's because of my father. He's dying."

There was a stunned moment, a flattened instant of time during which the mind of Eileen Waters faltered and fell through the gape of her mouth onto the desk in front of her. There was a soft plop just barely audible to Carol Blake listening at the door outside, and then nothing. The principal could not speak, the top button of her blouse was too tight. She was looking down at her desk, which was swimming like wreckage on the watery uncertainty of the moment. She opened her small lips and tried to smile.

"I'm very sorry," she whispered, and held on to the desk with her right hand. She was still grasping it a moment later when Stephen stood and left, walking out of the office and down the cool emptiness of the school's corridors, an inch taller than he was before, the line of his trousers falling perfectly, not rumpled, and the slap of his shoes crisp with resolve.

6

An hour after school, in the falling darkness, Stephen called at the front door of Moira Fitzgibbon's house. A small girl of about eight opened the door five inches and looked at him. When he asked for her mother, the girl stood motionless, as if she was looking at some strange colour radiating about the visitor. Then Moira Fitzgibbon was standing behind her, opening the door.

How one person's life touches upon the edge of another's and moves it like a wheel was a small mystery Moira had learned to accept since first hearing the story of Moses Mooney and his dream of a concert hall. So when Stephen Griffin appeared at her doorstep she sensed the role she was to play before she knew it and was not surprised when he asked her, please, to help him. Her husband was in the sitting room watching television. Cait, her daughter, was still standing in the hallway, gazing past her at the stranger, and Ciara was in the kitchen sprawled over the careful homework of six-year-olds. Like a set bomb, there would be ten seconds before one of them would call her, and so Moira did not invite Stephen in. She stepped forward and drew the door nearly closed behind her.

"I want to know where I can find her," Stephen said. "The woman who played the violin. Gabriella Castoldi, her name is."

"Who's there, Cait? Who's at the door?" Tom Fitzgibbon was calling from the sitting room. Cait's face was pressed like a mask against the opaque glass of the door. "A man, Daddy," she shouted.

Already Tom Fitzgibbon was rising in his chair.

"I don't know," Moira whispered quickly. "I don't know where she is. I'll . . ."

Her husband's hand was on the door lock.

"I'll try and find out," she said and, motioning Stephen backward with her head, added in a louder voice, "Thank you now, goodbye," before turning back to meet her husband coming out the door. "Some business of the Development Association," she said, and went back inside.

At ten o'clock that evening Stephen was sitting in the front room of his house awaiting the inevitability of fate. When he

176

saw the headlights move in an arc across the far wall, he did not need to turn around and look out the window, but knew that it was Moira Fitzgibbon and that the plot of his life was moving now in swift grand strokes that made little of great difficulty and certainty out of the improbable. He opened the front door as she was about to knock. The wind shouldered past him like a sea lord and banged the doors of the two rooms.

"I won't come in," Moira said. Her words were blowing back into the town along the road where Moses Mooney was listening for them. The car's engine was running, and its lights had been left on as if to illumine the murky turning of the plot and make clear the way ahead, for Moira Fitzgibbon was not sure why she had come, why the intensely burning figure of the man at her door had moved her so, or what it was in the disconsolate beseeching of his eyes that made her slip upstairs to her bedroom and go through the letters and papers she had until she found a mention of Gabriella Castoldi playing a residency in a hotel in Kenmare; she did not know why, other than that it was the response of her heart, which, like the purest of souls, felt the grief of another like the grief of herself, and by healing it could heal the world.

"I won't come in," she called again into the wind, for the door was still held wide open and the weather was running through the house like a party of drunken ghosts. "I found something," she said. "Maybe she's not there now, I don't know."

"Where?"

She held up a pamphlet that the wind-ghosts almost took.

"Kenmare," she said, "in Kerry. She plays there. Or did, anyway."

The teacher took the paper and looked at her. "Thank you," he said.

She looked at him, and then could not look at him, as if his vulnerability and innocence in dreaming of love were a sweetness so easily shattered that she dared not imagine it for long. "I have to go, Mr. Griffin," she said.

He reached to touch her shoulder.

"Thank you," he said.

And she was gone.

Stephen brought the piece of paper inside. He sat where the wind had been sitting in the low chair by the fireless chimney and greedily read the words until he found her name. Gabriella Castoldi. What it was to read her name. What it felt like to see the figuration in print and allow himself to imagine her now in the small gatherings of

178

those letters. He touched them, traced them, he sounded the name slowly, *Gabriella,* and then quickly, calling it softly at first and then getting up and walking through each room and calling it, *Gabriella,* as if summoning her there at the very moment that she was just leaving each room, as if her name was the first part of her that he could claim in the privacy of that house by the sea and the saying of it was a kind of company that admitted without rejection his outrageous declaring of love. *Gabriella.*

He read aloud: "Gabriella Castoldi was a member of the Orchestra de la Teatro de la Fenice in Venice until recently moving to Kenmare in County Kerry. She frequently performs in evenings of chamber music at The Falls Hotel."

He read it and felt lighter, imagining the hotel and the evenings of chamber music deep in Kerry. He took the piece of paper to his bedroom and lay down. He did not undress; he put his hands behind his great head and said Gabriella Castoldi, like a whisper to the wind. He said it like a message. He said it like a signal and a code, as if the sounding of the words might reach her wherever she was and that she might stop and turn her neck to the side, as if with the violin, and hear in the night air the soft beating of wings that was the incipient approach of his spirit. *Gabriella.* He said it over and over, clinging to it like the almost drowned, so that even Mick Clancy, his neighbour across the fields, heard it in mutated form in his dream and awoke to tell his wife, Nora, that the Angel Gabriel had announced something in Italian in his head.

7

The following morning Stephen drove the yellow car onto the flat-bottomed Killimer ferry to cross the river to Kerry. The old boat tugged at the grey sleeve of the Shannon. Stephen got out of his car and climbed up onto the viewing deck. Seabirds swung in the air overhead. As if by a conjuror's trick, Kerry in front looked no different from Clare behind. As if the ferry was forever to cross between two reflections, neither of them as frighteningly real as the places of the homeless and murdered on the radio. Green fields sloped sleepily to the grey river. It was late November. There were no tourists on the ferry, only a milk tanker and the washed cars of a couple of salesmen who were talking on telephones in the middle of the river. The crossing took thirty minutes, but seemed longer. Away from school, Stephen felt the slow energy of the countryside seeping into him like a potion. There was a gentle easiness, an unhurried ordinariness in the waving of the ferryman as he directed the cars off on the other side. Even the little line of their traffic moved into Kerry with the slow grace of wanderers, not business people. In the small town of Tarbert women were stopped and talking. A butcher stood at his doorway. Stephen slowed down. He had awoken that morning with the urgency of arriving in Kenmare, but now, when he had moved beyond the habitual perimeters of his own life, he felt the wonderful ordinariness of the market towns he drove through: the shopping and talking, the women who slipped like breezes from the church after weekday Mass, the buying of carrots from parked vans, the saluting of friends, nods and laughter, gossip, deals, and the talk of funerals that moved the world along. By the time he had driven fifty miles into Kerry, Stephen Griffin had begun to learn the small history of life, the unchronicled plain fable of the everyday in which until that morning he had not taken part.

When he stopped the car for petrol at a small station on the side of the road, a short man in a suit and hat came out to serve him. He was sixty years old, and the absence of any teeth gave his smile the air of a deflated football.

"Lovely weather," he mouthed, taking the pump.

Stephen looked up; it was not raining, but the sky was broken.

"Oh, it's coming," said the man, and moistened his sunken lips at the prospect. "Nice as summer this week coming."

"I see."

"Not yet you don't, but you will." He paused and grinned a gaping toothlessness at the sky. "I'm not wrong," he added cheerfully. "You'll be coming back this way?"

"Yes. I don't know. Well. I mean, yes, I will."

"You stop in and tell me if I wasn't right. Lovely weather." He turned his head at a slight angle to himself as if hearing an inaudible broadcast, and then resumed pumping the petrol.

The petrol gagged at the tank, and the old man stopped and hung up the pump.

"I'm Martin O'Sullivan. You never heard of me, I suppose?"

Stephen said nothing. The man smiled at the vastness of the world and the decreasing smallness of himself in it.

"No," he said, "you did not." And he left it at that, taking the fifteen pounds for the petrol and adding nothing of his own story, the fading fable of how once he had held the world record for holding his breath and imagined that the vast populations of everywhere admired him for it.

He waved off the car and watched it go into Killarney and the mountains. Then he walked back to the small seat inside the door of the shop, to watch the world becoming smaller and the wonderful weather arriving in the sky.

It was late afternoon by the time Stephen drove the winding road out of Killarney past the lakes and into the mountains. Here was a road with no shop or houses, a rising thread of grey through the thickening greenery and the rock. Streams ran across the roadway and fell farther towards the mirrors of the lakes below. It was a road in fairyland. A timeless way out of the pages of children's tales. It wound like a spell, climbing all the time through a green hush that was older than Aesop. That November afternoon there were no cars ahead of Stephen or behind him. He was driving so slowly that arrival seemed to move ahead of him uncertainly. He rolled down the window and felt the cool air like a damp lusciousness enter the car. It was as if he were moving barefoot in deep undergrowth, and the smell of pine had cleared his mind to a serene vision of Gabriella playing the violin. He did not know that he was driving now in the places where she had walked, or that sometimes she had played the violin high among the trees on the sides of those mountains. He did not know it, but heard nonetheless in the thin purity of the air the notes that she had left.

In that verdant and ancient loveliness the yellow car crawled on, moving through a place where it was less difficult to believe there was a spirit that loved the world.

At half past four in the afternoon Stephen arrived in Kenmare. He drove down off the mountains with a falling mist closing in behind him. By the time he arrived at the top corner of the triangular town, the mountains themselves had disappeared, like the toys of God. Drifts of soft drizzle moved in the air, dampened the pink faces of the townspeople, and made their radios crackle. He had no idea exactly where to go. He walked along the footpath, past the shops, his heart fluttering with the bird within him. He tried to amble, to walk with pretend interest along the street, while all the time anxiety roiled his stomach. It was only when he was already out of the car and walking in Kenmare that the possibility of meeting Gabriella on the street dawned on him. He stopped and tried to swallow the sharp pieces of his panic; he thought of retreating, acting a small pantomime of forgetting something and urgently running back along the path. Having driven a hundred miles, he was suddenly terrified to meet her. What if she was there in front of him, walking her shopping home? An appalling sense of the outlandishness of it froze him to the ground; of seeing a woman play a violin and then dropping everything, abandoning a life and driving off like a latter-day Lancelot into the mountains to see her again. He had a surging sense of the absurd anachronism of romance, of its implausible and obsolete currency in the world, as though it belonged to ancient history and, along with words like Valour and Hon-our and Truth, was credible only in fables. His black hair fell down in front of his eyes as he studied around his feet the running rain stains that looked like maps of lost countries. He stood there in his thick coat and told himself again that he was not there to speak with her, that he had come because he wanted to hear her play again, because he wanted to watch her, and in that watching was a kind of healing he could not explain. He reasoned it in a slow argument like a practising solicitor and tried to climb the specious rungs of logic until it did not seem absurd.

He was standing, arguing the case of himself, when Nelly Grant saw him from the vegetable market across the street. When he moved off the wet space he had been standing in and walked down the path again, she saw the strange hesitation in his manner, the way he shuffled along half-turned from the people coming against him, and was at once suspicious of his contorted energy.

A man like that, she thought, needs plums.

It was another twenty minutes before he arrived back up the other side of the street to her shop. Later, Stephen would tell himself that he had stepped in the door because it was open and not because he wanted fruit. But the moment he appeared before her Nelly Grant already recognized in the twisted shambles of his body the jangling and unaccommodated condition of his spirit. All his organs are in deep stress, she thought, and smiled at him as he fingered an apple on the side of the stack.

"Quiet time of year for a visit," she said across to him.

"I'm sorry?"

"Taking a small holiday? It's a good time for it. Kenmare is too busy now in the summers. Though I shouldn't be complaining, should I? But it's nice and quiet now. You'll

187

get a nice few days if the mist lifts. Which it will too, I'd say." She paused and looked at him. "Try a few plums," she suggested lightly, and raised her eyebrows with her voice as if approaching a delicate bridge between them. "Try one, they're lovely. Taste of autumn in them."

And he did. He bit the plum, and lifted his head for the first time as the juice ran down his chin.

It's worse still, thought Nelly Grant when she saw the egg-yolk hue of his tongue and the lifeless colour of his teeth. She had to turn for a moment to the shelf behind the counter where she kept the vitamin and mineral supplements. She moved two jars of A and E and recalled it was Tuesday last since she had checked her own tongue for the pinkness of her life force.

"I need . . ."

"Yes?" She turned, like luck.

Stephen scratched his forehead, and small skin cells flaked falling in the shop light. He looked to the right in a loop of hesitation, but Nelly Grant came forward and with her the affirming scent of cinnamon oil that was burning in pottery by the register.

The loop unknotted.

"I need someplace to stay."

"Oh yes," said Nelly. "Well, there's still a

few places that stay open all year round. I have a card here for . . ." She turned to the crowded noticeboard behind her, but stopped when the man behind her spoke.

"There's a hotel here," he said. His voice was skipping like a record and he had to swallow hard before he added quickly, "It's called . . . The Falls, The Falls Hotel."

"That's right." Nelly Grant turned and looked at him, detecting only now the burden of secrecy he carried.

"I don't want to go there. Not stay there. I mean I just — It's not far, is it?"

"Oh no. It's just up the street," she said.

"Right. That's fine. Thank you. There's em . . ." Stephen felt his transparency like a face blemish and half-turned towards the door while Nelly Grant blew the scent of the cinnamon softly forward once more. "There is, there are . . . em . . . concerts there sometimes?"

"Oh, there are," she said.

"Good. Good." He nodded and drew breath like the drowning, and it was a few moments before he realized that he was standing at a shop counter but had nothing to buy.

"Do you want this, it's Mary White's place. Very nice and comfortable," said Nelly Grant, holding out the card. "It's not far from the hotel," she added, already a half-conspirator in the plot of his loving.

Stephen took the card and thanked her, then tried to repay the graciousness of the woman by going over to the nearest stall and taking a bag of apples. Then a bag of oranges. Then a clutch of green bananas.

My God, thought Nelly as she watched him, he has hardly ever bought fruit. Plums, she knew, were the fruit for him, and she tried to guide his body towards them with the energy of her mind. This man has no balance, and plums are the fruit of balance; the softness of the flesh to the solidity of the stone hints at it, the perfect proportion of the stone to the fruit tells it even more clearly. Peaches work in the same way for people of southern climates, but it is plums, thought Nelly Grant, that balance the Irish. Pick a plum. Pick a plum.

She let the suggestion flow like a current to the back of Stephen's head. But his body and spirit were too out of balance to receive it, she decided, and so said, "I have a special on those plums this week."

"Oh yes, thank you," said Stephen, jostling the bags of apples and oranges against his chest, holding the bananas down with his chin, and reaching toward the basket of plums. Nelly came forward. When she moved across the small shop the oils that scented her body followed her through the air. She was able to fill the space like a large sound.

"I'll take these," she said, and unloaded the fruit bags and bananas, standing briefly next to the stranger so that the wholeness of her energy and the scent of lavender might soothe his embarrassment. He was the most awkward man she had ever seen, but that very awkwardness was attractive, too, for it broadcast an intensity of feeling. She watched him gather three more plums, and then the two of them moved back to the register. As if she would not allow him to buy them, Nelly put the other fruits to one side. She did not weigh the plums, but charged him two pounds.

Hurriedly Stephen reached inside his coat for coins. Even that, Nelly thought, reveals him.

"And the . . . em . . ." He looked over at where she had left the apples and oranges.

"These are very good," she said, ignoring his gesture, looking directly at him with the green compassion of her eyes and patting softly with her right hand the bag of plums.

"Oh yes, I'm sure," he said. "Well, thank you. Thank you very much." He nodded quickly, as if to an allegro, and then turned towards the door.

"Come back again," Nelly Grant said. "All my customers come back."

"Yes; yes, I will." He stopped at the door as if he had suddenly remembered something important to say to her. He turned. She was looking at him.

"Em . . ."

Then he sighed, nodded, and was gone.

8

Stephen stayed that night at the small clean guesthouse of Mary White, a woman of fifty-nine who had buried her husband and lost her children to the invisible places where only telephones reached them. She was a slender woman with fine white curls and thin legs who, since losing her left breast, had become a close friend of Nelly Grant's and believed without hesitation it was she who had helped her recover in the world. When she saw the man arriving at the front door with the bag of plums, she knew where he had come from and brought him forward into the yellow bedroom that had once belonged to her eldest daughter. Then she went and made him tea, calling him from the room with a gentleness he felt like a mother's hand.

"Perhaps you'd like me to wash the plums?" she asked as he sat down in the living room, where the extraordinary green beauty of her back garden rose before the window.

"Or just tea," she added, "and some biscuits." Then she left him alone there and went to warm fresh towels for his room. Mary White was a slight woman, but knew the enormous goodness of giving comfort. That it might be given to her, that she might deserve or need it, did not enter her mind. She warmed the towels, turned on the oven, and baked fresh scones and brown bread for her visitor out of that simple and immeasurable force of goodness that moved within her. When he finished his tea she brought him more, and asked him to tell her if there was anything he needed to feel comfortable.

That evening the mist came down into the streets of the town. A damp clothlike darkness fell, and when Stephen slipped out of the house within it he could smell the pine trees in the mountains. He walked to the hotel, feigning casualness and calm. His forehead shone beneath the yellow streetlights, and the moisture of the night glittered on his hair like a crown. By the time he had arrived at the wide gateway and the illumined sign welcoming visitors, he was breathing so shallowly the thin air of both fear and desire that he might have fallen down there on the pathway. He balled his fists inside his coat pockets, as if squeezing the life of his own timidity, and then headed up into the bright lights of the hotel. The stone steps were red-carpeted. A round-faced man in a black uniform and cap nodded to him as he entered and stood in the timbered hallway where a wood fire was burning. Stephen didn't know where to go. He had planned on getting to the hotel to see Gabriella play the violin, but now that he was standing inside the door, he felt lost. He ran his hand up over his forehead and hair, and then had to hide it momentarily in the collar of his jacket, until the drench of white sweat disappeared. The porter stepped over.

"Evening, sir."

The man had a way of making the greeting seem like a question, a way of looking with round brown eyes that declared he had seen the world in all its guises come through the doors of this hotel and now knew intimately, intimately, sir, the myriad vagaries of the visitor in Kerry. He knew Stephen did not belong there. Or so Stephen imagined, holding like a lip-tremble the impulse to hurry back out the door.

"Can I help you, sir?"

Stephen held his lower lip between his teeth.

"Sir?"

"For the em, for the music. I em was hoping to hear some music. Played."

Maurice Harty studied him like a new text, reading in him the plot of a simple mystery novel and noting the clues with a small satisfaction. "What music would that be, sir?"

"Here. I thought there was — a concert, of violin and . . ." Stephen looked away down the hallway towards a large lounge. Maurice Harty touched his arm and was startled to feel its thinness.

"That would be Friday or Saturday night, sir," he said, and watched Stephen Griffin's spirit fall like a shadow.

"Friday?" It was a breathy sigh. As if the swimmer had closed his eyes and made a hundred strokes, only to open them and see the shoreline had receded even farther.

"Or Saturday, sir."

Stephen did not move, he floated there on the harsh awareness that he was encumbered with some invisible baggage of misfortune which guaranteed the unease of his passage.

"You're not a guest in the hotel, sir?" Maurice Harty thought the visitor might faint. "There's tea served in the lounge if you'd care for it."

But Stephen did not move or answer. He

only nodded his head slowly, watching a place on the carpet, waiting, swallowing the bitterness, and then taking the decision not to be defeated, not to see as failure the dreamlike journey across the Shannon and through the mountains to see the woman who was not there, not to suppose these were signs or messages and that he should abandon everything and return to Clare. When he lifted his head and thanked Maurice Harty, he had regained some balance and, assuring the porter that he would return to hear the music on Friday, he walked out and down the steps of the hotel into the moist blackness of the night, returning to the yellow bedroom in the guesthouse of Mary White, to lie in his clothes on top of the blankets and eat slowly, one after the other, the dark and delicious fruit of the plums.

9

When Philip Griffin returned home from the hospital he wore the cancer like a suit of clothes two inches too tight in all measurements. His life was constricting about him, and although he played Puccini and left the lights burn through the night, he could not escape the feeling of things closing about him. He had three bottles of tablets, but only the white ones were painkillers. These he took three times a day, imagining them as timber ramparts against an advancing army of iron. Since he had been in the hospital the pain had increased enormously. Often when he was tailoring he had heard stories of men and women being opened in surgery and the doctors seeing the cancer almost growing in the exposure of the air and quickly stitching the patient closed again. Air makes it multiply was the given wisdom among the middle-aged men standing for their leg measurements, and Philip Griffin had believed them, taking the strange apposition of air and death as another of the mysteries of life and thinking on it no further. Until now. Now the pain that rode up his stomach into his heart seemed better for air, and he wondered if the ease of pain when he walked outside was in fact the approach of death.

Since he made the pact with God in the hospital, he had had little chance for good deeds. He had tried to do what the nurses told him, had eaten the mild-flavoured yogurtlike food that slid like wet paste in his throat, and not pressed the call button when Healy in the bed beside him stole his sleep by venting all night his repressed anger in urgent, snapping snores and bulbous farts. But Philip feared that this was not enough. It was when he was home again in the empty house behind the chestnut tree that he knew he must get under way a daily practice of goodness. What it might be, or how he might achieve it, he had no idea. Vaguely he supposed that it would be something to do with the people he would meet that he would see things in the course of an ordinary day, and that all that could be expected of him would be to react in as kind and generous a manner as he could.

On his third full day home he left the house in the afternoon with the painkiller still dissolving on his tongue and drove into the city centre. For the first time in years he did not drive the car with any impatience or haste, but motored instead through the be-grimed streets like a Sunday driver in the pastoral quietude of a country lane. He waved like a mad uncle at passersby. He touched the brim of his hat at a mother and child on a pedestrian crossing, and allowed cars to pull out of side streets in front of him. While the painkiller made numb his inner organs, he smiled at Dublin and softly whistled "Dixie" when the car in front of him took the last space on Stephen's Green. He wanted to park nowhere else, and so contented himself by driving around the green park repeatedly. When at last he found a space, it was the middle of the after-noon. Philip stepped out onto the path. Goodness, he thought. Acts of goodness. He moved along the path with pleasantness on his face. He prepared a kind of wordless greeting in his raised eyebrows and gave it continuously to the people coming against him, hoping that it was not misunderstood and that God was watching. When he had greeted a hundred Dubliners like this along the top of Stephen's Green, he took their lack of acknowledgement as a judgement and headed down to the crush and hurry of Grafton Street with a growing awareness of how difficult goodness was going to be.

When he reached the traffic light at the top of the street, the wind pressed on his back and he had to hold on to his hat. In that instant the light changed and the people hurried across past him. He was left standing there, and felt the pulling away of life. He didn't move, and the light changed again. It was a moment before another cluster of people gathered around him. He gave some of them small smiles and a parcel of nods, but they paid him — an odd little man holding his hat at the traffic lights — no attention. As the light changed once more, a woman with two young children was on the kerbside next to him. Philip Griffin offered a child his hand to cross the street, but the mother drew away the child at once and was gone.

Again he stood there and did not move. He watched the city, the city he was born in. He watched its grey relentless tide of forlorn faces, the figures of the windblown and harried, dispossessed of dreams, hastening along the street in the narrowness of shopping and getting home. He heard the noise of people and traffic and knew how each one was lost in the privacy of his own pursuit, not noticing one another. No hand reached out to touch him. The lights changed three times while he stood on the edge of Stephen's Green. Courier cycles flew past. A taximan paused his cab and waved the old man to cross, but Philip Griffin declined. He was stilled on the point of an epiphany, and as the first spits of rain hit the crown of his head, he imagined that he saw only for the first time the vast monstrosity of selfishness and meanness that had become the world. Across the street he could read the headlines of the evening papers: TAKEAWAY KILLING. FATHER RAPIST. The city he was born in was now this, and Philip Griffin had to hold on to the traffic light for something solid.

It was raining heavily now, and darkness was descending rapidly into the afternoon.

Philip's face was wet when he turned to walk back to his car, defeated. He had thought that if he walked into the centre of the city his footsteps would be guided to the person who was in need of his help. But nothing had happened. There was a woman sitting on the ground begging, not far from the top of Dawson Street. Another across the way at the gates to the Green, and a child with a cardboard begging tray was beyond. What was he supposed to do? When he reached his car he had still not resolved it. He carried the load of his ungiven goodness like a burden of treasure. I am un-used to people, he thought. I don't have the faintest idea how to approach anyone. He leaned against the top of his car. It was cold, and city grime soiled his face.

Then, abruptly and without further thought, he took out his wallet, drew out all the notes that were inside it, and walked over to the park railings of Stephen's Green.

He glanced around to see who was looking at him. But he needn't have. Men and women passed without noticing, and Philip Griffin was able to take all the money he had, place it on the ground under the bushes inside the bottom of the railing, and walk away.

It is not much, he thought, but it is some-thing. Let God direct whoever He wants to find it.

The following day he did the same thing. Only this time he chose a different railing.

That evening, while "O mio babbino caro" played loudly in the sitting room, Philip Griffin counted his money. He had been a prudent man. He had modest savings and investments, and lived his quiet life without show. The money he had saved had been put aside for a future that never arrived. Ultimately it would have been Stephen's, but now he reasoned that the sale of the house would be enough. Besides, obscurely, it was all for Stephen, the given-away money being the acts of goodness which would buy Philip the time on earth to help Stephen through the breaking of his heart.

He calculated the figures in a jotter with his reading glasses halfway down his nose, poring over them into the night like God's accountant, balancing the books of good deeds against the rest of his life. How many more weeks did he need, and how much per week, per day, did that require? His wife was beside him while he did the calculations, doing the figures as if budgeting the time and money for a holiday together.

They could be together in heaven in less than a year, he figured. "Is that all right, love?" he whispered in the lamplight. In a year Stephen would have survived and be returned to his ordinary life once more. In a year Philip could have given away all the money, arriving at a zero balance like a cleansed soul and hearing the trumpets coming to get him. He would be doing it for Stephen, doing it out of that most potent mixture of love and regret, as if he could now and here make recompense for the innumerable small failures of his fatherhood, the doomed and islanded silence in which he had left his son for so long, repairing in small measure the great gap that he had let grow between them.

Philip did not want to calculate the exact day, for he supposed that was a vanity and taking the control from God. It was enough, he thought, to know the rough time, and that when he had exhausted the wallet of goodness God Himself would not be long arriving to keep up His end of the pact. That night he went to sleep with the painkiller tasting like almonds in his mouth and the prospect of the year ahead brightened with visions of giving. He lay in the blankets and felt Christmas coming. He placed his hands on his stomach and sensed their heat travelling like a minor army to meet the cancer. He had named it Prendergast for the despised, low-sized, and sly figure of his first boss — a tailor at Clery's who had routinely ripped out Philip Griffin's stitches, saying butchers could do better, and had forced him to work long evenings on repairs when he should have been courting Anne Nolan. Prendergast was a bastard. But as the tablets took action he was masked and made invisible, erased until three o'clock in the morning, when he would come as fire in the old man's insides and reawaken the world to the certainty of suffering and woe.

The following day Philip Griffin drove to his bank on Merrion Square and withdrew £5,000. When the teller heard the amount he hesitated and disappeared. An assistant arrived, and Philip Griffin was drawn down the counter and asked what he wanted the money for.

"To give away," he said.

"I'm sorry, sir?"

"To get rid of, to give away," the old man said, "not that it's your business. It's my money."

"Yes, sir, only that . . ."

"What?" He shot the word so quickly and with such pointed indignation that the assistant manager withdrew. "I'll get you a draft, sir," he said.

"Cash. It must be cash."

There was a flat, beaten moment between them.

"Five thousand pounds? In cash?"

"Correct." The old tailor looked the other man directly in the eyes. How difficult is goodness, he thought, everything blocks it. And deep within him, Prendergast turned like a knife.

It was half an hour before he got the money. It lay neatly in a long envelope, and when he walked out the doors of the bank it conferred on Philip Griffin a sudden power of joy. He was exuberant with possibility. His small eyes flickered at the city, as if seeing everywhere now the chance to touch another's life. And, in a moment of beatific vision as he passed a bus queue, he wondered if many others were not secretly engaged in doing the same.

This time he did not wait to get the car, but walked directly towards Stephen's Green. It was, he had decided, the appropriate place, and would remind God of the reason for their pact, Stephen, Stephen's green. He smiled to himself at the small joke, although in fact the banknotes were less green and more the colour of bruises.

As Philip neared the park once more, he reached inside the envelope and took a clutch of twenty-pound notes. He kept them in his hand and walked on. Sweat gathered in the brim of his hat and he felt his trouser catch at the back of his knee. Three hours had passed since he had taken his morning painkiller, and now he was emerging from it like from a tunnel into the bright searing of the pain. God, help me. The money was wet in his hand inside his pocket, the railings made him dizzy, and he had to stop and lean and wait for a small group of schoolchildren and their teacher to pass by. Then, once they had passed, he took £480 and quickly slipped it down onto the ground between the railings.

He had to hold on for breath. He could have changed his mind and reached in and withdrawn the money. But he did not. He knew that it could be taken by dogs, eaten by rats, or befouled in any number of ways, that it could be found by the avaricious or the mean-spirited, any number of the evil or selfish undeserving as easily as by the needy. But that did not matter to him. For he trusted in God, and knew that the puzzle of His ways is beyond us, and only vanity leads us ever to imagine that there is more than only the smallest corner of the jigsaw perceivable at any time. No, the money would go where it was to go, Philip reasoned. His job was only to drop it off there, like a deposit of good energy given back into the universe. He watched the winter sky as if light might suddenly break through the heavy blankets of the cloud. But nothing changed, and he walked on. The city of Dublin trundled past, and the small man in the felt hat was lost in the crowds.

(It was only later, when he was back in the sitting room, looking at the set-up chess game on the small table and listening to the music of *Madama Butterfly* with the pain-killer blurry in his stomach that Philip Griffin could sigh and think of Stephen and wonder if the love affair was progressing now, if a father could touch his son on the other side of the country, if goodness travelled through the air like luck or love and could arrive unexpected and simple as a blue sky over Stephen's head two hundred miles away in the west.)

10

During the night the mist withdrew like an artist's drapery and in the morning revealed that the mountains had moved closer to Kenmare. It was a John Hinde postcard sky, a blue so intense that it seemed the unreal season of childhood memory. Summer had arrived in Kerry in time for Christmas, and while Stephen sat to the softly boiled egg Mary White had prepared for him, he heard birds singing in the garden. Mary came and went like moments of kindness. She brought him more toast, a fresh pot of tea, entering the room from where she sat for her own tea in the kitchen with the raised eyebrows and pursed mouth of gentle apology, moving around the guest in her own house with the air of being herself an unfortunate interruption. She did not enquire what Stephen was doing in Kenmare, nor did she hover in the room about him while he ate. When he told her after breakfast that he would like to stay until after the weekend, she said only one word, "Lovely," and allowed herself to smile at the simplicity of this small joy as she hugged with thin arms the long-felt loss inside her.

For Stephen there was almost a week to wait. He did not know whether Gabriella Castoldi had returned yet to Kenmare. The fear of actually meeting her tied the knots of his stomach. But finally, when Mary White knocked softer than a knock on his door and asked if she might tidy his room now, Stephen walked outside into the sunshine. When he reached the town he did not know where to go. He walked around the lampposts like a man looking for his dog. The morning sunshine saddled his shoulders. By half past eleven he had toured the triangle of the streets seven times and had already been noticed by all the shopkeepers. (Mick Cahill on the door at the bank had decided he could be up to no good and must have come over the mountain from Limerick or somewhere to rob them. Veronica Hehir up at the bookshop considered he was a renegade priest, exactly like the one in the book she was reading. When she told Kathleen O'Sullivan, Kathleen replied that he was the eighth that week alone. What was it in Kenmare that drew them?)

"You brought the weather with you."

Nelly Grant stopped him from her doorway. She had sensed the energy of his restlessness arriving in the town fifteen minutes before she saw him and had kept an eye over the shoulders of her customers for the confirming vision of him loping down the street.

"I'm sorry?"

"The weather."

"Oh yes," he said weakly, and then added, "Thank you."

"We get that here sometimes. Balmy as summer. Makes you think somebody has been looking through the books and decided we're due a few more good days before the year's end." She watched how he stood there, the mute tightened presence of him that bespoke imbalance and combustion at the same time. "How did you like the plums?" she asked him.

"Very well. Thank you."

His politeness barely contains him, she thought, like a paper cup of scalding water.

"Come in for more."

She was abrupt and jovial in the same moment, generous and insistent, and for the second time Stephen Griffin entered the fruit and vegetable shop to be given the plums of balance. Within five minutes Nelly had drawn from him that he was going to stay for the rest of the week, and while she weighed the plums on the old-fashioned scale on the side of the counter, she decided that he was in love. It was the gift of her character that she could be pointed without wounding, and when she told Stephen that he should visit Sonny Sugrue, the barber across the street, she was able to make it seem not a comment on his looks but a prescription for the health of his spirit.

"The growing of hair," she told him, "can steal our energy. Visit Sonny, and come back for your plums," she said, and raised her hands to relieve him of his coat before he was aware of it.

Sonny Sugrue was waiting. He was reading a newspaper in the spin-around red-leather chair of his customers and following closely the case of a murder trial in California. He was a man of mostly stomach. That and his hairless head gave him a double roundness that he imagined were comment enough on his pleasure at the world. He had been a barber in Manchester, New York, and Chicago before the arrival of muffled speech like cottonwool in his ears signalled the beginning of his deafness and forced him to return to Kenmare, where he did not need to hear his customers' requirements. His left ear heard nothing, and his right caught the distinctions of instructions only when his hearing aid was at full volume, something he considered an unnecessary waste of its battery. Sonny cut hair short, or off. When Stephen Griffin appeared in the doorway before him, he looked up from knife murder in California and smiled. There was cutting in this one, he thought.

Half an hour later Stephen's hair lay on the floor, and he looked with surprise at the mirror to discover that the centre of his pate was almost entirely bald. When he raised his head he saw the curved limit of himself like a passing moon and was aghast.

"I'm bald," he said.

Sonny Sugrue didn't catch him. He was sweeping the hair into the corner.

"I look like a clown."

Although he paused, Sonny missed the words as they passed him in the air, merely nodding the slow, wise nod of a man who had handled the heads of ten thousand, seen the vanity of youth, the diminishing of beauty, and the horror of age as the customer turned to the truth of the mirror. We are always a shock to ourselves.

"Five pounds, please," he roared across the small shop.

It was a moment before Stephen moved; he was transfixed by the changed image of himself in the glass, and then gladly realized that as he was unrecognizable to himself, he could walk the streets of the town with no fear of the woman knowing him. When he reached the doorway he felt the warm day cool on the top of his head and stooped out beneath the jamb as if bearing eggs on his crown. A small bubble of joy inflated in his stomach.

He went across to Nelly Grant. When she saw the white dome of his forehead coming, her heart lifted and she told him at once that he looked much better, and remarked to herself the dark health of his eyebrows. "You'll see," she said aloud before he reached her. "Walk in the sun this week now, and eat plums. You'll see." She paused in that moment before friendship, then added, "I'm having a mug of tea, would you like some?"

She sat him in the small side room to the shop and poured a tea that was not Indian. It was green in colour and tasted like the wildflower and grass teas of children playing house in the summertime. She had concocted it herself while he was in Sugrue's and now watched him drink. He has the embarrassment of those who feel deeply that they should not be alive at all, she thought, those who have survived where others who were better, more gifted or beautiful or true, have perished into death.

Stephen's face collapsed in a scowl at the dregs of the teacup.

"You don't have to finish it," she said. "But it will do you good. You'll see."

Nelly Grant filled a bag of plums and gave them to him. She took his money and then watched him walk out the door, telling him she would have fresh supplies in by Friday.

And so Stephen began the week of his wait for Gabriella Castoldi in the town of Kenmare, where the sun shone like midsummer and the farmers drove their tractors in shirtsleeves. Blue skies hung like canopies above the green mountains. The white flecks of the winter sheep ran and kicked air like lambs as the pulse of a midwinter spring beat beneath the earth. Yellow blossoms reappeared on the gorse bushes that week. The crown of Stephen's head burned pink, and for it Nelly Grant gave him oil that smelled like coconuts and induced the tropical dreams of warm seas and white sand that woke him with both eyes weeping saltily on his pillow. The town was lifted with the weather, as if a holiday had been declared without tourists. Nelly sold salads on the first of December, and fed Stephen Griffin the restorative fibrous lunch of raw carrots diced in muesli. Out of politeness he gagged mouthfuls of what seemed like horse food and listened to her telling him how his complexion had improved. He had begun to show a little of his life force, she told him. She had already detected that Gabriella Castoldi was the woman he was waiting for, but she did not yet know the extent of their relationship and imagined that at least they had met. Each sun-bright bedazzled day, while the flies buzzed back into Kenmare and the wild rhododendrons reglossed their leaves in the mountains, Nelly Grant plotted the return of Stephen Griffin to health; and he submitted. He was a textbook case, she thought, not that the characteristics of his symptoms bespoke a single remedy, but rather that the multiplicity of his ailments prompted Nelly Grant to consider giving him everything in the textbook. She gave him zinc for his skin and made comfrey tea, and then diced watercress in the salad sandwiches she made for him for his walks. For the anaemic condition which she feared was almost endemic to his character she gave him garlic and sunflower seeds, Brazil nuts and almonds, and offered him a soup of soya beans when he returned red-cheeked and pink-crowned from clambering all day in the lower slopes of the mountains. For the poorness of his respiration, a complaint common in uncertain lovers, she made a carrageen blanc-mange from the moss which was still growing in winter along the temperate shoreline of Parknasilla.

Four days was too short a time to change the habits of over thirty years, but Nelly was reaffirmed in her philosophy when she saw the clear improvements in the patient. Love, she knew, was simply the energy that bound us to the earth; and for it the energy of the earth needed to be administered. For love you need carrots, and Stephen Griffin collected four in a brown paper bag every morning before walking his lovesickness out into the green air of the mountains.

And so, that warm and close week of waiting. It was a week that Stephen had taken out of his life, as though he had torn the next page from a book and thrown the rest away, following the sentences down the page with no idea of what in the airy infinity behind it came next. Endlessly as he moved out into the mountains and walked the lower hillsides he read down the page to the end — how he had heard a woman playing in a concert, how it had moved him, how he could not stop thinking of her and had come now to Kenmare to see her again; it read as simply as an infant's text. But in the moment he reached the bottom of that page the limitless possibilities beyond it made him ill with a sense of freefall and the notion that he was being absurd and should drive on back to Clare.

But still, at the moment when he might sensibly have left, he stayed on, his resolve fuelled at crisis moments and his balance restored by the hundred plums and the tropical summertime that had softened the air between the mountains of Kerry like a pair of hands tossing a light pastry. He stayed on, waiting. Mary White brought him boiled eggs in the mornings, and when he discovered her small tape recorder she joined him sometimes in the evenings when he listened to Vivaldi in the garden-looking sitting room, where the saffron crocuses were already blooming. He listened to the music with his hands on his knees and his head back on the armchair, his eyes closed. He wore a white shirt with the collar open that gleamed in the low light. By the Thursday evening sleep had deserted him, and long after Mary White was lying in the familiar dream of her husband in the garden with the straw hat on his head and their camellia in blossom; Stephen was lying wide-eyed on top of the covers, where the moon spilled like mercury, aware only that his life had reached a precipice, and holding in his hands the yellow page that announced the Friday-evening concert in the hotel, with Gabriella Castoldi on violin and Paul Sheils on piano.

11

When Stephen Griffin walked in the doorway of The Falls Hotel on Friday evening, his breath scented with parsley and his head clear from the chewing of lemon balm, Maurice Harty was not on the door. And neither was anyone else. The front hallway was deserted and only a young girl clicked the keys of a computer at the reception desk. At first he thought he was early. He had been waiting all week for this moment and now imagined that his watch had moved ahead of Time in rhythm with his mind and that perhaps it was not yet eight o'clock. He walked over to where a wood fire was burning low and mimed the warming of his warm hands to hold off for an instant his gathering sense of foolishness. Then he went to the receptionist and asked what time it was. When she told him it was eight o'clock, he nodded as if in exact agreement with her. He was like a lost traveller, having voyaged on long, uncertain seas towards a land he presumed was there, but now, checking the coordinates, was vanished. Nothing was happening. He was there, clean-shaven and freshly scented, his eyes already glossily enlivened with the week of herbs and his head high, just above the sinking feeling of despair. But in a moment he might drown.

"I was wondering," he said to the girl, his voice so low in his throat that the words were marshmallowy lumps of nothing, "if there was . . ." He raised a large one with a small cough. "A concert here." It was as though he had declared the New World begins here and the men rushed to the side to see only the boundless watery horizon.

"Oh yes," the girl sighed, "there is. That's why I'm not gone to the bingo. Don't say you haven't heard? It's with your Man Who Releases the Balls, you know, on the lotto, on TV, he's here tonight, down in the hall. For the football team. They're raising for a pitch." And as if he could not already tell, she added, "It'll be brilliant."

Stephen was trying to contain the shaking that had started in his legs.

"There is a concert, then."

"Yes, in the O'Connell Room. Five pounds. I'd say it's just starting."

He paid her the money with the butter-flies of his hands and swallowed the air-apples that gagged him as he walked along the carpeted hallway to where the New World was and O'CONNELL ROOM was written in gold leaf above an oak door.

It squeaked when he opened it. No music was playing yet, he was in time, and it was only when he had turned to close the door that he felt the emptiness of the room at his back.

There were twenty-seven rows of chairs, fifteen chairs wide, and only seventeen people who had not gone to watch the Man Who Releases the Balls.

He walked into the middle of the room and sat down. Then Peter Sheils and Gabriella Castoldi entered, took their places, and began to play.

12

She wore a green velvet dress.

They played a Boccherini minuet. There was a light above her and he watched where it glanced upon the angle of her neck. She pressed the held notes and squeezed them for tenderness, her lips closed and her green eyes watching the invisible ghosts of feelings that she freed into the air. Her right foot appeared beneath the dress, and he watched it through the fullness of Brahms's Hungarian Dance no. 17. She played Kreisler, Elgar, Schubert, and Brahms. While she played, nothing else mattered in the world.

When the concert had finished, Stephen stood and applauded loudly, and was still standing there when the rest of the small audience had filed past and Peter Sheils had closed the piano and walked away.

Gabriella stepped down from the small stage.

"Thank you, thank you for coming," she said to him. She might have been about to walk past him, but she stopped, and Stephen moved a foot closer.

He stooped down. She smelled like autumn below him. He wanted to eat her voice, and for a terrible gaping moment said nothing, waiting for her to speak again. A driplet ran downward on his crown until he turned his head slantedly to the right.

"We appreciated your listening," she said.

Appreciated. It was like an Italian word when she said it, and he tasted it like a delicacy. He wanted to listen to her talk as he had listened to her play, but the fear of his pause growing overlong made him speak.

"You are . . . you . . . I think you are . . ."

She looked at him. She looked in his eyes and she touched his arm.

"You are very kind," she said. "I think I saw you before."

"Yes. In Ennis," he said. "And Galway." He wanted so to look at her face that he did not.

"The Interpreti Veneziani. Oh" — she stopped — "you are the man who nearly died." She smiled when she said it, but even then, he thought, there was sadness in her. Her hair smelled like autumn rain, and he stooped down deeper within it. "Only then you had more hair." Her face was lit with small laughter, and Stephen reached his hand to his bare crown as if covering the revelation of some inner secret. "You must love music," she said.

I have not listened to music for fifteen years, he wanted to say. I have been dead and woken up. I am shaking here in every particle of my spirit because of you. Please stay. Please stay here talking to me, he wanted to say, but the idiot in control of his body merely nodded at her, breathing parsley-breath on the single word: "Yes."

She stood there. She stood there in the green velvet dress, and he imagined he could sense the Adriatic and the sunlight in the skin of her shoulders. She was as different as Venice, and when she spoke again, giving him words like fruit in her rounded and softly bruised English, he had to try hard not to reach out and touch her.

"We play tomorrow," she said. "There will be maybe more people."

"I don't care." The idiot was making his words into flurried, pauseless gasps now. "I mean I don't . . . if nobody comes I will be . . . You might prefer to play with more people . . . but I could pay more for . . . not that it's the money, you . . . But I . . ."

And there the words ran out and he was tongue-tied and trussed with a glittering crown of sweat falling from his forehead.

"No." She touched his arm once more, as if she were a balm. "It doesn't matter. I like to play," she said, moving a step back from him, this strange, anguished man with the stiffly bent wire of his emotions piercing his insides. "Bye-bye."

She was already walking towards the door with her violin when the idiot freed him and Stephen could whisper after her, "I will be here," closing his eyes and lifting his heart to repeat it louder, "I will be here," and causing Gabriella Castoldi to stop at the doorway and look back at him one last time before she said bye-bye again and was gone.

13

She did not even know his name. And yet when Stephen rose from the bed he had not slept in the following morning and opened the window on the continuing blue-bright and balmy summer of the first day of December, he felt the force of goodness moving in the world. He sensed the sweet energy of regeneration and bloom, the tenderness of light, the majesty of birdsong, and all the rapturous gladness and wonder that were the familiar quick-pulsed delights of those who since time immemorial have fallen in love. He was the Hollywood version of himself, the more handsome, white-shirted, and well-proportioned man singing while he shaved and finding that the perfect clean lines of his blemishless skin revealed no cuts and only the immaculate smoothness of his own face. Everything was charged, loaded with a richness of sensation: the water he splashed on himself, the scent of the witch hazel and aloe vera in the lotion, the peppermint in the toothpaste. Music should have been playing. And was when he arrived in the small dining room, where Mary White was bringing him his breakfast.

It was a micro-season of happiness, a blissed-out moment of abandoned candlelight, and Stephen Griffin could sit at the table in the brief pleasure of knowing: This is joy, this is the richness of things, the brimming sense of the impossible becoming real, when the Hollywood version of himself might have danced about the table and taken Mary White in his arms, spinning her in loops of gaiety, fox-trotting and cha-chaing out through the French doors and into the garden that even then exploded with fireworklike blossoms of orange and gold. There was tenderness in the sunlight and, in the gentleness of the air of that house that morning, a kind of clemency, as if the past had been swept softly with a horsehair brush and the lines of grief, disappointment, and failure were blurred now into the faded and waterpainted corners of the paper.

She had spoken to him.

Gabriella Castoldi had spoken to him, and for whatever came afterwards, whatever lay in the crisscrossed double-knotted stitching of the plot, and despite the reflex habitual expectation he had of everything in his life ending like a useless, lost thread that fitted nowhere in the fabric, Stephen Griffin was that morning briefly illumined with faith and calm in his heart, though he balanced precariously on the fast and silver needle of love.

He did not think of the way ahead. The morning gifted him with a blind optimism that was partly the confusion of his body following the sleepless moon-night, and he did not consider anything beyond that evening and seeing Gabriella play again. No thought of the following week lodged in his mind; Mrs. Waters and the school were not there, nor the enquiries she had already made about his father's health and the growing impatience and suspicion that were mounting in her mind, causing her to hear the morning news on the radio with the stiff cold porridge of dread in her mouth, certain that her history teacher would at any moment be covered in a bright red scandal and discovered in bed with another man. Neither this, nor any of the dull cautionary counsel of ordinary life that scorns and mocks romance, tells you you cannot leave your job and get in the car and go to Kerry to hear a woman play a violin, that you cannot walk out of your life like that on a whim, on a feeling, no, none of this did Stephen Griffin consider.

When he walked into Kenmare that morning, Nelly Grant sensed him coming. The town was in the sleepy aftermath of the party for the Man Who Releases the Balls and no custom had yet arrived for the Saturday traders at the top of the triangle. Stephen's stride was slaphappy and easy, and when he entered the shop he radiated the manic intensity that is shared by the hopelessly lost and the recently found. Nelly had known sometime in the night that his spirit was well, for the stillness of the moonlight foretold it, she believed, holding to the fairy credo that the energy of her principal clients was always reflected in the skies that they drew like children's paintings above them. It was an unproven but certain fact, she reckoned, that people make their own weather, that you could hold a grey cloud motionless in the air above you simply by the predisposition of your character towards the negative ions of depression. Look, she would say, at Connemara, and tell me it's not true.

When Stephen was three feet in front of her, he smelled like lilies, and this despite the aromatic display of oranges and lemons that filled the counter and the burning oil of rosewood in the dish beside the register. It was the scent of Gabriella Castoldi. And when Nelly caught it, opening her eyes wide as she drew it in, she knew the depth of feeling into which Stephen had fallen and remarked silently to herself how she must sometime write down the wisdom of that mystery: how we come to smell of those we love and can carry them like the smallest ghosts in the infinity of our pores.

"You are well today," she said, raising a lemon to her face and breathing the sharpness of its fragrance for clarity.

"You are a wonderful woman," Stephen said. "I feel very well."

"The concert was good?" She did not need to ask him, but wanted to hear in the timbre of his voice the inflection of the spirit.

"There was almost nobody there. Ha!" He laughed despite himself, thinking about it. "Well, she was. They both were. He played the piano, she ..."

And the words were gone, vanished on the moment when he was about to speak of her and leaving him to fall into the whiteness of space, where his praise and yearning went, unsayable and vast. His Adam's apple, large as a Granny Smith, plunged and rose in the narrow and ropey confines of his gorge.

"Sit down in there. Drink this," Nelly told him.

"What is it?" he asked her as she was stepping past him towards the ash-blond and supercilious figure of Helena Cox, the forty-five-year-old wife of the twenty-six-year-old butcher, Francie, who was just then entering the shop.

"Water. Good morning, Helena."

"Isn't the weather so unpredictable?" said the butcher's wife, looking about for the disappeared man she knew was there. She had seen him come in all week from her window across the street and only now managed to arrive across in time before he left. Her face fell twelve years when she realized she had missed him.

"Like all of us," said Nelly, taking with the smallest of smiles the net bag of Brussels sprouts that Helena held and which she knew were not the vegetable that the bound bowels of the Coxes needed. When the customer was gone, moving slowly with heavy weights of suspicion about the thickness of her ankles, Nelly Grant returned to Stephen in the backroom.

"She thinks you're having an affair with me," she said, folding her arms on the warmth of herself and beaming at the man who was gulping the water and gazing on

233

the air. "She senses love, though she doesn't know it. She has not found it with the butcher and is afraid somebody else might have found some."

"I want something," Stephen said. "I want something to help keep this, this." He gestured at the air about himself as though there were visible a cloud.

"Strawberries," she said. "Fruit of optimism." And handed him a punnet she had bought at the morning market in Cork.

14

Darkness fell at four o'clock. It was the first day of December, and when the sunlight was thinned out like beaten metal in the mid-afternoon the fog floated in like fine wrapping. The air smelled of wool and herbs, and might have slipped the town into fairytale sleep had it not been for the iron clatter of Guinness barrels, the last delivery between the mountains, and the twin Keogh brothers carting crates of empties that cackled with remembered delight like false teeth come alive.

Meanwhile, the town readied itself for Saturday night; it held its breath and did the small jobs. It hurried around the yard, it checked the football scores and ate its bread and butter and its slice of currant brack, hearing the nightly tragedies on the news with mute and impotent anger, before washing its face, putting on a clean shirt, and going to stand outside seven o'clock Mass. By the time Father Moriarty was giving out Communion to the variously odoured breaths of his congregation, the pulse of the town had quickened, and for the first of the escapees, who had drifted away on the last word of the Gospel, the porter was already filling pint glasses on mahogany counters.

When Stephen walked out into the night, it was like walking into a pillow. He had to hold his face upward towards the obscured moon to find air. Scarves of fog entwined the mountains. When he arrived at the hotel, Maurice Harty on the door gave him a nod like a movie spy; the same girl was at Reception, and while she gave him his ticket she told him with deep self-pity that the crack at the previous night's computer bingo had supposedly been Unreal.

There were forty people for the concert. He sat in the third row in the aisle seat and did not take his eyes off Gabriella from the moment she entered in a blue dress.

While she bowed the thousand notes, she saw and heard nothing else, and neither the polite applause nor the coughing fit that took one of the elder Donoghue sisters moved her from the far country of the music. It was only between the pieces that she sometimes glanced down at the audience, turning the sheet music with her bow hand and looking briefly at the faces of those astonished to have found such a musician playing in the hotel. It was in those moments that she looked for the face of Stephen Griffin and found him there in the third row looking at her. She saw him and he looked away, and before she had drawn breath to begin the Kreisler, she was already moved by him. A quality of longing in his look pierced her, and as she pressed into her chin rest, she had to steady herself against the suddenness of feeling. (Although she did not know it yet, there was common ground between them, for Gabriella Castoldi shared with Stephen Griffin the expectation of failure and the familiarity of despair. Neither did she realize yet that grief is a kind of glue, too, that the essence of humanity is this empathy, and that we fall together in that moment of tenderest perception when we see and feel each other's wounds and know another's sorrow like a brother of our own.) She did not think of this yet. She played the Kreisler. She played the Elgar after that, and did not look down at him again until the concert was over. Then, as unexpectedly as life, Gabriella Castoldi walked down amongst the chairs and the departing audience to Stephen Griffin and asked him if he would like to walk out into the fog with her.

15

When the salt-smelling letter of Eileen Waters arrived at his house, demanding to know the whereabouts of Stephen and stressing his responsibilities to his students, Philip Griffin realized the love affair must be progressing. He felt the pain less keenly that morning and thanked God for keeping their bargain while he skipped the first tablet of his day. By eleven o'clock the pain that was overdue had still not arrived in his insides, and he stood by the front window looking out on the tranquillity of the suburban street for a sign of anything changed in the world. But there was nothing. The chestnut tree was bare and hung its limbs in the still air above the green pentagon of lawn. A few women and old men walked by to the shops.

"Well," he said at last to his wife. "This might go quicker than I thought, love." And then, with a sudden but muddled enlightenment that perhaps Christmas was to be somehow significant, that patterns ancient as creation make meaning of our days, he added, "I'll go to Toby Madigan's for cloth. I'll make him a suit."

And so that morning, without his pain-killer, Philip drove into Dublin and left God the extra bonus of £345 behind the railings, before walking over to the brown dust-snowed premises of Tobias Madigan & Son. It was Son he dealt with. Son was already a grandfather, but his son had decided to be the retail manager of a branch in a cheap clothing chain and the old shop had been left to fade into the line of other buildings that were the ragged endpieces of the street's memory moments before renovation took it away. Son answered the door when Philip knocked. He was all neck wattles and loose skin; he had an air of sagging, as if he were a cloth man or his bones had already preceded him into the next life. He knew Philip Griffin when he saw him and raised the shallow purses beneath his watery eyes as a greeting. "Ah, Phil," he said, "long time."

When the tailor told him what he wanted, Son drew him into the back room, where they walked across newspapers that Time had worked into the floor and reached the bolts of material that Son brushed left to right with a flimsy hand. He was famous once in Dublin for the quality of his cloth, in the vanished era when such things mattered.

"What about some of this?" he said, drawing out a yard of navy-blue material that was the fabric he had sold to his last customer, the minister, almost two years earlier and before his appearance at the first Tribunal.

Philip felt it for texture and made a few short tugs between thumb and forefinger, as if teasing the cloth for weakness, the way life does a man. He held the material sideways to the slant of low light that fell diffused through the grimy window and then said he would take it. When Son was measuring and cutting, Philip waited in the front room, which had once been busy enough to keep three salesmen when Prendergast had sent the young tailor across the river to buy more cloth. He stood where he had stood as a young man and felt the heaviness of the years. Then, as he took the cloth, folded in brown paper wrapping and tied with twine, he felt come on again the sharp pain of the cancer. He left the old shop quickly, saying goodbye to Tobias Madigan's son as if not wanting to delay the old man's imminent departure into ghosthood and squeezing gently the offered palm of his hand like a cool white handkerchief damp with tears.

The pain turned inside him as he walked back to his car. It seemed larger than his insides, in the same way that the immensity of our sorrows dwarfs the smallness of our hearts. His breathing was lumpy, his throat was swollen inwards, and he could not draw inside him the cool air of the December noon. He had to lean against a wall.

Oh God, he thought, not now. Not here. He saw his hand against the grey building, how it appeared like a freckled fallen bird, useless, trembling with last life. He turned and saw people walking past him. He imagined with brief cruelty against himself the thought of those who had found his money now passing by and his dying against the wall and falling on the cloth of Stephen's unmade suit. His faith wavered and buckled like thin metal in heat; was there no pact after all? Was nobody listening? He reached the knot of his tie with his left hand and pulled it back for air. His right hand clutched at his stomach. He was going to die right there, and then suddenly, like light breaking, the pain eased once more.

He made it to his car and drove home for his lunchtime painkiller.

In the afternoon, when the medication had twirled the air about him into a white fuzz like candy floss, Philip opened the cloth out onto the carpet in the front room. Then he lay down upon it. His son was nothing like himself, they were different as tweed and cotton, but in lying on the blue cloth the father could imagine its shape upon his son. He knew Stephen's dimensions chiefly in relation to his own and held out invisible extensions of his arms to the six extra inches in length that measured the unreachable hands of his son. He marked the cloth without use of a tape measure, turning over on the ground and bringing his face so close to the fabric that he could smell the shop forty years earlier, when he had gone there as an apprentice. To save his ruined muscles Philip rolled over to get up. This would be the last suit he would make, and in the silence of the empty house on that darkening December afternoon, he wished to make it better than any he had before. This was to be the last testament of his skill and craft, the final expression of the many years spent cutting and shaping cloth, suiting the city's men in the good-looking fabrics that not only dressed the body but, through some ancient magic of tailoring, bestowed grace, too. This was to be the last one, the last Philip Griffin, and he took the thirty-year-old scissors and slipped it like a surgeon into the thin veins of the cloth. He did not snip; he moved the scissors with an even confidence, making the first cuts with that quality of assurance that he knew transferred itself directly into the finished garment.

For Stephen, his father wanted the suit to be the shadow of himself. When he cut out the arms he wanted them to be his own and laid them in gestured embrace across the chest of the unmade jacket, hoping that the tenderness he felt in working on the cloth would become part of the suit and forever evident to his son, that the failings and remoteness of his fatherhood would be forgiven and redeemed in this tailoring that was to be his last gift to Stephen.

He switched on the light over his head and worked on while the headlamps of cars coming home arced across the window like searchlights for love. He worked on into the evening, lying down on his back when his knees locked and delivering a series of short blows to them with his two fists until they loosened and he could kneel like a priest to the work once more. He worked on until the pain knotted up again and he had to stop and wait for the tablet to work. It was while he was sitting there, feeling the now familiar dissolve inside him and the medication taking the pain to someplace beyond Dublin, that the doorbell rang.

Philip left the cloth on the ground and went to answer it. He was the kind of man who expected that only calamity could make the doorbell ring late in the evening, and was surprised when he saw the thin figure of Hadja Bannerje standing at the door.

"Mr. Griffin," he said, "I was wondering how you were doing."

The Indian was younger than Stephen. He had come from the hospital to find the dying man because he could not forget how the old patient had told him of his son being in love, and because the tailor had mentioned Dr. Tim Magrath. He had come, too, for reasons he did not yet understand, some part of that submerged algebra of our actions that makes obtuse and elaborate relation between X, the absence of his own father in India, and Y, the man wanting to live a little longer for his son. He came into the front room, where the cloth was cut out and the sewing machine had been uncased, and when Philip Griffin told him that he was making a suit for Stephen, Hadja Bannerje made a small bow, acknowledging the act as something true and correct in the unclear workings of the world. He sat down and saw the chess game laid out on the side table.

For a few moments the tailor said nothing. He sat in the chair across the room with the suit on the ground between them. He lowered his head and ran his hand up over it, as if smoothing the ghosts of his vanished hair. He was fearful for a while that the Indian had come to tell him the tests had revealed something new, and only when the silence had settled like old spirits between them did he look across the space. Hadja Bannerje was waiting.

"You have not heard the news of Dr. Magrath," said the Indian.

Philip felt a chill on the back of his neck. Here it was, calamity after all.

"He died this afternoon."

When I should have, thought Philip Griffin, when I was fallen against the wall and it passed over. Oh God.

Silence clotted the air with the unsayable sorrow. Philip Griffin was painted in a stained wash of guilt and put his hands beneath his chin to keep his head from falling. He felt the old unworthiness of those who survive and the loss of the man who had helped him.

"I am sorry to tell you," said Hadja. "I remember you mentioned his name."

"Yes."

"It was heart failure. He was dead in his home."

Tim Magrath's heart had failed so long before, thought the tailor. He held his head like an iron weight and breathed the short, shallow breaths of upset, until his visitor asked him could he make him a cup of tea.

"No. No, thank you." A small emptiness, and then, lifting his spirit with weary effort into the lightweight world of politeness, Philip asked, "Would you like one?"

"No. Not for me, thank you very much, Mr. Griffin."

"Right."

The two men sat still in the late evening. The doctor was wearing a pale green raincoat, and with his arms folded and his face restful, he dwelt in such apparent ease that it did not seem necessary to speak.

It was some time before the tailor noticed him looking over at the chess game.

"Do you play?" Philip asked him.

"This is a vulnerable position."

"Yes." He nodded to the truth. "My son is White. You can see what he is like. But he's a fine player most of the time." Philip stood up and went over to the board. "Would you like to play a game?"

"This is not finished," said the Indian. "You don't want to disturb it."

But already the older man was taking the pieces and resetting them to begin. "I have it memorized," he said, and lifted the suit cloth from the floor and laid it aside and drew his chair closer.

And so they played. It was past ten o'clock. A glittering cold was falling on the unwalked paths and stilled driveways of Dublin, where the windscreens of cars went blind with ice. Television light died away and families were curtained into sleep while the doctor and the tailor played a game of chess. Hadja was an accomplished player; he had been gifted with that quality of deep patience and forbearance which characterize the ultimately victorious, and which allowed him to suffer many losses without ever losing sight of his long-term goal. He took the capture of his king's knight without the slightest expression of sorrow, and neither did he rejoice when, almost an hour later, he won Philip Griffin's queen's bishop in a forked move on the king's side. It was the game and not the men that spoke. Positions and counter-positions of the pieces flowed between them as its own language, and in that exchange both men got to know each other in a way that would scarcely have been possible in the three hours the game lasted. In that playing each man revealed his own suffering and small triumphs; the chess game mirrored perfectly the pattern of life, and showed in the gradual dwindling of pieces the ceaseless exhausting of energy that is the action of time.

When Philip Griffin could see more board than pieces, it was already one o'clock in the morning. He was a slow player who did not believe in the constraints of a stop-clock. Although, by that hour, he was aware of the hopelessness of his position, he did not consider resigning. He liked the game played out to its end, for even the coming of the inevitable had a certain beauty. His only gesture at resistance was that, with the Indian about to checkmate him in four moves, he took longer and longer over his turn, gazing down at the checked timber forever, until at last Hadja Bannerje looked over at him and, seeing the transfixed expression of a dream, realized that his opponent was soundly asleep.

16

Gabriella Castoldi walked with Stephen Griffin into the night, unaware that it was the transforming moment of her life or that the farfetched and wildest happenstance could sometimes be the inevitable. She took his arm when they reached the night air. He is shaking like a tree on fire, she thought, and steadied herself against him, walking out through the grounds of the hotel to where a river waterfall was lit brilliant and white, the last expression of mountain streams as they jabbered in the swollen throat of the river running down into the free translation of the sea.

They were mismatched: his long legs and arms, the extra foot of his stride he had to keep shortening, the loom of his head over hers that made him seem craning, crooked, slowing and then towing her, all combined to make them seem oddly paired, a knee- and an ankle-sock out walking. The spray came up to meet them. Immediately their faces were wet.

"I love this," she said and, letting go his arm, stepped towards the bank of the rushing water and opened her mouth wide to meet the spray. She was a slight figure in a grey wool coat. Her hair was pulled back and lost in the collar, and the light off the water found the vulnerable places above the angles of her cheekbones. She stood and he waited three feet behind her. He had no idea what to do. Gabriella looked back at him.

"What are you thinking?" she said.

"That you are beautiful."

She turned away from him.

"There is a walk down here," she said, and stepped ahead.

She was still not sure why she had come, why she had invited him, or where one moment would lead the next. Gabriella Castoldi had abandoned the fantasy of true love; the rigour and perfectionism of her character, which had been gifted her by her father (a man whose ceaseless but muted anger at the world had found expression only in the three warts that ran in a line on the left side of his forehead), meant that she could not envision happiness for herself longer than an instant. So, as she stood by the river's edge in the late evening, where the falling fog smelled of the mountains, she did not think of love; she did not imagine that the awkward man with the long arms and bare head could have a long and lasting role in her life. She considered none of this. She was there with him simply because of the way he was, because of how he had listened to the music, because of that quality of intensity and seriousness in the white puzzle of his face that suggested a dumbfounded amazement and wonder at the same time as the long-suffering knowledge of woe.

Gabriella walked ahead of him down the gravelled path by the river. She heard his footsteps crunching unevenly behind her. It was dark and drizzling. They had moved beyond the reflected light of the floodlit waterfall into a place where the pine trees grew thickly and the scent of the night air was held low upon them by the overhanging branches. Gabriella stopped and Stephen came close to her.

"Shush. Listen," she whispered.

"Yes."

Nothing. Stillness. Their breaths slowed until the entangled sounds of the woods and the water rose like raised volume, those soft crashings and whisperings that were the life of the night, revealed and shared like a secret.

"I love this," she said. "This is why I like to stay here, in Kenmare. In the mountains."

They stood a time with nothing to say.

"The world is simple here, isn't it?" Gabriella said at last. She looked into the darkness of the river flowing past the trees. She looked at the outpouring and onrushing river that was the river of her own life and felt its sadness teem; here was her childhood in Venice, firstborn of the policeman Giovanni and Christa Castoldi, the child of their earliest loving, upon whom fell the unsaid yet subtly broadcast disappointment that she was not a son, and whom her father, Giovanni, could not hold for more than five minutes without passing her back like a strange fish netted in the murk of the lagoon; her mother, who was always pregnant and miscarrying, who passed to Gabriella the understanding that girls clean and cook, and who made her from age six the second in command of the narrow brown rooms of the house in the Calle Visciga, where already her two brothers were lords; how her duties mounted, and how frequently she stayed in the kitchen with the caged bird that did not sing to prepare the meals which might garner love in her returning father's quick praise as he gorged himself closer to death; how she had heard the violin teacher Scaramuzza when he moved into the apartment below them and managed to persuade her mother to let her take lessons; how there, too, was reinforced the already solidifying belief that nothing she could do would ever be good enough, and that the brutal music she made was a sorry and discordant insult to its composers; and yet how she had continued, playing only when her parents were out of the house, and then, when her mother, after six miscarriages, was taken to bed with the early stages of liver failure, gradually daring to bow the notes in diminuendo in the farthest room; how she had become the mother then, years before she had been a lover or known anything but the dreamt caresses that visited her sleep like the princes of fairy tales; the years of her father's pent-up and brooded-upon horror as his sons became vivid and frightful mockeries of his once most cherished machismo fantasy of the Castoldi boys, who were to be policemen like their father, cleansing the plaguey corruption that soured the air of Venice like grey spores, but who became instead the very same small villains with open shirts and silver chains whom he spent his life jailing; how Giovanni Castoldi did not get to retire, but whose spleen had ruptured and exploded inside him with hot rage in the police motor launch on the Canal Grande when he found himself chasing the slippery and evil shadow of himself that was Antonio Castoldi, who had fired three shots at the man he did not know was his father before crashing at full speed into the *vaporetto* station at the Ponte Accademia; how the music had taken over then for Gabriella; how the violin had become her father and her mother and her family; and how even Scaramuzza had admitted her progress, scratching the dryness of his right ear and clearing the wet cloud of his chest phlegm to acknowledge her with the single word *bene;* the years of her university then and the approach of those not yet men who saw in the cool remoteness of her playing something to be conquered, a woman too much in her own kingdom who they imagined needed bringing into the tight prisons of their smaller passions, and whose fumbling and filmy-sweated version of love left Gabriella Castoldi feeling there were no emotions as pure as those she played in the music; and then the poet Pollini, who arrived in her life with the surprising abruptness of grace, when beneath her eyes was already the colour of pale plums; the season of that happiness that then like everything else fell down and withered. And left her there in Kenmare.

She saw it in the night river. She saw it and felt the grief and loneliness of her world grow immense and cold inside her. She stood motionless, and Stephen stood behind her. There were no stars. The mountain fog lay on the treetops. Thin veils descended wetting their hair. Gabriella turned around.

"I don't know your name," she said.

When he told her, she nodded, as if the sounds of it revealed something that she had already known.

"Stefano," she said. "Hold me."

17

Early the following morning Gabriella lay on the bed with the covers half across her and her feet hanging over in the cool air. She was midway between waking and sleep, and lingered in that warm place where time slows and holds still the not quite vanished dream-like quality of the night. She was lying on her back and her hair fell to the right across the pillow. She kept her eyes closed and held behind them the astonished and rapturous kisses of the night, the white tremoring of Stephen's body when he was undressed, and his loving that was first infinitely hesitant and slow, each touch like a terrifying adventure — this place on her bow arm, this firmness in her neck where her violin fit and where his mouth tasted her — until, in the clockless time of two bodies learning each other like a language, he had loved her more wildly, and they had rolled back and across the bed-clothes in each other's held embrace, in a way that had sometimes seemed as if from the unseen and enormous tide of loss, grief, and despair, each was rescuing the other.

Gabriella was not in love. She was not ill or delirious for his presence, she did not feel she needed him to be able to get out of the bed and imagined she could live through the day without seeing him and have no balloon of longing inflate in her chest. She had nothing of the schoolgirl's flushed excitement and ran no fever. But the emotion she felt for Stephen Griffin was the baffled and uncertain beginnings of love nonetheless.

She lay in the bed and listened to the sounds of morning. Stephen had gone to the shops for milk for her coffee. When he returned with the milk and two punnets of strawberries, he entered her cottage with the deep hesitation of a man unsure if this was the place where he had left a dream. She stirred in the bedclothes, and he went to her kitchen, opening her presses like privacies and finding that she drank no tea, only coffee from grounds. He looked at the cups she had, at her sugar bowl and milk jug. He ran his hands on the countertop, as if fingering a hidden keyboard where there played the music of all her time there in Kenmare. He looked at everything that was hers, and then made a muddy coffee without a paper filter, carrying it in to her bedside and then sitting down in the chair beside the window like a visiting uncle, with his hands on his knees.

Gabriella sat up, and the bedclothes fell down. She looked at him and laughed.

"You are so sweet," she said, smiling at his attendant heart sitting beside her and passing through another wave of her own disbelief that such a man existed. She held out her arms to him, and in his jacket, shirt, and trousers he stretched himself across; he did not reach for her with his hands, but closed his eyes as he craned forward like a finishing sprinter and was an instant there in that invisible place of long-imagined arrival, until her fingers touched his face and drew him toppling onto the bed. She was laughing. She drew him against her breasts and rose her body against him, caressing him with the fullness of her so his face travelled the length of her skin and tasted the perfume that was herself and did not come in bottles. He shook again in spasms. He clung to her as she moved now beneath now above him, now turning him over like a shipwreck in the churned-up waters of a passion that she could not fathom. She undressed him with a quick and flashing urgency, not thinking that her actions were like those of a saviour or that the dampness of her mouth finding his was the ageless, time-honoured way in which the world was resuscitated and gasped anew the miracle air. She thought nothing. She kissed the white and shaking wreckage of his body and swallowed his tears that spouted and rolled; he wept and tried to cling to her, embracing in this woman for the first time in his adult life the possibility of happiness and feeling at the same moment that the wave might crash, drowning him in that strange foreknowledge and expectancy of suffering which every day had taught him. He held her so tightly she arched and cried out, the breath squeezed from her in a thin red-and-yellow ribbon, and she was pressed onto him like a transparency. Their loving was thrown about; it rose up and fell down, it tumbled off the bed and arrived on the carpet among Gabriella's shoes. It squirmed and burned. She took handfuls of his skin and closed them tightly within her fingers, letting go and taking another even as he held hers. He hooped her, she enwrapped him. She rolled him over and shook him. She pressed his face hard to her breasts, she pulled his shoulders against her, as if the wholeness of himself might enter there; as if each of them had somehow forgotten their sex organs or forgone them as some hopelessly inadequate apparati of conjoinment, as if they wished not to be joined at all but to be one another, to blend. They wrestled and tumbled within each other in a way that sought transcendence and to make their bodies one as air or spirit.

"I love you," Stephen said.

Gabriella touched the smooth moon of his bare head where he lay across her. But she did not say she loved him.

18

And so there was then a brief season before Christmas, a time which glimmered with the quality of fables and made for Stephen Griffin and Gabriella Castoldi the single most enduring memory of what happiness could be like on earth. The sun stayed between the mountains. When Gabriella told Stephen that the cold dampness of the weather in winter depressed her, he made the characteristically rash promise of the first-time lover that he would not let it rain on her. Within a few days, when the pine needles of the town's Christmas trees were drying and falling and the sun still warmed Kerry like Maytime, he began to believe, like a child, that love had more powers than he supposed and that the force of wishes sometimes made things true. His gift was one of pure sentimentality and he wanted so deeply for everything to turn out right that, in that brief season of sunlight, he imagined it would. He lived at Mary White's and visited Nelly Grant and carried to Gabriella's cottage the bags of fruit, honeys, and jams that fed pleasure and rapture. Sometimes she played for him. She stood beside the bed, and having bargained that he lie long and naked while he listen, she bowed a light quick music whose notes came like birds and sang through the cottage air. She played more easily than she had ever done, not yet knowing that the quality she had discovered was forgiveness and that in the secrecy of her spirit a healing had begun.

It was a season of love in the afternoon; of slow time and long caresses, of strawberries (that had been flown from Africa and bought in a market in Cork) passing from mouth to mouth like the wet ripe and softly bruised essence of pleasure itself. It was a season of nothing else; the world had been made small and sunny. Everything else had been lopped away, had in a single kiss been rendered meaningless, and while the days passed by, Stephen did not think of returning to Clare. He did not think of the letter that he must have known would come (and did) from Eileen Waters, the threat she did not quite have the authority to make that unless she heard from him at once he would be dismissed from the school, and that further, he would not get work from the department again; he did not consider tomorrow nor the diminishing funds from which he paid Mary White as Christmas approached. But neither did he hear the voice that whispers insistently beneath the surface of all our happiness, that urges you to gather each moment like a small stone and store it in the deep pockets of your soul, that knows what lies ahead and offers only the wisdom of living fully and cherishing like the briefest dream this season of loving, for these are the instants of passion which will later become those diamonds of memory that will cry out: Here, there, look, in these moments I lived and knew a boundless joy, I loved.

Stephen did not hear it. He did not think, A day will come when this will end, when I will sit in a room and turn over these moments like the story of another man's life. But rather, in those three weeks before Christmas, he awoke and loved and listened to music and clung to the thin belief that the things of the heart endured and mattered and were the secret magic which could entangle the varied and ingenious knots of life like the fingers of an ancient mariner. At thirty-two years of age, in love for the first time, Stephen was an early model of romance. He withdrew money from the bank and bought flowers from Mary Mungovan's shop on the lower street, which specialized in wreaths and funeral accessories. He carried the chrysanthemums in the crook of his arm like an infant and brought them to Gabriella as a lesser declaration of the inexpressible. It was in the character of his love that he could not describe it and tried instead to deliver it through an entire inventory of small gifts and gestures: he made her thick, undrinkable coffee every morning and brought it to her in her bed, he washed her dishes, he tidied the clothes it was her habit to leave on the floor, he brought her the Cadbury's chocolate bars she said she loved, leaving them in half-hidden places about the cottage, and telling her she was beautiful when she stood before the mirror and mockingly said he was fattening her into a Madonna; he wrote her small notes, he bought books and left them by her bed, he emptied Nelly Grant's shelves, buying every kind of fruit and fresh juice, carrying bottles of elderberry wine up the hill to the cottage in a string bag that Gabriella had brought from Venice.

Stephen did not suffer greatly from the fact that Gabriella Castoldi did not tell him that she loved him. He had the visionary blindness of a saint and wanted only for her to let him love her. He did not expect nor even imagine that she might requite his love.

Life had imbued him with a deep humility and then nourished it with a Catholic sense of his own unworthiness. He was the lesser for not being beautiful, for possessing no gift, and for the flawed understanding with which he had grown up that fate had chosen him for misfortune. He was dazzled by her, and did not care how he appeared to anyone in the town, carrying her groceries, bringing her flowers, hanging her strawberry-stained sheets on the line. It was enough for Stephen Griffin that the great airy burden of love he had discovered inside himself could be given to Gabriella. He felt she was the saddest woman he had ever met, and wanted to heal her, to caress her, and to remake the world around her with tenderness in that earliest and most redeeming of our instincts that is the deep-felt and inexplicable longing to make another happy.

They took walks in the December mountains. They told each other's lives like stories. She dared him a dozen dares and he took them on for her, taking off his clothes and sitting screaming in the icy stream while she laughed and clapped, rushing to him with their blanket and drying him gently like some astonishing new proof of God. He jumped off rocks and climbed trees, clambering slippingly among the wet branches, losing his footing, cutting his chin, triple-scratching the top of his head, and arriving forty feet above her, where at last he could answer her question and tell her what the view was like from up there. Neither did he mention his fear of heights, nor the swimming world below him, where her face seemed to bob and waver like a watery moon.

A season of tests and provings. To Gabriella Castoldi it was the unlikeliest thing; her experience of passion had taught her mistrust, and as she did not believe that she was beautiful or truly gifted, she first imagined Stephen Griffin's loving as something with the tender insubstantiality of a dream. It would pass in its own time. But when the days ran on and the strange sweetness of his presence lingered longer, Gabriella found herself waiting for the moment when he arrived at the door. He had left his kisses in her imagination, and they lived like exotic roses, blooming wild.

Five days before Christmas, when the people of the town had begun complaining that the sunny weather had robbed the season of its spirit, Gabriella lay across the body of Stephen and decided she had to break the back of love.

If it would break.

Nothing that is good in the world can last long, she believed, and the sweetness of those days and nights in the cottage had brought her to a frightening vulnerability.

She lay where Stephen could not see her face and she told him that he must go back to Clare.

"You must go back to your job," she said.

He said nothing. He touched the top of her head and stroked her hair.

"I have no job," he said.

"You have. You will get it back." She was still not looking at him. "Then you will be going to your father for Christmas."

"I have sent him a card. I told him I was going to ask you to come."

"I won't," she said, and then, while moving her right hand slowly across the pale softness of his belly in a gesture that would lodge in the underwater sand of his memory, she took a firm blow at love and said, "I am leaving. I am going back to Venice."

Silence. Her back was to him. When Stephen spoke, his voice cracked like glass in the blind air behind her.

"How long will you be . . . Will you be . . ." He didn't want to say coming back, he wanted the small room hope needs to survive.

"I don't know," said Gabriella, "I have to go. For now. I have to," she said, weeping onto his skin, kissing it gently like a farewell, and wondering why she felt the brutal necessity of testing love, of bending its back towards breaking, and trying to bring on before time the grief she imagined was inevitable.

Slowly she ran her hands down the length of his legs in last caresses. Then she turned over and saw the vanquished ruin of his face, and without telling him that she already suspected that she was pregnant, or that she could not herself dare to imagine as true and durable the love he was offering her, she reached out and touched his wet cheek and said, "Stefano, make love to me."

1

It was Christmas Eve when Stephen drove across the country once more to the house of his father. A misting rain was falling and the still unrepaired rubber of his windscreen wipers smeared it on the glass like fingers at the blood of a wound. He peered forward, but drove into unseeable country, his heart leaking the disconsolate acid of lost love. Three times he was stopped at Garda checkpoints, where big-shouldered men wore the rain like a stain on their backs and dripped it from the brims of their caps, leaning down to check the Christmas drivers for drunkenness. Stephen told one of them he did not drink, but his words came out warped with emotion and he was Breatha-lyzed all the same. When he was closer to the city, driving down the last part of the motorway into the four o'clock darkness, he almost crashed, as in a disturbed dream, into the white flanks of a wild horse.

In all, there were nine of them, galloping like a bizarre vision across the thrown lights of the cars and taking off down the motorway ahead of him. They flashed across the darkness, charging before the headlights into Dublin. For a mile the horses kept to the motorway. They trotted past the lights that changed green before they got there and disappeared, like ghosts of themselves, into the places where had once been fields.

Stephen drove the first car behind the horses and thought of Gabriella. He had already realized without shock that when you give yourself completely to someone else you see the world through their eyes, and easily imagined her own delight at the strange wildness of the scene. But then, when the horses took off to gallop to the left along the toll road to the airport, he turned right and felt the leaving of Gabriella like phantom pain in a lost limb.

When he arrived, the house lights were on. He found his key and walked across the wet lawn and was on the point of opening the door when Philip Griffin did it before him.

"Stephen," he said, briefly looking into the space where the woman was not with him and, with the strange awkwardness of those facing unfamiliar mechanics, reaching suddenly forward to embrace his son.

Together, after ham sandwiches and Mr. Kipling's mince pies, Philip and Stephen Griffin drove to Midnight Mass, which was at ten o'clock. Earlier that afternoon, on the numbing tide of his third painkiller, Philip had slipped £600 between the railings of Stephen's Green, and had gone home hoping to see in his son's expression something of the fair justice of God. He had now deposited £5,387 in the green place of the city centre. He had never put the money in the same place twice, nor had he ever gone back to see if it was gone.

The Griffins drove into the city beneath the lights of Christmas. They did not speak, but instead passed small comments on the lights, the traffic, or the rain, making use of that ancient code like spies burdened with the secret vulnerability of the world. They arrived at the Church of the Blessed Sacrament and hurried across the black weather into the organ music and the rising hum of the Rosary. They knelt and said nothing. They were two men missing women, and until the priest arrived they stayed on their knees and were, like everyone else, lost in the privacies of their own personal longing and beseeching, silent voices ascending to unknowable heaven.

The Mass began. The priest was an old man. He had said Christmas Mass in eighteen parishes, including three in Africa, and, like Philip Griffin, fully expected this to be his last. He said the prayers slowly, as if journeying back on each one into the memories of the past. And when he came to the small stand of the pulpit for the sermon, he looked down at the faces of the congregation with the serene and beatific expression of a man who has at last made peace with himself.

"I wish each of you a happy and joyful Christmas," he said, and then swallowed his breath and lost the rest of his sermon, realizing he had reached the tranquil and easeful end of words, saying nothing, just holding out his hands for a long moment in front of him, as if passing to everyone an invisible gift of joy.

To the surprise of his heart Stephen Griffin received it. He felt a strange and spreading lightness, and by the time he was sitting and watching his father go to receive Communion, he discovered he had somehow been gifted a piece of white linenlike optimism. He rose and passed his father coming back along the aisle. He took the host in his mouth for the first time in years and felt it taste like the memory of goodness. He returned and knelt down and prayed for his mother and his sister in the prayers he did not know were the echoes of his father's. Then the Mass was over and the old priest left the altar a last time. The Griffins stood up at the same time, moving from the church with the melted Communion still lingering like grace and their spirits joined with something rare and fragile as faith.

Things could still work out. Believe it.

Stephen put his hand on his father's back, and when they reached the church door he raised an umbrella over the old man as they walked out beneath the dark and starless heavens that spilled with rain.

When they returned home, it was half past eleven. Inside the house, where all his Christmases had been, Stephen made tea while his father sat in the front room and put on *"E Lucevan le stelle."* The music travelled through the house like an old guest and became, in the metamorphic magic of notes and rhythm, the true expression of those two men. It contained the full and varied complexity of their separate longings, and when they sat to have their tea, they did not speak across it. It was only when the disc had ended that Stephen picked up the opened letter that had been put by the side table for him to find. It was the angry missive from Eileen Waters, a slightly less bitter replica of the three others which Stephen had found inside his front door when he had returned to Miltown Malbay. It was school holidays and he had driven directly to Dublin without going near the principal. Now he read the letter she had sent to his father demanding to know where he was, and across the faint humming of the stilled music player, he said, "You know I was in Kenmare?"

"Yes. I got the card," his father said. The old man raised his small face to pass his son only the slightest encouragement to talk on.

Stephen was looking away. The rain sounded on the windows and made a muffled dullness of the distant ringing of churchbells.

"I mentioned bringing a friend," Stephen said, and paused and sighed and breathed the scent of lilies that was expiring from the pores on his neck.

"Oh yes, I was wondering."

"She plays the violin."

"Is that right?"

"Yes. Her name is Gabriella Castoldi. She is from Venice."

He could not tell it without half-smiling now. He said her name and felt wings opening in his chest. Then at last he told his father all. He spoke without pause and began by saying the three words "I love her," and then spinning out the tale of his loving across the midnight of Christmas like the newest fable in the oldest book of stories, telling the remarkableness of his own emotions as if they were so entirely unexpected and even unimaginable gifts that unknown friends had dropped at his door, telling the sunshine and the cloudlessness, and making his father smile away wet smiles towards the window, where the narrative of love was the certain and indisputable proof of the listening ear of God.

When Stephen had told him everything, silence fell like snow. It gathered about their ankles and rose slowly. When it was threatening to leave them frozen on the opposite sides of love, Philip Griffin raised his hand and pointed to the old chess game. Despite the sharp ending of the tale, he was not discouraged by what he had heard: goodness had travelled to his son, only it was clear now that Philip needed to do more.

"Do you . . . ?"

Stephen joined his father's eyes on the chessboard.

"It's a mess," he said. "I . . ."

"No no," said Philip, pushing the board

into place between them, "I thought that, but no, your position isn't so hopeless at all. One move changes the game."

2

On Christmas morning Stephen awoke to
find the suit his father had made him. He did
not put it on until late morning, after he had
already given Philip Griffin the new discs of
three Puccini operas and four of the violin
concerti by Vivaldi which were playing constantly in his head. When, later, he appeared
downstairs in the suit, he looked like a newer
version of himself. The cut of the cloth was so
perfectly made that for the first time in his life
he experienced the naturalness of clothes and
wore them with confidence. His father in the
downstairs hall eyed him with a scrupulous air
of self-examination, and then nodded, acknowledging that transforming moment in
which the son passes the father like opposite
but identical travellers on the up-and-down
elevators of life. Stephen was going on, Philip
thought, and renewed in himself the difficult
faith that after so much that was ineffective
and muddled and wasted in his life, this much
was going to be right. He saw his son with his

wife's eyes and felt her pride in him, too, and then led Stephen out the door of Christmas morning to drive together to the graveside.

In the days that followed, Stephen stayed in Dublin and visited Venice in his mind. When the bookshops reopened, he drove across the glitterfrost of the New Year and bought a life of Vivaldi and three histories of Venice. He came home, and while his father paced on the creak of the upstairs bedroom floor and wondered what God would want him to do next, he sat in the front room and read. He read the shadowy insubstantial version of the life of the composer, of his birth in Venice in the bleak March of 1678 in the sestiere of Castello, his father a barber who gifted his son the red hair which was startling enough to name Vivaldi later as the Red Priest of Venice, when he was already teaching violin to orphaned girls at the Ospedale della Pietà and earning in the autumn of 1703 a salary of five ducats a month. He was Maestro di Violino, the priest who did not say Mass, who left the altar with chest pains and said he could not return to it, who lived his entire life as a priest, but whose only sacrament was music, writing notes quick-handed on roughened parchment, as if taking dictation from God.

Stephen sat in Dublin in the frozen first days of January and read himself into Vivaldi's Venice. There, in fragments and hints, oblique suggestions, was the composer's relationship with the singer Annina Giro, the daughter of a French wigmaker, for whom he wrote now forgotten operas, and the all but vanished music for a voice none but he thought was so fine. Stephen played the discs he had bought his father and then read hour after hour the gilded and glorious fable that was the history of Venice, of its flamboyant past made of silks and cloths of gold, of spices and scents, of galleons and golden gondolas, the palace and power of the Doge and the ever-lapping green waters of the lagoon across which came, like rightfully returned sisters, the potent and influential magic of Arabia and China. When Stephen read of Venice, he read of Gabriella. Like every lost lover, he sought in the large room of her absence the smallest continual reminders, the dust of her presence. It did not matter that Gabriella herself had left Venice and preferred the mountains of Kerry to the bridged and watery maze of the city where she was born, when Stephen's eyes travelled the pages and read the names of streets and squares, the *calles* and *campos* that gathered

281

like excitement in the long S of the Canal Grande, he was closer to her.

When in the evenings he played a half-hearted and uninspired chess with his father, he played with a map of Venice at his feet.

"Here."

Philip Griffin was standing inside the door of the front room, having just returned from the city. He had business to attend to, he had told Stephen, leaving his son in the diminished dream that was his condition in the first cold days of January and which his father saw with increasing panic was each day undoing the good of December. He had gone into Dublin with a new withdrawal, and telling God that it was just this once, he bypassed the park railings and went instead into the travel agency of Jimmy Galvin, a man who had played soccer for Ireland and once bought from Philip Griffin four suits of blue green purple and grey tweed with specifically tailored elephantine flared trouser legs and twenty-nine-inch waists. Jimmy Galvin did not remember him. He bought his clothes off the rack now and wore them with a thoughtless monotony that reflected his life since glory. He had three girls working for him at the counter and sat in the back room behind a window, where he lived on the phone, untying the knots of foreign agencies, commissions, and airport pick-ups, and all but forgetting the moments only his legs remembered when he had scored twice against Spain.

Philip watched the top of his head and wondered if Jimmy would recognize him. He didn't, and a small loss smarted in the tailor like a sudden discovery in the death notices. He held out his money to the girl at the counter and paid in cash for a ticket and a hotel room. Then he drove to the hospital and spoke with Hadja Bannerje.

Finally, he arrived home with the envelopes in his pocket, like the folded certificates of his fatherhood. He stood inside the door and gasped as the pain roiled and made his eyebrows rise involuntarily, as if making room in his face for new suffering.

"Here," he said, and held out the envelopes.

The first one Stephen opened was the headed notepaper of Dr. Hadja Bannerje and the declaration in slanted blue ink that Stephen Griffin was currently the patient of the undersigned and that he could not return to work at the present time, for his condition necessitated monitoring under the care of yours sincerely, Dr. Hadja Bannerje.

Stephen finished reading it and looked at where the grey slump of his father was leaning against the door.

"Well?" said Philip Griffin with a breathy inhale. "That's her complaints fecked. We'll send that off to the old bitch tomorrow. Open the next one." The father nodded, he touched his tongue to wet his lips and half-grinned half-grimaced at the madcap and wild plan, its rash and foolhardy nature that was not in his character, that was the reversal of his previous position, but to which he had given himself with a kind of sweet and feckless madness that made him imagine, against all the evidence of his life and amidst the broken and long-smouldering ruins of his own heart, that here now, at last, for his son, he could play the angel of love.

Stephen opened the second envelope and found the ticket to Venice.

"Go," his father said, and did not move, speaking with that purity of motive that makes men saints, and hearing himself say the words he wanted said to him and which instead, for another while at least, stayed suspended in the lonely silence of his eyes.

"Go," he said. "Go and find her."

3

By the time Gabriella Castoldi had arrived back in Venice, she knew she was carrying Stephen Griffin's child, and bore it with sour bouts of illness up and down the steps of the Rialto and through the fish-fumed air of the narrow streets to the house of her spinster cousin, Maria, in the Calle dei Botteri. Maria Feri was fifty years old and still worked in the *papeterie* in the Calle Piovan where she had first earned wages as a girl. She welcomed Gabriella on the day before Christmas, when the grey dampness seeped through the air of the city like the cloths of drowned ghosts, and the seasonal efforts of the inhabitants to hold off melancholia was mostly manifest in the quickened movements down the alleyways and across the bridges, a hastening towards the year's end, urgent with shopping and the little clusters of families hurrying to and from visits with unbearable relatives.

Maria Feri had prepared for Christmas alone, but the unexpected arrival of her cousin visited her like a secret blessing. Her heart fluttered, roses shot out in the pale powders on her cheeks. She sat Gabriella in her only comfortable chair and tapped the cage of Goldoni, the yellow-feathered bird she had named with an endearing lack of originality, who was her truest companion and could, she said, flushing with shyness, sing finer than Pavarotti. While Gabriella sat with the bird, Maria made more welcoming the guest room where no guest had ever stayed; she carried through the sitting room extra blankets, a jug of fresh water, two apples, and the potted lemon plant which was dying in the kitchen, all the time struggling to keep the deep joy of her visitor's arrival from showing beneath it a half century of loneliness.

Gabriella sat with Goldoni. Sickness came in waves, and when she went to the window for air, the familiar mildly bitter scent of the canal water turned her insides with a swift churn. She gasped and held on to the rail, feeling both the illness of her pregnancy and the stronger, older malady that was the returning loss and disappointment of her childhood. She caught the air and gagged as if it were brown water. There she was, herself at nine years of age going to the window as if it were a portal of escape from the sharp censure of her father, who sat at the table asking questions of geography and knuckling her brothers' heads when they failed to answer correctly. Gabriella had only just slunk back into the armchair when the angular face of her cousin reappeared through the doorway. Maria saw the pallor of the other woman and supposed it to be sisterly shock at the news of Giovanni. She sat down on the hard chair opposite Gabriella and gave her a glass of mineral water.

"They arrested him last Tuesday," she said.

She was a thin yet strong woman, whose bones might have been made of an assemblage of the wooden handles of farm tools with skin drawn over them. Her lips were so used to tightness they held her expressions unfreed in a clamp which dared not release the yearning for all the unlived love her life had missed.

"I didn't think it was right," she said, "Christmas."

Gabriella smiled a half-grimace. She had not known and took the news like the latest in a long line of defeats above which the ghost of her father was laughing bitterly.

"They said Giovanni had done terrible things. He has been implicated in . . ." Maria stopped when she saw the wound open in her cousin's expression.

"I cannot help him," said Gabriella, "it is his own life. I don't know what I could do." She raised her hands and let them fall with uselessness.

"No, of course," said Maria Feri, and reached with the large fingers of her hand to touch Gabriella's knee. "You must be tired. Will you come and see if the room is all right? I can change anything you don't like."

And then it was Christmas in Venice. Rain that was falling in Dublin fell, too, into the Canal Grande and emptied the narrow streets, bathing them in a flowing melancholy until they seemed sometimes awash with the waters of sadness. The buildings perched lofty and aloof from each other, as if they could ignore entirely their lower beginnings and the certainty of their sinking to the victor of Time. The city closed in on itself, and in the sitting room of the house of Maria Feri the two women sat on either side of despair. Gabriella had not told her cousin of her pregnancy. She had given her as a Christmas gift the two bottles of bath powders that Nelly Grant had concocted as a complement to love, but Maria had put them safely away in a dry press, where all her treasured things awaited the arrival of happiness. She sat and made coffee and read long novels and fussed over her visitor. She fed Goldoni French biscottes and carried his cage away from the draught of the window when she realized he had not sung in three days.

Gabriella did not know what she was doing there. She did not know yet that she could not repair the past, and so her mind brooded on the failed pregnancies of her mother, the miscarried sisters who, like some treasured but lost luggage, had never appeared, and left her gaping at a revolving emptiness. Gabriella questioned herself with the rigour of her father. She interrogated Love until it could not answer and broke down in choked-up confusion that could only mean there was none: she did not love Stephen Griffin. Time and again, she sat under the glare of examination and, while her cousin whistled at the bars of the caged bird, she turned over in her head the impossible questions. What should she do? How could she be in love with that man? He did not love her either, did he? He loved her violin. He loved the idea of her, and had fallen in love with his own imagination.

But now the child, the child was not imaginary, she heard her father chide her: "It's irresponsible and stupid. You're a fool like your brothers. There are laws, there are rules for living and we follow them," he said, "whether we like them or not." He stood across the room from her and leaned his disgust against the wall. He held his head angled backward to aim the shot of his anger like spit.

"Andiamo a pranzo?" Maria Feri asked, and at once he vanished.

Under a black umbrella then, they went through the grey and green wateriness of the city for lunch. The air blew cold. Many places were closed, and they had to make do with the *brasserie-birreria* of Antonio Renato, who had opened for the few tourists and to escape the madness that was his family upstairs. He served the cousins a pizza primavera with a small nod and a kind of quiet and restrained decorum, as if attempting to make himself invisible. He polished the counter and gazed regretfully at the street outside.

"Will you be staying for long?" Maria Feri dared at last to ask her cousin, and then flushed with embarrassment. "Of course you are welcome for as . . . I mean, well, I am very glad."

"And you are very kind."

Maria smiled and looked down at her

lunch, hoping that her schooled air of politeness concealed her desperation for Gabriella to stay.

"I don't know exactly. I have to decide some things. I would like to stay a few weeks if I could."

"Oh, a few weeks, yes. Of course." The older woman lifted her glass of wine with a shaking hand and held it tight against her lip, lest it show her disappointment.

While the rest of the city greeted the New Year with a mixed response of religion and carnival, the cousins lived with the quietness of convalescents and waited for the cold rain to lift. Gabriella played the violin for herself, and in the other room Maria listened and experienced the astonished awe that those with undiscovered talent sometimes feel for the gifted. The music was played not with sweetness but with a sharp and quickened intensity that even Goldoni the bird recognized was the playing of the heart. Gabriella played it for herself; she played it in the city where her music had begun, and in the playing revisited the rooms of her home; she played it for the child not yet born, and for the thousand unanswerable questions of its future. She played the music for its own order, for the pleasure of its form, which was in itself the one perfect thing in her life. And when she had finished, and the door of her cousin's room creaked and the bird began to sing, she lay on the bed in the kind of exhaustion that makes do for peace.

It rained on. When the rain lifted, the mist clung in the sleeves of the streets. Venice dripped into itself. Short damp days passed moments after they had begun. Gabriella awoke with the door closing behind her cousin going out to work. Then she turned over in the deep blankets of the bed and it was afternoon and the grey light of another day was sliding softly into the waters. She rose and walked around the apartment in her nightgown. She watched from the window, throwing a cloth over the birdcage when the manic gaiety of his chirping stitched like a needle along the soft rim of her brain. Gabriella returned to her bed. With her hands on her unborn child, she turned into the pillow and became her mother. She became the woman giving birth to grief, to loss, and to the failure of hope. Sweat ran down her face, her hair matted in wild short ropes, her mouth dried, and her tongue wore a white fur. She cried without tears and, in that room in Venice, felt pressing down on her the terrible loneliness of those who seek like saints to know and do the right thing. Oh God, she thought, closing her eyes for clearer vision and looking in the darkness for a sign, Oh, God, what am I to do?

4

When Philip Griffin waved Stephen goodbye
from the edge of the front garden, he felt a
weight lifting in his spirit and looked down to
see that his shoes were still touching the
ground. It was the day after the Feast of the
Epiphany. There was a sense of slow waking
in the drizzling air, as if Christmas like a re-
luctant guest was only now leaving the sub-
urbs; the streets were drowsy with aftermath.
Knowing that Stephen was leaving for
Venice, both men had woken up mute and
spent breakfast with the studied concentration of wordless monks. Stephen wore his
father's suit, with the tickets and his pass-
port next to his breast. The bigness of his
feelings kept colliding within him. The
round enormity of his gratitude rose in his
gorge like a ball cock. He could say nothing.
His fingers twisted in knots of yearning that
kept coming apart beneath the table and
leaving him feeling the emptiness of air with
a free-falling panic. He thought of Gabriella

vanished into Venice and, in the suit of Philip Griffin, was briefly courageous, balanced on a thin and heroic belief like some latter-day Icarus moments before he chanced the waxen wings and leapt into the air. I will find her, he thought. I'm sure I will. He gulped his tea. The sweat ran off his shoulder blades into the small channel of his back. He took leave of his father with the delicate and mismatched embrace of a crane above a small building, then walked out across the weather to his car.

Philip watched him drive away. He watched the emptiness after the car had gone and then let the wordlessness of his morning escape in a low groan. He opened his mouth to let his relief float out and followed it immediately with the quick prayer: "Oh God, Anne, I hope it works out." Then he went back inside the house, where he climbed the stairs to his bedroom slowly, gripping the bannister like the nearness of his last days, ascending, going to take out the bank book, where he could recheck the balance of his account and calculate anew the cost of living.

5

Beneath the powders with which she tried to smooth away some of the wrinkles of her life, Maria Feri's face bloomed crimson. Her cousin was pregnant. Gabriella was sitting in the dim light in such a fallen torpor that Maria had to disguise her delight when she was told, and she turned instead to Goldoni in his cage. She tapped him the news until his heart was fluttering. She wanted to share with him the extraordinary vision of it: a child, a child could be born here, right here. And in the vastness of her loneliness a pure joy flew, white as a dove. Maria did not think of the father, of the missing man; she had lived her life in the company of that absence, moving from the days of promise, when any moment he might appear, to a slow, sad reckoning that was like the slow and unannounced fall of petals from last week's flowers; she did not think to ask Gabriella. Instead, she turned her back momentarily and tapped the birdcage to see if Goldoni could sing her mood. Her cousin had come to live with her and now was going to have a baby. For Maria Feri it seemed as if everything in her life might have been waiting for this; it was the arrival of significance. Here was a meaning that washed clean the smudge of ordinary days, weeks, and years. Here, after all, was discovered purpose; she was to be the child's other mother. Goldoni sang. Maria regained the composure that was her learned manner with the world and turned to her cousin.

"You are run down," she said. "We must take good care of you. Of course you should have told me sooner. My bed is much more comfortable. I will move you in there tonight."

"No, please."

"Yes." She touched a fallen ash-grey hair back from her eye and had the brief dizzy sensation of feeling pregnant herself. "*Mia cara cugina.* Gabriella. You are my guest here. Please let me make you welcome. It is my happiness."

She left the room and went to the kitchen, from where she could still hear the bird singing. Then she cooked the first of several meals that were her prescription to enrich the iron in her cousin's blood. The scent of liver with onions and polenta travelled the house like an upbraiding nanny.

Gabriella had told Maria only when the weight of her uncertainty threatened a kind of madness. She had told her she was pregnant to explain the discourtesy of not wanting to go out to hear concerts or visit relations. She had told her in desperation, not with shame or upset, but with the calm resignation of those who have no idea what is supposed to happen next. While the pots were clattering and the onions sizzling in oil, Gabriella lay back in the armchair and drifted in a half-dream of Kenmare. How unreal it seemed now. The days and nights of loving blended in a blue memory. What had happened? She turned to the long, narrow window that looked across the street at the ochre wall of the Passinettis' and tried to see there the face of Stephen. Then she shut her eyes and held her lips tight together, as if one kissed the other.

And there he was. He was that long white figure standing by her bedside. He was the man she had reached out to in the morning and who had come onto the bed and been careful to keep his shoes sticking out in the air not soiling the covers. He was the man who shook like tin foil when she touched him. Gabriella's heart opened with memories of him: how he looked at her with disbelief, how he reached across the space between them each time, as if the journey of his fingers towards her skin were the sailing of some intrepid armada voyaging towards a dream continent. She lay back in soft memories all afternoon, until darkness fell, and then, for no reason other than that it was the learned habit of years, her mind sliced into them like a knife: she diced them into nothings. Love wears off like cheap perfume, she heard her father say. A child, marriage, a life together, these were different things from a passion in the Irish mountains. Gabriella heard her father, she heard the harshness of his voice and saw the vanquished look of his eyes, and then with a sudden chill understood that his voice was her own. It was she who was unable to believe in love. She had been able to sustain no relationship in her life thus far; there was some flaw in her, she believed, some fracture that ran deep below the surface of her soul and made the reality of loving seem a fairy tale. Stephen loved her, she knew that, and knew, too, that she had loved him in Kenmare. But in the dull melancholic weathers of Venice, trapped in the dry rooms of the apartment of Maria Feri, Gabriella lost belief in the future.

A return to Ireland seemed suddenly impossible. She could not imagine herself a mother, and fell into naps feverish with nightmares of miscarriage and blood. Her hair matted and her eyes burning, she woke in the dawn with pressure on her soul and banged on the birdcage to get Goldoni to stop singing.

6

When Stephen arrived off the airport bus in the Piazzale Roma, he had no idea where to go. The afternoon was chill and grey and empty. He had less than fifteen phrases in Italian and had never been out of Ireland before, and yet with the blind innocence of lovers, imagined he would find his way to Gabriella. He did not have an address for her or the slightest clue other than the name of her old music teacher, Scaramuzza, who he knew might be dead. He stood in the *piazzale* with his bag and waited until he could sense the unseen canal to his left, and then he crossed to the floating platform to await the *vaporetto*.

Venice on that January afternoon was unlike the pictures of itself. When the *vaporetto* came and took him in a steady tugging round the bends of the Canal Grande, Stephen saw the palazzi grimly shuttered against the winter and had a sense of the city turning its back on the progress of time.

Greenly brown watermarks lined the lower walls of the buildings; the colour of everything was faded, there was a worn air of enormous fatigue in that winter afternoon, as if some long and brutal enemy had been exhaustively endured and barely defeated, leaving the stonework of the city itself cracked and dismayed in a way that to the summer tourists would seem antique and elegant with grandeur. Still, it was Venice. It was like nowhere else, and as the *vaporetto* moved down the green waters of the canal, the very frailty of the city, its watery divisions and myriad narrowly bridged islands, struck Stephen as being clearly the city of Gabriella. He could imagine her there. He could imagine the childhood she had described to him in those narrow ochre buildings that rose from the waters. He could see her as a girl and felt in the foolish hopeful way of the romantic that in some way he could heal her past by coming. He leaned on the side rail of the boat and watched the slender streetways they passed as if he would suddenly see her.

He got off at the Ponte Accademia and found his way with the small tourist map in his guidebook to the Hotel San Stefano. His father had chosen it with the same purpose he had chosen Stephen's Green: to remind

God to keep an eye on his son.

After Stephen had settled in his narrow room and opened the shutters that looked out on the Campo San Stefano, he got a phonebook and checked the listings under Castoldi. He knew that Gabriella's parents were dead, but imagined that he might find one of her brothers or relations and learn where she was. On a small piece of paper he had written down the phrases he needed.

"Mi scusi, sto cercando Gabriella Castoldi."

He rang seven different numbers and grew familiar with the exasperated tones of Venetian voices telling him he was calling a wrong number.

"Ha spagliato numero."

"Gabriella Castoldi."

"Chi e? Non l'ho mai sentita."

By the following midday he had called them all.

There was no violin teacher Scaramuzza either.

It rained coldly. He had come ill prepared for the weather and wore a sweater beneath the blue suit his father had made for him while he walked through the chill city looking for her. He began after breakfast. He crossed the empty square of San Stefano, where no pigeons flew, and took different *sestieri* each time, walking through the labyrinthine alleyways, stopping to read carefully the posters of concert performances, and then pacing on while his symptoms of flu worsened. His nose streamed. The cold made his ears burn and his eyes water. Within five days of pursuit through the puzzle of the city, he was a shattered, wild-looking shell of himself. He imagined the awfulness of chance lurked everywhere, that he might miss the opportunity of meeting her if he stopped somewhere for lunch, that if he rested for the afternoon she might be that very day passing by the hotel. It was the madness of the unrequited, and in the city of Venice for ten days that January Stephen Griffin succumbed to it, walking from morning until night the twisted street system, where the sudden turns and blind alleys might have been invented for avoidance and secrecy.

For ten days Stephen searched for Gabriella. He asked for her and said her name at shops and fish stalls, and then, in desperation, visited damp candlelit churches, where he prayed that he might find her, until at last, his coughs choking in his chest and his body releasing a kind of rheumy film of sweat and anguish, he surrendered, took the *vaporetto* back up the canal, and returned to Ireland.

7

On the twenty-third of January Philip Griffin
awoke with no pain. The morning was bril-
liantly lit. It was as if spring was being pre-
viewed, and so when he got out of bed he
chose the light fabric of his green trousers
with the blue blazer that he had worn in the
summertime. He breakfasted with Puccini.
He played the music so loud that down the
little street Mrs. Flynn and Mrs. Hehir listened while they cleaned their windows and
hummed the airs without knowing them.
(The music slipped inside their minds like
birds in trees, and within two days both of
them had bought discs of *Turandot*.) Philip
left the music player on Repeat and polished
his shoes to the infinite sweetness of *"In
questa reggia."* When he had finished, he
looked at himself in the mirror and was suddenly himself forty years younger, looking at
the fresh face of his youth before going to
meet Anne for the first time.

The music soared through the rooms. He

almost wept with happiness. His pain had died away. At last, he thought. At last. Stephen was in Venice. And Philip had given him the ticket, had urged him to go. If it wasn't for me he mightn't have gone. But now he will be all right. He will be there and have met her, and she must love him, after all. He shook his head with the surge of gratitude he felt, that his son's life would turn out well in the end, that Stephen would not be left abandoned again, and that God had been listening, after all. Suddenly the logical formula of his life was made clear: while love progressed in Venice, the cancer grew in Dublin. The fact that that morning he felt no pain meant that there was nowhere else for the cancer to go, his healthy tissue had been eaten up. This he took to be a good sign. Now is the time, I must be ready to meet her now.

He walked out the door, leaving Puccini playing as the best defense against the daylight thieves that robbed the houses on the street in numerical sequence. He took his car and drove to the bank with the excitement of a youth on his first date. He called for the manager and withdrew everything he had left in his account, taking the cash and putting it in a plastic shopping bag before heading for Stephen's Green.

The morning had a soft quality that Philip Griffin imagined had been prepared for him like a bed. Sunlight danced across the windows of buses. The perfumes of spring were awakened and mingled beneath the leafless trees of Stephen's Green, catching the moving crowds and teasing them with a sense of rebirth. At the first railings he came to, Philip stopped and reached in the bag. He let his fingers clutch the money blindly and looked up at the blue sky, as if he could see there the face of lost love. The brim of his hat dribbled a small sweat. With only a half glance about him, he took a fistful of twenty-pound notes and stuffed them quickly into the bushes at the muddy bottom of the railing. Then he walked on. He didn't hurry. He had a lot to get rid of, and knew that when the last of his lifetime's savings had been given away, he would have exhausted his source of good acts and at last death would arrive. He would fall down in the street, and his wife would be there.

He had no pain. The sun pressed its palms on the back of his blazer. He smiled, thinking of Stephen in Venice, and wondered if that was where the weather had come from. He stopped and leaned against the railings, letting the city pass him for a few moments. Then he reached into the shopping bag and drew out another thousand pounds. He was about to make the second down payment and had turned to put the money through the railings when a blow struck his head.

His hat fell forward onto his face. A man wrenched his arm backward. He cried out, but his cry was short and went downward instead of up, so that the sound was lost. There were two men. They were not men, they were youths, he thought. He was expecting angels. A woman walking past was looking at them. "Hey," she said. And the second blow landed in Philip's stomach, and his head fell down and he vomited on himself. For an instant he clung backhandedly to the railing behind him as he was swaying over, holding an instant as if there was still some chance the world was reparable and he could catch the ship of death.

"Hey, stop that!" the woman called from another world. This brought another blow, hasty, more urgent. Any moment there might be rescue, he thought. Help me, please. Still, Philip did not let go of the bag. Not until he felt teeth biting into his hand. They grated on his bone and a searing pain ran through him, so he screamed and let go. Then the men were running away, and the money was gone.

The world hung and swayed in the sun-light. The old tailor slid down the railing to the ground.

8

To his later regret, Stephen did not call his father when he returned to Ireland. He could not face the disappointment he would bring him, and so instead slipped into Dublin, took his car from where he had left it at the airport, and drove across the country to Clare. In the cottage by the sea he lay on the bed, with no music playing, and waited for his flu to pass. He lived in the hollow emptiness of the lost and did nothing. When, after a week, he was able to move around without betraying too blatantly the evidence of heartbreak, he drove to the school and asked if he could return to teaching.

Eileen Waters was astonished. She did not believe his excuses; she eyed him distrustfully, like the vision of her own misjudgement, and was not prepared to be caught off guard again. She kept the interview going longer than necessary, leaving Stephen in the office and visiting her bathroom where she took time to examine her facial expressions for signs of weakness. Only when she was convinced that she looked severe, that she was not a woman to be trifled with, did she return to the interview.

"Your condition," she said, "the one this doctor referred to, is it passed?"

Stephen looked at her across the emptiness of the world. "Yes," he whispered.

Eileen Waters paused. "Probation," she said then. "I can take you back on probation." She fixed her eyes on him like grappling hooks and tried to hoist herself up inside the shadowy mystery of him. What the hell was this man's problem? What was he hiding from her?

"I've had to take your classes myself," she said. "We couldn't get a sub. We've all had to cover. A situation like this is hard on all the staff."

"I'm sorry."

"Yes. Well." She paused and stopped herself from going on. It was a trick she had learned: use pauses. Silence is a strong weapon. Let him feel my silence now, she thought, and turned her tongue along the front of her teeth.

"Well?" Stephen said.

"I was very . . . very . . ." She paused again. She released her hands from each other and placed them flatly on the table, as if just

311

keeping it from floating upward. "Very disappointed."

Stephen just sat, slouched in his father's suit, his spirit too low to make a stronger case. He felt he was deep in ashes. When he moved the slightest muscle, they blew up into his eyes.

"As it happens," Eileen Waters told him, "it would not be possible to replace you for the remainder of the school year, in any case. So you can be on probation until June. I will expect full attendance until that time." She announced rather than spoke, obscuring the weakness of her character with performance.

Secretly she longed for Stephen to break down, to slide onto his knees and weep, to confess and reveal to her there in the office exactly where he had been and what terrible turbulence had left him like this now. She wanted to be the rock he clung to and, despite herself, turned her most compassionate gaze on him as he stood up to leave.

"It has been unfortunate," she said. "But it is now behind you." She held the doorknob but did not turn it. For a brief moment the hope crossed her eyes and she imagined one last time that he might stop and truly speak to her. But it passed and she composed herself, readjusting the face of consternation as she drew open the door and let the ashen figure leave.

And so Stephen's life resumed. He taught classes in history. He walked the beach with the great weight of nothing pressing his footsteps deep into the sand. He had lost love and accepted the harshness of the winter storms as if they were a personal judgement. On his first day back in the school he waited for an eruption among the boys, but it did not come. It was as if the pallor of his complexion, the tone of his voice, or the general aspect of his demeanour all broadcast the same message: Here is a broken man, leave him alone.

He went home in the last light of the afternoon and was lying on his bed fifteen minutes after finishing work. He lay in the suit that was coming apart a little more every day. He did not know yet that his father had been robbed of his lifetime's savings or that he had told the doctors his son was unreachable in Venice and was spending days in hospital while Puccini played on in the empty house without him.

Stephen did not know the half of it; he did not know that Gabriella Castoldi lay like him on a bed of diminished hope, that she waited for a sign that did not come, and balanced on the edge of new life unable to move. For the plots of love and death had stopped altogether. It was a time when nothing happened. A cold, strange, wind-and-rain-beaten season of its own. It arrived in off the Atlantic and smashed on the rocks with destructive gladness. Hail fell out of the night skies into the churned-up waves. People hurried from their houses to their cars; they held their complaints closed on their chests and then gasped with released curses and coughs when they stepped inside shelter. A brutal weather held the towns of the west captive, and in it nothing grew. Gorse and white-thorn bushes slanted east-ward and the cattle huddled beneath them. Caps blew off. Puddle-mirrors loomed in the yellowing grass, and everything waited.

9

When Gabriella Castoldi awoke in the dawn light on the morning of the last day of January, she smelled smoke. She rose from her bed and opened the window to be sure it was not a fire in her dreams. It was not. The sky above the red rooftops wore a grey smudge and the air of Venice smelled bitter with grief.

It was half an hour before she discovered what had happened. She dressed quickly, prompted by a sudden sense of urgency. When she stepped into the street, the disappointed light of the January morning met her like a returned memory from childhood. She drew her green coat across her chest and walked toward the smoke. When she was crossing the Campo Manin, she already feared what had happened. Others were walking talking in the same direction, hurrying along like blood to a bruise.

They crossed the Campo San Angelo and were stopped by *polizia*.

They stood, the gathering excited crowd,

and heard the truth of their fears confirmed. The Teatro la Fenice, one of the most spectacular opera houses in the world — the building, it was said, was like being inside a diamond — had been burned to the ground again.

Gabriella heard it in disbelief. *"Non si credo."* She gasped a shallow breath and felt the blood rush to her face. *"O mio Dio."* She looked away and back again at the billowing smoke and thought she would fall down. The vision struck her forcibly like the phantasms of nightmare, and her heart raced with the distress of it. She wanted to cry out and run away, but stood with the others staring at the dark swirls rising and smudging the sky. She watched, and though she could not see the *teatro* itself, she felt the loveliness burn, she felt the stage she had stood on crackle with the licking flames and herself falling through it, downward into the darkness. And in that moment of freefall, even while she was standing there in the bitter fume-soured air of the Calle Caotorta and seeing burn so much more than the *teatro,* seeing the burning of all her yesterdays in that city, Gabriella thought suddenly of Stephen and knew that to go forward she had to go back to Kerry, and that the puzzle of love was that the pieces did not seem to fit but lay in the palm of your hand like some insoluble cipher, until at last you let them go and saw them fall, gradually, into place.

10

When Philip Griffin opened his eyes he did not see the face of God.

He saw the round, mobile face of Michael Farrell like a placid moon hovering beside his hospital bed.

There was more of Michael Farrell than God intended. He sat beside the bed in a chair that did not fit him. He wore an expanse of grey cloth with a white shirt and a yellow tie. He was immaculately groomed and kept his hands on the great globes of his knees. The absurd smallness of his shoes squeaked on the polished floor like minor jokes.

"Well," he said.

"Well well well," he said. "There you are now." He leaned forward, the chair drew breath. "You don't know me, of course." He blinked his eyes together. "I work for Fitzgerald & Carey. The solicitors," he added, struck as he always was that the name brought no recognition and that as a large man his junior capacity diminished him. He brought the very tip of his tongue peeping out between his lips and kept it pressed briefly, stoppering further announcement.

He looked down at the small broken figure of the tailor in the bed and thought that the lack of reaction was perhaps nothing but fear. So, withdrawing his tongue, he threw up the eyebrows to say, "No no, there's no trouble. Nothing wrong. We sent you a couple of letters, Mr. Griffin. They're at your house waiting. In any case, we learned about your misfortune, and well, I live across from the hospital here and I thought I'd check up on you myself . . ."

He waited a moment to see if any light dawned on Philip Griffin's face. But it did not. The old man just watched him with a kind of frozen bewilderment.

"Yes indeed," he said. "Well, you know the late Dr. Tim Magrath?"

Philip Griffin made no gesture or expression. He lay motionless in the deep confusion and abandonment of those who feel God has not heard their calling.

Michael Farrell paused a final time, took a white handkerchief from inside his jacket, and dabbed at the damp leakage all over his face. "Well," he said, "it's Mr. Considine who will tell you, but Dr. Magrath had no family as such, and well, you've been named prominently in his will." He paused. "Very prominently," he added, and then leaned forward to pat a huge hand on the tailor's shoulder, saying, "Now, isn't that good news?"

11

From the moment Gabriella returned to the apartment, Maria Feri knew that her dream of being the twin mother of the child had burst. Gabriella would not stay in Venice. When she walked in the door there were ashes in her hair, her eyes burned with a kind of wild indignation as she paced in the living room and would not sit down. The bird flew about in his cage.

"They have burned down La Fenice," she said.

"*Santo cielo*. Oh, Gabriella, be calm. Calm yourself. Sit down."

"No, I can't. I don't want to. I feel like . . ."

She thumped the back of the armchair hard. The acrid smell of destruction rose in the air, and the ashes spun from her head in a pale beam of sunlight. She could not be still, and while her cousin leaned against the press that displayed the serene blue glass of Murano, Gabriella kept moving back and forth across the light, twisting like a fish on a grim hook.

The disaster of the opera house spoke to her personally, like a moral fable; and it was less than an hour before she had discovered the sharpness of its meaning inside her: we cannot remake the past nor build a new life on the ruins of the old.

It was so obvious, and painful. The city was spoiled for her now, and even though it was long before she heard the faintest rumours that her brother Antonio had in some way been involved in the fire, that Giovanni had laughed in his cell so loudly when he heard, that the jailors had gagged him, Gabriella knew that she would leave Venice for good. She couldn't fathom the murky depth of that evil, to destroy the glittering place of music.

"I can't believe it," she said, and struck at the wing of the chair.

Maria felt the glasses tremble in the press behind her and saw anew how one grief impacts on another. She raised the sharp angle of her nose as a precaution against tears and held on to the press with pale, hidden hands. The bird watched her and did not sing.

"It is barbarous. It is, you know. It is . . ."

"It is very sad," said Maria from the shadowed side of the room, her voice low as a sigh in an ancient chair as her spirit subsided into it.

"It was like a jewel, La Fenice."

"Yes."

Gabriella lost her words. She leaned on the window, and at once the full force of man's stupidity, meanness, and malevolence caught up with her and crushed the energy of her rage. She could say nothing. The two women stood in the room silently apart and the light diminished. They could not speak. It was as if the room were flooded to the very rims of their lips with the despair of mankind and to utter another sound could only drown them. Maria Feri felt her own frailty and the great sudden pressure of the world. She told herself to concentrate. She made a mental ladder of prayers and thought of her favourite story of Venice, of how once, when the city had a plague, the population had prayed so fervently that their prayers became a wind that reached Mary in heaven, and how when the plague had passed, they had built her an impossible church on water. It was her favourite story, for Maria knew intimately the quality of that beseeching and could easily imagine the force of yearning transformed into something elemental. While Gabriella looked out on the smudge of man on the Venetian sky,

Maria Feri held herself stiffly against the press and longed for what she already knew was impossible.

Then perhaps time passed the two of them by. The light was lost in clouds of smoke. Gabriella and Maria sat there silently, with the strange unity of people waking together to the disappointed endings of their separate dreams. At last Maria spoke.

"It is not the city," she said with the sudden bravery of the vanquished.

"What?"

"It is a sad thing, but that is not the pain in your heart." She stepped away from the press towards her cousin. Goldoni flitted onto the high bar in the cage. Maria reached the place where the shallow bar of light fell, and almost at once the things she had come forward to say were unsayable, were swiftly rendered mute and unnecessary as Gabriella turned towards her.

"Oh God," Gabriella said. Instantly her hands flew like birds to her lower lip, and in that strange way that one tragedy trapezes to the next, she was torn apart by the terrible uncertainty of her ability to sustain love.

"Oh God, Maria," she said, "what am I to do?"

And in that moment, as Maria Feri approached to put her arms around her cousin, becoming briefly the mother of the child, and held her with strength and tenderness in the nourishing faith that mothers know, Gabriella Castoldi changed her life and surrendered to that embrace, and wept. Her face flowed, the way water might flow from a rock. In Maria's arms her ferocity was gone and she allowed herself to be gently guided into the big armchair.

"I'm sorry," she whispered.

"Stop. Please, Gabriella."

Maria knelt down beside the armchair and stroked her cousin's hair.

"Do you love him?" Maria said.

"Oh God. Oh God Oh God Oh God."

"Gabriella, tell me." Maria could not see her face. She stroked her hair. She drew a scented paper tissue from the sleeve of her beige cardigan, but Gabriella did not take it.

"Gabriella?"

"How can I know? I can't. I might. I think I do. I don't know." She raised her wet face and swollen eyes. "I don't know."

"Does he love you?"

Gabriella brought her fingers to her cheeks; she touched them as if she were another.

"He thinks he does. If I go back, if I tell him I have his child, he will tell me he loves me, he will marry me. He is a good man. His goodness will love me."

"And what is wrong with that?"

In the cage the bird sang six notes in echo.

"Look at me, Gabriella," Maria said. "I missed my chances. I did not know. I waited. I waited, thinking, A day will come, Maria, and you will know. And do you know what? It did not. It did not come and he went away."

"Maria."

"Listen, Gabriella! I know. I have missed out. I have missed love because of pride, nothing else. It was my own fault. You think I don't know, I do. I know. I know what I am and how I am and how my life will be. I have given up thinking a day will come and I will know. For it will not come now. No matter how many prayers climb to heaven or how deeply my knees mark the floor. Please, Gabriella. I won't speak of it again. But please, don't wait to know. Go."

Maria pressed on the armchair to raise herself from the floor. She walked away from Gabriella, put on her low-heeled brown shoes, and powdered over the pale face of sorrow with another that was rouged with hope. When she looked at herself in the mirror she was ten years older, but respectable with a reserve that was a finer mask that any made in Venice. She practised a thin smile. Then she left the house in her sensible shoes and entered the streets that smelled of the burned opera house, raising her chin from defeat and redeemed in the not small triumph of knowing herself so well.

She went on her way to work.

It was the middle of the morning.

12

Twelve hours later Gabriella phoned Stephen.

He was lying on top of his bed in the blue suit. When he stood in the moonless dark, the right sleeve of the jacket came loose and fell down his arm.

His phone had not rung in days. He had returned from Venice two weeks and had not yet called his father. He had imagined the disappointment the old man would feel and waited each day, hoping to find a way to tell him. Finally, he could wait no longer and decided he would drive to Dublin the following Saturday.

The phone rang. In the time it took him to cross the bedroom to answer it in the blind dark of the hallway, the certainty that it was bad news made his throat tight. He was stooped forward, guilt weighing his shoulders, and imagined even as his hand found the cold receiver that it was his father or, worse, news of him.

Then he heard her voice.

"Stefano?"

The sound came from so far away it might have been the next world. He could not believe it was his name in her mouth. He opened his lips to it in the darkness. The wind that came beneath the front door chilled his ankles. He held the receiver with two hands and listened deeply to the sound that was the sound of underneath the sea.

"Stefano, hello?"

His lips moved soundlessly and his eyebrows lowered as if he was concentrating on the most difficult puzzle in the world.

"Yes," he said at last. "Yes. Gabriella."

He could say nothing else. The tenderness of her voice moved him. He felt he would fall down, and with the loose-sleeved arm, he reached to touch the wall.

"I had to talk to you. I have something to tell you," said Gabriella.

She waited. The deep ocean of the darkness between them crackled down the telephone line. Stephen said nothing. He listened to her breath as if it were language.

"I am carrying your child," she said, "and . . ."

And his breath went, as if someone else needed it and took it. He put his forehead against the wall to balance himself; life came pulsing through the darkness and lit him like a charge. He was exhilarated yet extinguishable. Gabriella was talking, but his ears were humming. He pressed his head against the wall.

"I love you," he said.

"Stephen."

"I love you."

"I know. I know you do. But . . . Well, I mean this is different. It's a child, it's . . . I don't know what I feel. I don't know what I will feel tomorrow, the next day, the day after . . ."

"Please, Gabriella." He said it like a demand. "I want you. I want to see you. I want to be with you. Oh God, Gabriella, I can't . . ." He stopped and thumped his forehead on the wall. His face was wet. "I love you." He had nothing else to say and imagined for a moment if he repeated ceaselessly the three immemorial words, then the enchantment of language would bring her to him.

"You are kind and good. You are too good for me," she said. "You love me even if . . ." She paused, as if a wave were rising, then said, "I don't know if I love you, Stephen."

The one who had taken his breath now took his voice. The truth was like ice on him. Then Gabriella said, "I mean I do. I did. It's just me. I am so wretched. I . . . I don't know.

Can I love anyone for my whole life? I don't know."

And Stephen's voice returned: "I was in Venice."

"What?"

"I came to find you. I . . ."

"Oh God, Stephen . . . Where did you, when did . . . ?" And the questions fell away into nothingness, and the air hummed down the line between them.

Please, Stephen thought, please, God. And he closed his eyes tightly on that deeper darkness that was the darkness of all the disappointed days of his life, the darkness of that all but defeated spirit that skirted the shadowy edge of dreams with the expectation only of their failure. Then he heard her say:

"I will come back to Kerry."

He wasn't sure he had heard her.

"I will come next week to Kenmare," she said, as if she were telling herself to see how it sounded.

There was silence. Their lives hung in the baffled air; then Stephen said, "Play something."

"What?"

"Play something, please."

"Now?"

"Yes."

"I couldn't. I haven't played since . . ."

"Gabriella."

The sea rushed into the phone.

"Wait," she said.

And while Stephen held the phone in the darkness, he imagined her crossing a living room in a building just across the Campo San Stefano from where he had looked out on Venice, and he joined her there in imagination as she found the case and opened it and rosined the bow and walked back across the hardwood floor, making the footsteps that he could hear approaching (as Maria Feri heard them, too, behind the shelter of her slightly ajar bedroom door). Then Gabriella was playing the violin beside the telephone, a passage from the A Minor Concerto of Antonio Vivaldi.

The music travelled, invisible as love, into the house by the sea. It returned, and was like some simple and ancient language between them, the one playing, the other listening. The quick notes in the upper octaves were the music of human ache and flurried down the phone the unsayable, timeless message of all our yearning, the never-ending, indefatigable, and desperate need to believe love like God's exists on earth. It was a message beyond telling. Yet it travelled the three hundred years from the Ospedale della Pietà, where Vivaldi had scored the music in black ink by waxen candlelight, all the way to that moonless night when Gabriella Castoldi played it to the shores of the Atlantic. It played and pierced Stephen Griffin like an arrow.

Then it stopped, and as if the natural closure of that playing was a coda of silence, the phone line hummed between them for a time. They said nothing, and then replaced the receivers.

As if he had just returned to the world, Stephen opened the front door. The loose sleeve of his jacket fell off and he caught it and put it on, patting it back in place like a plasticine limb and going along the gravelled pathway into the big blowing of the night wind.

"Gabriella," he said softly, letting the gusts take her name like a bird and blow it down the road. *Gabriella.* Clouds blacked the stars. The sea was in the air and spat saltily at the back of the house, but Stephen did not care and walked down to where the land fell away to the rocks and the waves. His heart was racing. He felt as if, out of the infinite vastness of the unknown, a hand had reached for him, and he had been given new grace.

He walked down to the sea, because he

felt she was nearer to him there. Though he faced west, he imagined her there before him in the water. His shoes sunk in the soft sand. The white of the waves greyed and vanished in the darkness and made the sea seem smaller than it was. Stephen felt a buoyant whiteness rise in his spirit, and remembered his father. He thought how Philip Griffin thought he was still in Venice, thought that he was with Gabriella walking the Fondamenta delle Zattere allo Spirito Santo and taking the air of the New Year like a blessing. He thought of it and thought his father's gift was not in vain, for she was coming now.

Stephen opened his arms wide and held back his head. And he sat in the wet sand and looked out. "Thank you," he said to his father, who was just then passing him across the waves in a floating dream.

13

It was early the following morning when Stephen was awoken by the phone once again.

He walked into the hallway in the dismantled suit, and down the clearest line heard Hadja Bannerje tell him that his father had died during the night.

IV

1

Gabriella returned to Kenmare on Saint Brigid's Day at the beginning of February. She travelled by bus from Dublin in slow stages, and arrived on the road through the mountains as the darkness fell over them. In the headlights the road gleamed and vanished like an eel, the way ahead and the way behind only briefly present as the bus plunged on, its three passengers clutching the waywardness of their unsteady bags as if they were straying children. When the bus arrived in Kenmare, the brakes hissed and sighed and the driver, Mike Mahony, turned an uneven grin backward to the ones who had survived with him another day. God was good, his face implied, and hadn't toppled us into death yet. With true but brief pride he watched the few souls get off, as if he knew that he had delivered love back into the town.

If he had, it was well hidden. Gabriella was sick. The journey had been wrenching; the sorrow of leaving Maria Feri in the apartment in Venice where the bird sang dementedly and had to be cloaked like a funeral all day and night had left Gabriella filled with the emptiness of new loss. She travelled with the infinite introspection of uncertain lovers, and by the time she had reached Dublin, the oily mixture of regret and hope had spread. Now nausea floated to her face like a sourness rising off her soul. The hair at her forehead was dripping a cool trickle, and when she touched her cheek the flesh was damp and unforgiving like the underside of a cold tart. A chill made puppet shudders of her shoulders, and as she stepped back into the town where her new life was to begin, she almost fell over with the weight of expectation.

It was seven o'clock in the evening. Kenmare was stilled as a town in a bottle. Shops had shut, only the small supermarket that was the glorified Honan's grocery threw light out the door onto the street. Gabriella stopped and leaned on a car and breathed the mountain air. She breathed the sweet familiarity of that timeless scent that was the smell of the trees in the darkness, the primal air tangled with the invisible presence of all the innumerable and nameless streams that ran forever down those westerly mountains, the scent of water over rock and under trees that filled into the night town. She breathed it and welcomed it like encouragement, then spewed her anxiety and the anxiety of the child within her out over the front of Paudi O'Dwyer's car.

"Gabriella, is it you? Here, let me help you."

A hand touched her shoulder and held it firmly. And when Gabriella Castoldi turned about on the street of Kenmare she saw the face of Nelly Grant.

"I knew you would come back," Nelly said. She was whispering to the air and had the glad expression of a reader who looks up and smiles, having re-encountered a favourite character deep into the book. "Easy now, just lift your head a little and breathe. That's it," she said, "breathe." She supported Gabriella's head until it faced the heavens, then announced: "It's a baby. Of course. Nelly Grant, you old fool." She shook the wild wool of her head at the plotting of the stars, then led Gabriella across the street to her shop. "Everything will be all right now," she said, in a tone which Gabriella could not decide was either predicting the future or warning God.

The arrival could not have been better timed. For a week Nelly Grant had been studying the energy of the new year. Years earlier she had chosen to live in Kenmare for the purity of its air and the translucent quality of the light through the passes of the Kerry mountains, for the feeling of arrival she had felt the first moment she came down through Moll's Gap. But more than this was the certainty of her belief that such places were the last sanctuaries of an ancient spirituality. She had read widely books of Celtic folklore, studied the uses of all the indigenous plants, eaten wild haws and sipped sloe wine, learned to read Old Irish texts, and recite prayers, enchantments, and spells that addressed the souls of woods trees and rivers, until at last she had grown to believe that in the mountains and valleys of west Kerry there existed a kind of spirit world contemporaneous with this one. It was beside us all the time. No corner of Kerry was without its ruined cottages, roofless stone places where the dead had left their names, where O'Connell's Crossroads existed one hundred years after the last O'Connell died, and where the presence of the vanished lingered like an afterscent in the great emptiness of the landscape. The spirits, Nelly knew, were there all along. They had no inclination to leave and coexisted in the brambles and ditches, living through all seasons without remorse or age but taking from winter and spring alike the same joy in the turning rhythms of the world, living as it might have been intended without the regret of time passing. The spirits lived on like the mountains and the streams, and by the time Nelly Grant had passed her fiftieth birthday, she had begun to feel in Kenmare the comfort of their acquaintance.

Saint Brigid's Day, she told Gabriella, when she had settled her in the humpy couch and knocked alive the low sods of turf in the hearth of her house, was the beginning of springtime in the old Irish year. It was the feast day of the favoured saint who was patroness of cattle and livestock, who had promised fine weather and the bounty of a good season. It was not her saintliness that Nelly loved, she explained, but the real woman whose presence she felt beyond the veils of legend. That first Brigid, who was a woman so in tune with female energy, she imagined, that the earth itself had responded to her and released the first larks of early Irish spring in premature excitement. Brigid was a kind of pagan figure; she was in the moon's rhythm and felt the ripeness of the soil underfoot for the fall of seeds. She was good tidings, and the fact that Gabriella had arrived on her feast day was interpreted by the herbalist as an indication of the goodness ahead.

"It's a juncture, a doorway today. It means," Nelly told Gabriella, "that we have come through the winter and now have a little feast of thanks."

In the low light of her cottage and the burning of scented candles Nelly cut into a thick cake made of carrots, seeds, and raisins and served her visitor.

"There is this little prayer," she said, "*Teighidh ar bhur nglunaibh, agus fosclaidh bhur sula agus leigidh Brid isteach.* Go on your knees, open your eyes, and let Brigid in." She paused; her eyes glinted with the candles as if seeing visions of the Holy Ghost. "I think it's lovely. Let Brigid in. What it can mean, do you know?"

"Yes," Gabriella said weakly, and the Englishwoman and the Italian said together the fragment of ancient Irish. They ate the cake and drank strong herbal tea. Nelly scattered pieces outside the front door for the passing spirits and the ones that took the form of birds.

Gabriella slept that night in the house of Nelly Grant and in the brittle frosted starlight was revisited by dreams of the dead.

Her mother was pregnant as a moon. She lay on the bed with the blankets pulled down and the doctor listening to the white orb of her belly for the secrets of the unborn's future. He was tapping on her skin with pink fingers whose fleshy tips betrayed the richness of his asparagus risotto diet and made a softened, muffled popping with each tap. His stethoscope he removed and clipped about his neck, raising his chin and then lowering it at the odd angle of a violinist, until his ear touched the moon belly and he listened. He told *la senora Castoldi* to breathe deeply and then hold her air like some inflated cartoon, so that he could hear nothing but the secret life of the child inside her. He tapped. He tapped quavers in quick time, he tapped in diminuendo, and then switched rhythms until he was pulsing with his fingers the flurried notes of a new allegro.

"What are you playing at, Doctor?" la senora asked him.

"Vivaldi's 'Summer,'" he said, and tapped on, his face against the creamy smell of her skin and his ear listening on the other side of where Gabriella was hearing that first music and flicking about her tiny body in response.

"Play music in the room, you might save

this one," said the doctor when he stood up at last. "Her spirit dances."

He walked out of the dream from where Gabriella saw him in the womb, and she thrashed in the blankets and hummed broken music, until at last she stopped and heard it playing, and it was her father playing his fingers on her mother like a bow on strings, making a music both harmonious and discordant in turns, a music that rose and filled Gabriella's sleeping until she dreamt she could feel the child inside her dancing to it.

In the morning Gabriella awoke to the tender February light with a new feeling of calm. She had told Nelly the night before that she felt she could never know the reality of true love or the certainty of goodness sometimes given to the sainted or the insane. There was no answer to that, Nelly Grant had told her, but she herself had learned slowly, stubbornly, and with the deepest resistance that at last we must trust the energy of things, to wait and feel the tug of the planet as it swings round and carries us all relentlessly forward.

"Everything," she said, "is not up to us. The thing is, Gabriella, to care for the child. Yes?" she said, and sounded almost in echo of Maria Feri as she pressed her warm palm on the woman's stomach.

Now in the new day Gabriella sat in the kitchen, where the door was open to the view of the mountains and the birds came and went across the dew-silvered grass. The air was fresher than in Venice, and the pale blue of the sky seemed the colour of mercy. The calm Gabriella felt was like the furled bud of the season, and for the first time that morning she dared to imagine it flowering. Imagine, she thought, imagine just for a moment it could be perfect.

She opened the case of her violin and, as if for many children, born and unborn, she played her music out the cottage door.

2

There was a small congregation at the funeral of Philip Griffin. Snow flurried in the air. The roads were iced and the limbs of the trees beseeching. A little cluster of old men in well-cut coats and felt hats stood at the graveside like last sentries, watching the disappearance underground of another of their world and time. The son of Tobias Madigan was there. He gripped Stephen's hand with gloved fingers and held his eyes with his as if he glimpsed there the retreating figure of Philip Griffin skating away across the immaculate ice of the heavens. Then he released the hand and said, "He was a good man. A lot of good men are gone now."

One man was not wearing a long overcoat. Hadja Bannerje was muffled in wool hat and scarf and a thick anorak. He stepped forward only when the others had gone.

"I know you very well," he said. "I am so very very sorry, Stephen." The snow fell across them. He held out a hand and Ste-

348

phen took it, and in that moment Hadja Bannerje felt he understood something of the mystery of our connectedness, of how the old man's life had longed for some redemption, for the passing to his son of an immeasurable and secret grace, which now, at that moment, by the crazy mechanism of the world through which one person's life touches anothers, Hadja Bannerje himself was empowered to bestow.

"I must tell you how your father loved you," he said simply.

The light snow flew about. Stephen looked down at the fresh earth and felt the loss grow huge inside him. The last time he had seen his father was when he left for the airport in the blue suit. "He wanted you to be happy," said the Indian. "It is what all fathers want. You should not be sad."

Stephen stood there. He looked up into the snow sky and felt the pieces of it fall into his eyes.

"I am sorry I did not come to see him," he said quietly. "I did not even know."

"Don't regret it. He saw you," said Hadja. "He saw you in Venice, he told me so in the hospital. It was better you did not come. He died a happy man."

Later, they returned to the house, and the

Indian doctor sat in the room where the last chess game was still apparent. Stephen brought him tea as if Hadja were his father, and was astonished to find that since he had last played, his position in the game had been greatly improved.

"Your father played your moves," said Hadja. "I am afraid I played his."

Stephen sat in his usual chair, and while the clock ticked in the hallway, the tears fell down his face. They fell in the dead stillness of the early afternoon in that suburban house where a long, ordinary everyday tale of grief and longing and regret had finally ended, where the last shadow seemed to have fallen. The queen's knight's pawn, which had been unremarkable and forlorn, was now moved forward, until it arrived at the seventh rank of the board, threatening to transform defeat into victory.

"He kept on moving that white pawn," said the doctor. "I was distracted from it. Now it is hopeless for Black." He smiled and tapped the palms of his hands softly beneath his chin.

The afternoon died away, but Stephen Griffin did not turn on the light. The companionship of the other man touched him in a way he had not experienced in his adult life. The silence was soothing, like the deep blankets of a morning bed. And in the dying half-light of the snowy afternoon, gradually, almost imperceptibly at first, the figure of the other man across the chessboard became the figure of Philip Griffin, as it became, too, for Hadja Bannerje, the figure of his father, whom he had heard from his brother in Bombay was dying now from a slow disease in his bloodstream.

And in that time, that grey and easeful afternoon while the two men sat after the funeral in the old armchairs and said almost nothing, there was something like peace shared between them. The pawn at the seventh rank did not need to be moved forward. The board faded into the dimness and floated away, and the snow fell. It fell forever out of the Dublin nighttime, and was falling still when at last Hadja Bannerje stood up and shook Stephen's hand again and said goodbye and that they must see each other again. And Stephen agreed and said that he would like that very much, and then opened the door and watched the muffled doctor print his footsteps out the driveway and away, vanishing into the blown and falling flurries of the snow, and (although Hadja did not know it yet) out of Stephen Griffin's life forever, as, three days later, Hadja would leave Dublin to return to his father in India.

3

In the days that followed, Stephen lived in the house and journeyed through the places of regret and loss, until he became aware that he was gradually feeling more love than grief. The face of Gabriella appeared in his mind, and he knew now that the loving of her was centrally connected to the meaning of his world. The air lightened. He opened all the windows, and the house whistled with a steady music. The clarity of the notes was remarkable, and as the wind rose and fell in the giddy and capricious games of early spring, the spirits of the dead Griffins danced. All the memories of the house nudged Stephen as he came and went on the stairs and in the hallway, carrying boxes of books and papers. He paused a half dozen times on each journey, bewildered, until slowly he became accustomed to the presence of the reunited family, the strange harmonious sense of them all together there in the house. He remembered more than he remembered he had forgotten, then discovered for himself the truth that nothing of life vanishes completely but can be recovered whole from the past. It was like memories of kisses on the skin. So, in three bright, wind-polished days of early February, when light snow came and went on the air and the music of Puccini played without being switched on, Stephen was joined in the house by Mary his sister, Anne his mother, and Philip his father. The many persons of himself were there, too. He was himself at age four watching his father in the hallway on the evening his parents were going out to the Rathmines Opera. His father wore a black suit and a scent of sweet oil as he hummed an air to the hall mirror. His mother's shoes came down the stairs, slipping slightly on the carpet, they were so light and thin and silvery. He was himself at eight looking at his sister sleeping; he was ten and at the kitchen table while his mother served skinless white boiled potatoes and peas alongside slivers of roast beef that were islands in gravy; he was hearing the first cello notes from Mary's quarter-sized cello in the front room, where the wallpaper was the same still and where the family had smiled watching her, and he had passed jealousy and rivalry and felt simply the visit of a communal happiness. All of himself was there in the house, and all of the others, too. And the more they were present, the lighter was the burden of grief, until it lifted up and floated away altogether, disappearing down the road like a noxious yellow cloud, to be blown into another household, visiting it like a sour priest and smelling of bitter lemons.

4

Two days later Stephen left the house. He took his father's car. He put the Puccini in the boot and the folded-up, faded chessboard with the little box of pieces.

For a week the snow had dusted upon the windows of the house, but when Stephen came out and walked down the garden beneath the chestnut tree there was no whiteness on the ground. For a moment he thought it might be some weird meteorological condition and that the snow was falling only about their own house, but then realized that the snow was falling only, it was not alighting. It lived in the air and vanished into the ground, like a spirit.

Stephen drove away from Dublin a last time and headed west on the road where already he was thinking of Gabriella and where the air was too warm for snow. He drove the Galway road towards a bright sky, and in the early afternoon turned off at Loughrea to head down into Clare. Past noon the day had begun to leak a little of its brilliance, the colour thinning and the line between land and air blurred. Bits of sky had fallen on the fields. And by two o'clock on the road out of Loughrea there were low white spumes of mist scattered here and there inside the stone walls. In that sleeping landscape Stephen thought of Gabriella and in his mind played a passage he remembered of the Vivaldi "Summer." By the time he passed the sign that welcomed visitors to County Clare, the interior of the car was deeply perfumed once more with the scent of lilies.

Then, by the bad bend at Crusheen, Stephen misjudged the sharpness of the curve and briefly threatened to hit the wall of the bridge at speed. At the last moment he managed to save himself, just. He pulled the car over beneath the hedgerows. His face glistened, and he brought his hands up over it to cover his eyes, where briefly he was seeing the vision of his father and mother and sister in the backseat behind him. Philip Griffin had his arm on his wife, guarding her around the bad bend. It was the briefest moment, and gone by the time Stephen had palmed the cold sweat from his forehead, but it broke like a dawn inside him, nonetheless, and made him fully understand a simple truth about his father: Philip Griffin had loved Anne with his life; he had loved her so entirely with himself that when she died, there was little left of him, only the corner he had kept alive for his son. She was everything to him. She was the figure behind all that music that rang out and sang through the little house in her absence, she was behind each of those infinitesimally aching arias that Philip Griffin listened to year after year with his head back and his eyes shut and his hands holding the armrests, as if taking off after her into the heavens.

And with that understanding Stephen drove from Crusheen and left the grief behind him, and felt newly the resolve of life that for him was the loving of Gabriella Castoldi.

5

Eileen Waters was warned by her secretary when Stephen arrived in the carpark. She looked out and saw him alight from his father's car and come quickly up the driveway. What she did not see was the zeal in his eyes or the sense of mission that carried him forward and bounding up the school steps.

"Tell him to wait when he comes," Mrs. Waters said. "Tell him I'm on the phone, I'm busy." She went back inside her office and examined her face. She moved the files into neater piles that they might establish more clearly her power. She pared two pencils and placed them lead upright in the green beaker before her. Then she looked across at the timetable on the wall opposite her, to remind herself of all the staff that were under her, the numbers enrolled, the size of the building, and the full and varied dimensions of her power. She waited fifteen minutes. Finally, she brought the largeness of her soft self forward so that no vulnerable space existed between her and the desk, and then placed her two pink hands together in a mime of tranquil forbearance.

"Carol."

Carol Blake opened the door.

"Will you bring me in the attendance book for 3A?"

"I'm sorry, Mrs. Waters, Mr. Griffin is here to see you."

"Really?" She enjoyed that, and said it louder to be sure he heard. "Really, Mr. Griffin?" She said his name as if it were an antiquated appellation from the Old Testament.

"Will I bring him in?"

"Do."

Outside, the class bell sounded and the corridors of the school echoed with the jostle and rush of the students.

"You are back with us again," Eileen Waters said to Stephen as he came in the door. She pursed her lips and narrowed her eyes. "I had thought . . . I had thought you might have been back last week. Or even the week before. I had thought — while of course a family bereavement is — I had thought, a week, a week or ten days tops." The pink hands floated up before her and palmed the underside of the air, as if fondling amorphous bosoms of power. She weighed them like moralities and looked gravely. "I have to tell you, Mr. Griffin," she said, "you put me in a very difficult position. I have been forced to make allowances again, and some of the other members of the staff . . ."

"Mrs. Waters."

The principal was vexed to stop mid-sentence. It was not even the end of her paragraph. She opened her mouth and shrank three inches smaller. Her eyes were blurry with unease.

"I didn't come to hear your lecture," Stephen said. "I want to say something."

"If you think a brief apology . . ."

"I have nothing to apologize for. Mrs. Waters, I'm not here for apology." Stephen looked directly at her and saw the fright freeze her expression. "I'm here because I've reached the end of this life, I'm not going to be back here anymore, I'm stopping teaching."

Mrs. Waters's face dropped; it fell on the desk with the powdery softness of marshmallow. It was a moment before she could recover it.

"Well," she said, having no idea what to say next.

"I'll tell you the truth: I'm not really a teacher anyway, I don't care enough about codes of discipline, acceptable standards of uniform, punctuality, all that." He waved his hand as if clearing a desk. His eyes were burning. "I care about the history and the few who want to learn it. But what I have discovered is this: it's not my life. It's someone else's life that I'm living, that I just fell into, the way people take wrong turns and don't know it and just keep going because it's too hard and frightening not to, and then they find themselves years later in some place they never wanted to be, with the regrets eating them up like cancers."

The air in the room throbbed. Stephen's words came quickly and the passionate fluency of his expression flooded the small world of the woman and drowned the minor armies of her objections. She could not imagine this was happening. She could not imagine such rashness.

"Someone else's history is the coming and going from here every day," Stephen said, "not mine. Staff meetings and test results and . . ." He raised his eyes to the ceiling, where he knew his family were watching him. "Anyway, it's over. Thank you for giving me the job, but it was a mistake. I won't be coming back."

Stephen stood up. He was a different man from the one Eileen Waters had reprimanded earlier. He was already unstooped and taller, and met her eyes with the strange defiance of those who imagine they have suddenly seen the plot of the world. She stared at him as if he were visiting from another planet. Her blood pressure pounded along the hardening arteries of her heart, her eyelashes felt cakey and weighted with the falling dust of years.

"What are you going to do?" she said. Her voice was as faint and whispery as the turning of pages in an old copybook.

Stephen raised his two hands into the air, and then he smiled. It was the first time she had seen him smile. It became a small laugh, and then he said; "I don't have the slightest idea." The smile kept circling around his lips and made glisten his eyes. "I'm in love," he said, saying those simple words there in that office and not even realizing that they sounded to Eileen Waters strangely childish and unreal, as if they belonged to some outmoded and tarnished notion of romance that no longer had any place in the country she lived in, which by the end of that millennium had been hardened by a thousand revelations of abuse and corruption and greed, until the very notion of a man declaring such a thing out loud in an office seemed as farfetched as a fairy tale.

"There is a woman, she's in Kerry, she

. . ." He stopped. He seemed to be seeing someone else in the room. "Well, goodbye," he said then, and walked out of the office, never to return, leaving Eileen Waters stunned and wordless and diminished as she watched the empty space after him and tried to repair and close the chasm that had opened between the life she was living and the one Stephen Griffin had briefly shown her.

6

The following afternoon he headed south into Kerry. The stillness of the landscape did not mirror his heart. The fields were like the fields painted on a plate. Thin light glistened on the hedgerows and made the first yellow blossoms of the gorse luminescent with the re-emergence of springtime. The hidden verb of life pulsed in secret, and the country-side was made gentle with obscured sunshine. Winter was over, and the precarious existence of bulb and root beneath the soil was made easier now; it was that kind of afternoon. The cattle nosed the wire that kept them from the spring grass. They smelled the alluring and sweet sticky scent of regeneration and moaned softly with the satisfaction of a favoured dream.

The light held for a time. Even before Killarney he could smell the trees and the mountains; the smells returned to him like visions of Gabriella, and by the time he passed the silver lakes, the air in the car was sharp with impossible yearning. Upon her rested his life's happiness; it was as clear as that, and if, once, the enormity of risk might have fractured his resolve and turned him around on the road, it was no longer so. He blinked at the light that came through the mountains, and drove on into them, feeling only the central most basic and human emotion that makes meaning of all our days: the urgency to love.

(He did not know yet the counterbalancing necessity of allowing himself to be loved in return, which would require a more difficult faith, and the passage of time.)

He drove the car into Kenmare and out to the house of Mary White. Both car windows were wide open now, and the scent of loving escaped everywhere and announced his return even to those who did not know his name.

Mary White was at home. She received Stephen with a brief pleasant rise of her thin eyebrows and brought her two hands together before her to clutch the happiness.

"Welcome," she said, "welcome," she said again, beaming a great contentment and nodding, as if she saw spirits entering with Stephen and was delighted with such elevated company. "You're back with us again," she said, saying "us" even though she lived alone.

"If it's all right?"

"Oh yes," she said. "I was so hoping we'd have you back." She paused and looked at him, and felt the way people do when a corner of the jigsaw has come together. "Now come on," she said, "I have your room ready."

And so Stephen followed her back into the room where he had dreamt so vividly of Gabriella that the presence of her was still in the corners of the ceiling. He felt it was right and proper to begin again; there was something fitting about returning to that house, as though life moves in spiralling circles and we arise along invisible tracks that were laid in the air. He felt the sense of it without knowing why, for it was not until he sat to tea with Mary White and told her about the death of his father in Dublin that she asked him if he was the son of Anne, who had died in the crash years ago and with whom Mary White had once been in school.

7

When Stephen awoke the world spoke with birdsong and the buzzing of spring flies. He smelled the sweet tang of the garden's annual resurrection, the slow stirring and secret life of the flowers not yet opened but breathing nonetheless in the open bedroom window. It was the morning of the declaration of love. When he opened his eyes, he caught the tonic air of wild rhubarb and was sharpened in his awareness that this was to be the beginning of new life. He would give himself to Gabriella and the child, and if she would not marry him, he would take any job he could get and live near her and be whatever he could to her for the rest of his days. He was filled that morning with such innocence. That morning, while he lay in the bed breathing the spring, he had a view of a world beautiful in its simplicity: that we act on our hearts and follow the things that move us. That it was outlandish and naïve and impractical, that it was the kind of thinking once expected of a child up to the age of twelve, then ten, but now, in our days, no more than the age of eight, that innocence had diminished so and the world become so old and weary that belief in such things had all but vanished did not bother Stephen Griffin. He lay on his bed on the outskirts of that town in Kerry and dreamed like a saint of a selfless loving.

When he rose he saw Mary White hanging clothes on the line in the garden. The soft wind billowed the white sheets.

Down in Kenmare that morning the streets were lively with men and beasts. Cattle trailers and wagons moved slowly, and the trapped cattle bellowed and stomped in the traffic. People watched them passing on their way to the spring mart and took the soured air of the dung and urine as another emblem of the new season, the countryside awakening and descending on the town. Wisps of straw litter were about the place, and there were children late going to school who had been drovers at dawn, leading cattle with hose-pipe sticks to the loading. There was a buzz of excitement, the noise of engines and the salutes and waves and cries of those leaning forward in their tractor cabs to call down to a neighbour some news of animal or man.

Into this throbbing Stephen walked. The

streets of the country town were alive about him. Before he had reached the corner where Nelly Grant kept her shop, he knew that his footsteps were bringing him to the doorway of his new life. He sensed the enormity of it with the freshness of a child facing First Communion, and by the time he had arrived at the fruit and vegetable stalls outside the shop, he had begun to shake inside his clothes. He took a moment to master himself. He raised his head, opened his mouth, and swallowed full the host of redemption. Then he stepped into the shop and saw Nelly Grant raise her eyebrows.

"Stephen!"

She was holding two Seville oranges, and with them in her hands came forward and embraced him.

"She's here," she whispered as she held on to him, taking the opportunity to smell the uncertain blended aroma of his hope, anxiety, and love. "You have a new radiance," she said, and stood back to admire his aura.

"Gabriella!" she called out before Stephen had even said a word to her.

And then, through the beaded curtain that separated the shop from the small back office, where the geranium oil was burning and choral music playing, Gabriella stepped out.

"Stefano," she said. She said it like a whisper. "Oh, Stefano." She brought her hands to her mouth as if to hold in a cry.

8

And in his bed that morning, quietly, while the rain that first seemed to fall only in Clare and then only in Miltown Malbay spilled down through the broken roof of his cottage and pooled on the floor and made the cats come from the cupboard to the shiplike dryness and comfort of his bed, while the water was filling so steadily across the flagstone floor that he laughed to think the nearby hurley stick might be his oar and his bed once more a sailing schooner off the distant shores of Peru, easily then, like moorings loosened at last or notes rising in that supernatural music that rose from the throat of Maria Callas, Moses Mooney closed his blind eyes in the falling spills of weather inside his house and saw the lovers Stephen Griffin and Gabriella Castoldi and knew what he knew and wept like rain, and softly died.

9

"I cannot marry you, Stephen. I cannot."

They had left the shop of Nelly Grant and, like people carrying heavy burdens, walked mutely from the town. They had taken the Killarney road towards the mountains instinctively, as if the bigness of their emotions demanded the otherworldly landscape of rock and wood silvered now with the torrents of the season. Water was everywhere running and made a noise louder than the birds. Stephen and Gabriella did not touch. They walked two feet apart up the slow incline, and by the time they had left the close cattle smells of the town behind, the air was thin and blue and clean as pine. The bread van passed and stopped and offered them a lift to Killarney, but they waved it on, not meeting each other's eyes but moving like figures in a romantic painting, as if to a prearranged spot in the vastness of that green wilderness.

There was no such spot; a car with four

swearing singing bachelor footballers raced past them on their way home from the night, and Stephen stepped into the verge and slipped and almost twisted his ankle, but caught against Gabriella. Her face was white. "I'm sick," she said.

"Oh God, I'm sorry. Why didn't you say?"

They sat down on a ledge of rock, the mountain behind them.

And for a moment, nothing.

They breathed and looked away. The valley was below, and deep within it the thin morning smoke of three houses rose and vanished in the air.

"Are you all right?"

"It passes."

"Here, do you want my jacket?"

"No no, keep it."

Stephen looked at himself for something to offer. He was suffused with a desire for giving to Gabriella, and was only just understanding that singular characteristic of love, that the impulse to do something for the other reached a point of such immediacy that it almost erased him entirely and left only the urgency. He looked at the side of her face with a dizzy desire to put the palm of his hand against it.

"I am so glad you came back," he said.

"I wasn't sure I would," said Gabriella,

"not when I left. And it's not because of the child."

"I know."

"I wanted . . ." She stopped, and her face briefly frowned, a frown that travelled down from her forehead to her mouth like a wind rumple in a sheet and flowed on then into Stephen. "I wanted to know. I want my life to be, you know, to find a kind of certainty, it's stupid, I know, but just not to fall into things, you know, to feel that . . ."

"I love you."

She turned her face towards him, and he saw the pain he had put in her eyes.

"I know that, Stephen. Oh, I know."

"I want to take care of you. That's what I want to do for the rest of my life."

She lowered her head until her chin rested low on her fists. A car travelled slowly up the hill and stopped five yards away from them to look down at what the driver imagined the two people must be looking at. It was not until the two tourists had looked all around for the spectacular view they couldn't find that they got back in the car and drove past. They waved at the tall man and the woman sitting on the rock, but no greeting was returned. Gabriella's brown hair fell forward across her cheeks, the pink whorl at the top of her ear appeared through

374

the strands. Stephen held on to his knees. He looked down as if from a precipice at the life he wanted to plunge into. He looked at Gabriella's clothes, her walking boots, the corded wine trousers, the thick woollen coat, and like a demented disciple, he loved them, too. If she had taken off her coat he would have hugged it to him and breathed its scent.

"Gabriella?"

She turned to him. "There's no need to say anything, Stephen," she said. "I know. I know I know." She touched his face and felt the emotion buckle him. "I am terrible," she said. "I am mean and hard."

He had turned his mouth to kiss her hand where it touched him.

"Please," he said.

"Don't."

"Please."

"Stephen." She brought up her other hand and was holding his wet face. "I cannot marry you," she said. "It wouldn't . . . I would always feel that I had forced you." She stopped and held back her head to face the sky. "I love you, Stephen Griffin. I do. But I am not in love with you. I cannot marry you."

"Don't, then. Don't," he said, and now held on to her hands at his face and did not let them go. "Don't marry me, but just let me . . ." He ran out of words and let the pleading rush from his eyes with the force that runs rivers into seas.

"You are the best man," Gabriella said, and shook her head in disbelief that such a man existed, and then she reached forward and pressed herself against him with such force it might have been for healing or to be healed, and then she kissed his face and then his mouth that was salty like the sea.

10

Nelly Grant knew when she saw them return into the town of Kenmare. She read their aurae like an ancient book whose pages have worn and yellowed from the feverish finger grease of a thousand readers. When they re-entered her shop and Stephen knocked against the Granny Smiths and sent four tumbling green globes onto the floor, Nelly could read the aftershocks in him and feel the trembling that had not yet subsided and that had brought the strange clamour from the birds in the yet unleaved sycamores behind Sugrue's. Gabriella stooped to pick up the apples at the same moment as Stephen. They are like twin clocks, Nelly thought, but do not realize it. She smiled and said nothing and watched them replace the fruit. The relation-ship is so unbalanced, she told herself, he loves her so much, that at any moment things might fall off shelves, spark, combust. Watching them standing in the small free space of the shop was like watching springtime in fast forward.

"Well?" said Nelly, and smiled. She watched the light from them radiate across the ceiling. Then Gabriella stepped forward and embraced her.

It was one of the qualities of Nelly Grant that she could become different people at different moments; and in that embrace on the shop floor, she was briefly the mother Gabriella had wished for. She was wise and knowing. Her body in a chunky blue sweater felt like a lifetime's bulk of warmth and hope, and Gabriella held on to it. While she did, Nelly Grant winked at Stephen and almost toppled him. She took Gabriella's thanks with soft protest, and when the younger woman told her she was moving back into the house she had left before Christmas, Nelly clapped three small claps for this minor victory of love and then went to fill a fruit bag for the two of them. While she circled the stalls, drawing oranges and grapes and a sweet pineapple, she watched out of the corner of her eye where Stephen's hand dangled dangerously in the air, charged with the imploding desire to reach and take Gabriella's fingers. He did not do it.

"Take these with you," Nelly said then, coming forward quickly with the fruit, before anything else could happen, and standing so close to Gabriella that the younger woman had to step backward and brush into the chest of Stephen. His hands landed like large birds on her shoulders, and the relief softened the line of his mouth. "And a little of this," said Nelly, bringing them a small bottle of a kind of milk made from the flour drawn from roots of the early purple orchids and spiced with nutmeg and cinnamon. "It is good for everything," she told them, "especially to keep resolve of the spirit." Then she placed her hand on Gabriella's head and let her go. "Call to see me."

"I will."

"We will," said Stephen.

The lovers walked out of the shop, and fruit rolled off the shelves. Everything is energy, thought Nelly, and laughed to watch the bananas twirl on the S hooks.

That afternoon, while the farmers slowly returned from the mart and the money began to surface on polished counters in all the pubs of the town, Gabriella moved back into the house she had left before Christmas. And whether it was the burgeoning spring, the relief of animals sold, the excitement of animals bought, or the radiant spirit of loving returned, by early evening the town was singing and smoking and swallowing pints in that strange mixture of celebration and hope and reminiscence that is the true hallmark of the end of winter.

In the house on the hill, when darkness had fallen, Gabriella sat on the floor before the fire and Stephen sat in the chair to the side of her. Their music was not the music of the town below them. It was a recording of Puccini's *Tosca* that Stephen had brought from his car and played for Gabriella when he told her of his father's death and that this was the music his father had listened to for thirty years. While the sweetest arias played they did not speak. They ate the fruit Nelly Grant had given them and listened, and it was not until the third act that Gabriella lifted her head and raised her hand and met Stephen's fingers and drew him so swiftly down to her on the floor that the turf smoke billowed out over them in a cloud. And in that moment, while the town below them was singing and the heavens above were thronged with spirits and stars, while the diva sang *"Vissi d'arte"* and made the small room one with others in different places and different times, Gabriella Castoldi kissed the man who loved her and took his head and touched his wet eyes and held her fingers upon his lips.

"Why am I so difficult?" she said beneath the singing, shaking her head as if to escape her father's knuckling fists landing upon her.

And for once Stephen did not remain quiet, but in a low voice answered her and said, "Let go, just try and let it go."

And in the simple, brief, and yet momentous way in which a life is decided, in which the hold of the past is released and the future arrives like new skin, Gabriella closed her eyes and at last surrendered to that impulse that was as timeless, inevitable, and relentless as spring itself, and was the subject of all the songs the men were singing in the town below.

11

Stephen stayed that night, and the one after that, and after that again. He brought his things from Mary White's, who bade him goodbye once more, this time with the gentlest of smiles and a wave of her hand, telling him he was welcome always and holding herself in her thin arms as if embracing some of the loving that glowed off him.

The easterly winds that were the harbingers of March and were nightly forecast did not arrive in Kenmare. The season was mild and the earth became tender. The soil moistened as it unfroze and released a sweet scent everyone seemed to have forgotten from the year before. Old women warned that good weather should not be trusted and wore their thick coats into the town with the sour wisdom of life's disillusioned. They stood at butcher counters ordering the cheapest cuts of meat, and when the new season potatoes arrived from Israel they looked at them with scornful downturned mouths and went home to enjoy the thick-skinned bitter gnarled potatoes that God had spared them in the shed since last July. But for others the softness of the beginning of March came as a blessing, not a curse. The worst winds that were sent from Finland whispered and diminished over north Tipperary and did not reach the Kerry mountains. The sun rose in clear skies. Among the lifted spirits of the town Stephen bought the groceries and things for the house. That he had no skill for carpentry or repairwork did not stop him buying hammer and nails and screwdriver and gazing fixedly at the closely packed shelves in Donoghue's hardware shop, wondering but not asking what things were. He returned to the house, where Gabriella was writing a letter to her cousin, and with a determined kind of manliness, he hammered lumps out of the doorjamb that was loose, and screwed crookedly new screws into the mirror frame that was falling forward out of the dressing table, and now only toppled backward.

He had moved into Gabriella's life like a kind of deferential giant; he wanted to be useful for her. He wanted to make her life easier, and in everything he did he thought first of what she would like. In that way in the mild spring days and nights of that year Stephen Griffin made vanish his own will, and instead shaped his life like a suit of clothes that would fit and shield Gabriella Castoldi from the brute vicissitudes of life. He fell in love with the idea of being her hero. He imagined that in all her life she had never come across anyone like him, that the men she had known were a selfish crowd of louts who had only deepened her grief and furthered the belief that men were weak spirits who sought nothing in women but the banishment of loneliness and a reflected proof of their own power. I am not like them, he told himself. He looked at the grey shadows underneath Gabriella's eyes and each day renewed his vow to make her happy. When she awoke he brought her tea in bed, and not coffee; he lit the turf fire downstairs and turned on the music. When she stayed in the bed and did not get up, he brought her soapy plates of stiff pasta with a jar of tomato sauce poured over it. He cooked fried eggs flecked with bits of shell and mistimed the toast so that the butter would not melt.

He had told her of the money he would inherit from his father and that he was not returning to teaching. But he did not tell her his work was there in the house about her, for even he feared that incredible declaration, and instead stood by her bedside and smiled the uncertain half-smile of those who are just beginning to trust in enduring goodness.

Meanwhile, Gabriella slowly moved beyond the time of morning sickness. In the soft and tender weather the child grew within her and lent her a deep and sensuous laziness. She lay in the wide bed and felt Stephen wrap around her through the night, and in the mornings after he had risen she walked her legs into the warmth he had left in the sheets and kept her eyes closed so that she might linger there forever in the glowing afterheat that was the small proof of a comforting humanity. She had swift sudden fits of gaiety and high spirits. Noontimes, when the sun flowed as a stream through the window and Stephen peeped around the door to see if she wanted lunch, she saw the white moon of his face and burst out laughing.

"What is it?" he asked her, stepping a half-step inside the door and smiling like a man who does not see the bucket falling on his head.

But Gabriella could not answer; she giggled and turned her face into the pillow, laughing, laughing in relief and disbelief, with the first gradual easing of the tightness in her spirit.

"What is it? tell me," Stephen said, emboldened by the laughter and the sunlight, and coming forward to the bed to grab on to her where she was wriggling and he was already tickling her.

"Nothing! Nothing! Stop, *o grido!* Ahhh!"

It became one of the things she loved about him: how she could erase the terrible seriousness of his face, how the pale earnestness of his expression inspired her to sudden small acts of rebellion. He could not tell the difference yet between her real and her fake reactions, and as if she was compelled to continually test the strength and limits of his love, she delighted in teasing him. She watched the instant and deep furrowing of his brow when she told him she had a pain, and only when he had come to her side to ask her where, did she giggle and point to different parts of her body, moving her hand across herself in the bed and drawing up her nightgown until her giggling was wilder and Stephen was travelling her with kisses. She was amazed by him. She did not tell him again that she would not marry him, but the boundaries of the relationship were always there nonetheless, and in those bright and hope-filled days at the beginning of spring Gabriella danced along them. She asked for ice cream when he brought her breakfast, then lay back on the pillow and listened to the ignited car engine as a metaphor of love, while Stephen drove hurriedly into the town for three kinds of ice cream cornettos. In the afternoons she did not rise, but rolled softly from the bed, believing that the carrying of the child to the sitting room was work enough for one day and, in thick red jumper and elasticized sweatpants, sat with Stephen to watch one of the many video films he brought her from Kenmare.

"Do you think it's any good?" he asked her.

"No."

He stopped the machine and stood up. "I'll go get another one."

"No, don't."

"I will. I don't mind."

"Stephen."

"I'd be back in ten minutes."

"I could have killed myself by then."

"What?"

"Yes. You better not leave me. Ten minutes and I could have . . ." She mimed an elaborate knife across her throat and rolled her eyes.

"Gabriella!"

"Or perhaps." She put her forefinger into

her mouth and cocked back her thumb to make a gun. "Bang!" She flopped her head dead. Then from the side she opened her eyes and looked at him. When she spoke her voice was soft: "Don't, Stefano. Don't go. I don't need another one now. They are all such rubbish, I shouldn't even watch them, but" — she paused and smiled at how indolent she was allowing herself to be — "I like to sit here on the couch with you, passing the afternoon. Is it so terrible?"

Stephen stood there, and gratitude warmed him like red wine. "No." He shook his head. "It's not."

One afternoon, from the small collection of his things, he brought out the chess set.

"Oh," said Gabriella, sitting up like a child, "you are going to teach me."

And so he did. Through the rest of the days of March they lived in the house above the town of Kenmare, dwelling like people on a private island whose hours are not dictated by the weariness and drudgery of work or the dread exhaustion of spirit in the tedium of life. They existed as if in another country. They did not hear the news, they did not listen to stories on the radio or television, of corrupted government or the revealed brutalities of Christian Brothers, of elderly women knocked down the stairs for the fifteen pounds in their purses, or the scandals and court cases and tribunals that were ceaselessly unpeeling the skin of the country like a rotten fruit. Instead, Stephen and Gabriella loved and lived in a sweet innocence and ate their meals and listened to music and played chess. Even when the post office in Kenmare was robbed in daylight and Helena Cox was struck on the face by a man with a gun as she protested at the counter, the news seemed never to actually arrive in the stopped time of their world.

12

By the beginning of April all but the ash trees were leafed; the wildflowers and berry bushes in the hedgerows moved towards early blossom and lent the air a seasonal gaiety. Big skies opened and let the light of the high heavens fall down on the town. Gardens were dug over and seeded. Men got their hair cut and drove in their tractor cabs with the scalped, white-necked look of plucked fowl. The landscape buzzed. Birds flew down out of the shelter of the trees and shat on the cars beneath the telephone wires a bright confetti, celebrating the return of April.

At last, after some persuasion, Gabriella agreed to leave the house and go shopping in the town with Stephen. In the comfort of the bedroom she had grown slightly fearful of the outside. She distrusted her own happiness and imagined that at any moment the world would crush it. How perfect it was in their own place beneath the mountains. Whatever guilt she felt in seeing Stephen do everything — washing shopping and cooking — was absolved in the evenings when she took him inside her arms, loving him more carefully and tenderly now, with the kind of kisses the rescued bestow upon the rescuer. In their weeks together Gabriella had grown accustomed to this strange rhythm of their relationship. She had allowed Stephen to take over, and banished for the time being all thoughts of what their future might be. She was, she even admitted, almost happy. Why change anything? Then, that third day of April, when Stephen told her he was leaving her briefly to buy the fresh rhubarb Nelly Grant said she would have set aside for them, Gabriella said she did not want him to leave her.

"I won't be long."

"No, please, Stefano."

"What is it?"

"Don't go."

She was sitting on the bed in her nightdress. Her body seemed smaller as her pregnancy grew. She was strangely more frail the larger she became, as if the part of her that was herself was each day subtracted from and was added instead to the child. Her face was flushed.

"What is it? What's the matter?"

"I don't know. I am foolish," she said.

"But sometimes . . ."

"What?"

"Nothing."

"Tell me."

"I feel that it won't last. That something is waiting to happen."

He sat down on the bed beside her. The brilliance of the April noon was at his back, letting the light fall like infinite pity into her eyes. She was briefly blinded. Though he asked her what exactly she feared he did not need to. He, too, had felt the fragile quality of each day and knew the awful expectation of loss that was the most enduring and reliable trait of his thirty-two years. The difference now was that since the death of his father and his own return to Kenmare, Stephen had begun to feel he was in a new life. He felt blessed. So when Gabriella curled on the bed and could not quite explain her fear, Stephen Griffin already understood and imagined, like some delirious saint, that the blessing that had fallen on him would now protect her, too. He leaned down and stroked her head softly like a grandfather.

"Come with me," he said. "Come on out. Come down to the town."

And so she did. They arrived in the town that had already been speaking about them. Gabriella walked linked on Stephen's arm, her green coat open and the child just visible ahead of both of them. It was not so bad. The sun was warm and welcoming. The first tourists had already arrived at the wool and tweed shops at the top of the street, and a constant jig and reel music was blaring out from the loudspeaker set above the shop in a broadcast of authenticity. Beneath the music Germans were buying bargain sweaters from Michael O'Keefe in his one black suit. He nodded across his dealing at Gabriella and Stephen. "Morning to you." His eye caught the curve of the child. "Beautiful today," he said, and turned back to the Germans.

Stephen and Gabriella went to the bank. The money that he had been willed by his father had not arrived yet. Stephen had little idea how much it would be after duties and fees, but knew that the sum was substantial. He was living on his savings from his teacher's salary and needed to transfer his account from Clare and tell the manager the funds would be coming.

The teller asked Stephen his name.

"Just a minute so, Mr. and Mrs. Griffin."

Moran, the assistant manager, was called from his desk to the counter to meet them.

"Well," he said, "good morning to ye." He beamed and reached out a pumiced pink hand. "Mr. Griffin, Mrs. . . . ."

In a moment he noticed the absence of a wedding ring and took a sideways glance away to show that he had not been looking. "Yes yes. Now, Stephen, isn't it? That's right."

Moran had, he knew, the gift of weighing situations, and when money was concerned, the balances were never even. There were always hidden weights, obscured feelings, fears and motives. The pregnant woman without a ring caused him to reweigh the situation swiftly and temper his approach. So, with his most liberal expression and a face that declared the only and absolute value in life was hard currency, he took the hand Gabriella offered and shook it once as if it were a wet fish.

"This is Gabriella," Stephen said.

"Yes. Yes," said Moran, looking at the tall figure of the fool. This woman was too beautiful for him. Could it be that she was not with him for his looks? He leaned on the polished wood of the counter, but did not invite them to enter. Moran was a man of a time, and it was a constant irritation to him that it was not this one. In his view, the situation was compromised by the presence of the woman.

Stephen told him of the money that he expected to arrive. Moran pressed his two hands on the counter. He asked Stephen approximately how much money were they talking about.

"More than ten thousand?"

"Yes."

"More than twenty?"

"More than a hundred."

"I see." There was a pause. "A good deal of money then," Moran said, and waited, and raised and lowered his hands on the countertop lightly as if playing the slow chords of the third movement of Disaster. "You need to come in sometime yourself," he said, "and we can have a talk about it, what best to do and so on. Sometime when you have a minute, when you can come in when em . . ." He stopped and nodded a tight smile. He could not say what he wanted to. He could not say: Come in when this woman is not with you. He could not say: This is a matter between men, though he thought it and tried in vain to let his expression say so. Moran offered Stephen the form to sign to open the account in his name, and winced inwardly, watching the fellow push it over to the woman for her to sign, too. The assistant manager looked at her with a pained smile. He endured her with a thin tightness in his lips and harsh judgement in his eyes. He would tell Mrs. Moran about her in the evening. He would reaffirm the main lesson life had taught him: money comes to the coarse and undeserving, and it was his unlucky lot in life ceaselessly to serve and assist those more wealthy than he. He nodded at the two of them. All the greatest fools in the known world, he told himself as he returned to his office, are ruled by the heart and not the head. For them there should be no such thing as money, they don't deserve it.

Martin Moran was not the only one who let himself be haunted by their visit. Mickey Hayes, standing in his Wellingtons in the queue at the counter, saw the way the assistant manager had leant over to talk to them. He could see the look of pound notes in Moran's eyes, and craned his neck and allowed the gambling addiction of his lifetime to make him think he overheard what he most feared: another's fortune. "They've won the fucken' lotto," he said in a cracked voice too far above a whisper for Maggie Saunders not to hear it and turn at once to watch Stephen and Gabriella walking contentedly out the door.

From that moment the word travelled like an airborne virus, so that it seemed to move and arrive in every house and business in the town as quickly as human greed. Mickey Hayes carried it to three pubs. He allowed the bitterness that life had long ago lodged in his bloodstream to inflate the terrible tale of the two, not even married, flaunting their fortune in the streets of Kenmare. Narrow-eyed and with Guinness froth moustaching him like a banderillero, he described them as walking mockeries. He said they had hidden it from everybody. They must have won the fucken' thing weeks ago and hidden themselves up in that house. Not even one drink on the house anywhere had the feckers bought, not the steam off their piss were they thinking of donating to anyone.

"That's nice carry-on, isn't it?" he asked Donal Mungovan on the stool next to him.

"Christ, but it is," said Donal, and shook his head in slow wonder at what the hell God was up to, letting the likes of them win instead of him.

Even before Stephen and Gabriella had passed Cox's butchers midway up the town, Helena had heard. She was still bruised on her left cheek from the business in the post office and was unsure yet that her cosmetic covered it sufficiently. She stayed indoors upstairs and received callers. When Maggie Saunders told her, her heart sank. Love *and* money, she thought, and had to tilt her head back to stop the involuntary spasm of her tears from streaking across the covered bruise. There was a silence bitter and heavy and thick in her sitting room, where women's magazines were scattered gaudily like unfulfilled promise in an empty heart.

Then Maggie Saunders said, "Well, all can't be well in paradise." She nodded and half-closed her eye, cocking her head at the invisible lovers. "They're not married. There's no ring."

This seemed to console Helena Cox slightly. She went to the window and looked out across the street, to where Stephen and Gabriella were talking to Nelly Grant at the stall of cabbages. In the tender spring light even she could see the love glowing from them; it smote her like a cold iron and made her think of Francie downstairs at the butcher stall, with his dumb brutish kind of passion that subsided into nothing. With Maggie behind her, she bit on her cherry-painted lip. "I have to tell some people," she said. "Father Dempsey will want to know." Then she turned and walked away, lighter and suddenly eased with the plan of spreading her sourness.

By evening everyone in the town had heard. It was talk with a life of its own. By the fall of darkness people who told the tale of the lottery win could not even remember whom they first heard it from. It was a fact. New details emerged in each telling and clung to the tale like wasps in flowers. Just so came the story of how Stephen had first tried to hide the fortune from the people of Clare, how he had failed to tell his principal and simply disappeared, pretending all kinds of elaborate ruses, even inventing his own father's death, so that no one would discover the money. Gabriella was no better. She was carrying some Italian fellow's child. She had dumped him and gone off and come back only when she heard, and was now pretending the child was Stephen's. The fellow was such a fool, his own greed was so thick that he could not even see hers.

Not everyone in the town that night was bitter with envy. The German silversmith laughed and clapped; he loved to see fairy tales in Ireland, he told Helena, and his blue eyes twinkled above the mass of his beard like cloudless azure. Nolan and McCarthy & Son, undertakers and builders, took the news as a sign of the nearness of luck and bought double scratchcards; the two O'Connells, solicitors, shrugged indifference and beeped the automatic alarms of their Rovers. There were others, too, to whom the news when it reached them had the quality of grim fable, and so slipped into their lives only as a chastening reminder of how terrible money can be.

Nonetheless, from the few the sickness of greed grew. And by the time the light died on that April evening, the story of Stephen Griffin and Gabriella Castoldi had spun a kind of thick yellowish brume out of the window of O'Loughlin's and Coughlan's, and O'Siochru's pub, too, and the air was so heavily scented with the exhaled bitterness and envy that it choked the lungs and browned the stars and half obscured the moon itself, so that it hung over the town like a gouged eye.

13

The following morning brown rain was falling. As if some malignancy were weeping, the water seeped off the sky from early dawn. It fell steadily and screened the mountains and made the town seem small and miserable. In his morning sermon at ten o'clock Mass, Father Dempsey scowled at the small gathering of weekday Massgoers and told them sometimes we have to feel God's Own Disapproval. Helena Cox had already told him of the illicit lovers and their fortune, and the news had arrived like acid in his stomach in the middle of his breakfast fry; why must the ways of the Unjust prosper, O Lord? he asked, and had taken some comfort when he walked out into the deluge.

And still the rain fell. It fell heavily, like regret, and flooded gutters and drains that by mid-morning were spilling over like the eyes of new widows beyond consolation. The streets of the town were awash in brown water. That the suddenness of the deluge was part of the capriciousness of west Kerry springtime was briefly overlooked, and in half a dozen shops old men and women were already gloomily discussing the vanishing of seasons and the nearness of the end of Time.

It rained. It sheeted down all that day, and the next, and the one after that, too. It rained so hard that television cameras appeared on the streets of Kenmare to film it. It rained on the rivers that were the streets of the town and which coursed along now at the speed in which a heart can change its feelings. It rained relentlessly, until the falling of the drops themselves seemed redolent with meaning and were interpreted variously on the radio and television programmes that mushroomed on the airwaves. But none of the callers who phoned in read the gloom of the weather as Gabriella did. None of them saw it as a colder vision of Venice, as the nightmarish return of murky uncertainty and the washing away of love.

While the rain fell Gabriella stayed in her bed and suffered a new form of her old despair. Her pregnancy now brought her so low in her spirit that she had not the energy to get up. She had seen the disapproval in the face of Moran when he looked at her, and knew it to be the look of her own father, too. When two men called in Wellingtons to tell Stephen at the front door that they had heard of his lottery win and wouldn't he like to donate something to the football club, Gabriella knew at once that the town must be speaking of them and that the islanded paradise of their house was destroyed now.

"There'll be no peace for us here," she said.

It did not matter that there were hundreds of others living around the town who, when they heard of the imagined lottery win or saw the ringless hand of Gabriella and the curve of her belly, thought nothing of it and understood and accepted that even their country was in a constant flux of change and that those notions of transgression which had made sinners of all in the past were faded now to the easier morality of only the endeavour of human goodness. To Gabriella it did not matter. The rain beat down. She could not sleep. She lost concentration and threw the chess pieces at the curtains. When Stephen tried to comfort her, she lowered her head and hit her fist into the side cushion of the couch, and hit the memories of her father in the house in the Calle Visciga, the sharp cold air of intolerance and judgment.

Stephen brought her cocoa. He was stunned and wordless, and as the wet evening deepened into drowned night, his face expressed a mute horror. He put turf on the fire. He sat in the armchair across from Gabriella by the ruined chess game and tried to tell her everything would be all right. But Gabriella just stared. And so he did not say any more. He sat in the chair, long and thin and defeated, and in the dim light that glowed from the flames watched his happiness burn away like fire.

An hour passed. The rain fell.

"I love you," he said in a small voice, when the light in the room was too diminished for him to tell whether Gabriella was awake or asleep and when the telling of those three words seemed suddenly impotent. There was no answer. Eight feet away Gabriella lay motionless. Her eyes might have been closed. Stephen did not know; he said the words again and immediately wished he had not, for in the loneliness of no reply he faced the cold, undeniable truth that Gabriella's happiness was not in his power, nor could he change the world for her. He sat and listened and the rain fell. At last he moved over beside her and reached and stroked her hand, and was still not certain that she was not sleeping, until finally the smallest movement of her fingers curved onto his and held.

In the darkness at the end of that night, when it seemed the world's sourness had slipped beneath their door and made the house of loving frail and unprotected as a china doll, Gabriella moved her face close to Stephen's, and in a voice that held the ceaseless yearning of her own childhood to make real and lasting the existence of love, she whispered, "Stefano, take me away from here."

14

It was the small hours of the morning. Rain was still beating against the windows when, with the tenderness of those who care for the wounded, Stephen took his arms from around Gabriella and rose from the couch where she was lying and began to pack. He did not discuss it. He did not explain his plans or try to reason with her or say that perhaps it was the rashness of her pregnancy speaking or a bright morning would see a change of heart. He rose and packed. Within an hour there was an assemblage of small boxes and vases, an Italian hilltown, inside the front door. When he opened the door to bring them to the car, the clatter of the rain made Gabriella stir on the couch. She raised her head slightly, the way sleepers do to look at dreams, and then lay back again.

Whether she was awake or not in his coming and going Stephen did not know. He gathered her clothes from the chairs and the end of the bed, where she had left them, and folded them into the brown case she had brought from Venice. Although there was space, he did not put his own clothes with hers. He took the case of her violin and the few books of sheet music she never travelled without, one of which had been given to her by Maestro Scaramuzza and was now like some yellowed covenant carried into the future. In his own case he packed the chess set, going around by the curtains on his hands and knees to gather up the pieces Gabriella had thrown aside.

At last he had packed everything that was theirs, except for the small black music player and Vivaldi, Puccini, and Mozart.

"Where are we going?" Gabriella whispered without moving. His long figure crossed the darkness to her.

"To make a home," he said. "I am going to make you happy. I am."

"Sssh," she said, and raised a finger to quiet him. "Play the music, kill the rain."

And so he did, and they lay in the last darkness as the rain fell in a world somewhere outside the otherworldly singing of Kiri Te Kanawa; Stephen and Gabriella held to each other and closed their eyes and escaped on the music away from the questions of tomorrow. They did not sleep. They drowsed on the disc that had been set to Repeat, and stirred on the fourth singing of "*Dove sono*" with paralyzing cramps and Gabriella's bladder bursting. Once she had rushed through the empty house, the mood was broken. She returned to where Stephen was hopping, trying to straighten the locked muscle of his thigh. He leaned on her shoulder. "My saviour," she said as he hopped, and she smiled.

In ten minutes they were in the car. They drove into Kenmare in the dawn and saw the flooding waters of the street part to either side in the headlights. Gabriella wanted to leave word with Nelly Grant, and through the steady spilling of the rain she hurried up the small garden path while Stephen held an umbrella over her. She knocked twice, but there came no answer. She knew from her own nights in the cottage the deep dreams that Nelly Grant nightly explored and did not knock a third time; instead she wrote in pencil: "We had to leave. We will let you know. Thank you. Gabriella." She did not add "Stephen," nor see the small pain the absence of his name alongside hers caused him.

They drove out of Kenmare through empty streets and throttled the engine to climb into the mountains. Stephen told her they could go to Clare, and hurried the car as if to outrace the uncertainty of finding happiness there. They sped into Killarney and arrived in Tralee when only squat lorries and milk bulk tanks were travelling the road. The rain was still pouring down as the dawn came up, so that the grey light and water mixed to make the day the colour of despondency. In the emptiness of the long north Kerry road Stephen and Gabriella said almost nothing. Gabriella watched the landscape flattening out in pale greens towards the Shannon and wondered if the dry scent caught in the car was cardboard boxes or desperation. They arrived at the ferry dock in Tarbert a full hour before the first sailing, and waited and watched the morning struggle to separate from the dark waters of the river. When at last they drove onto the ferry, Tom Blake, the ticket collector, came and looked in at them across the falling rain. When he saw the collection of their belongings packed into the car, he knew they were not tourists and was at once disconcerted by the impression that they were people taking flight. As the boat pulled away, he watched the road down to the pier as if expecting pursuit.

But there was none he could see. For what they were fleeing was not visible; it was the condition of their own disbelief, a long, enduring, and dogged sense of defeat so deeply buried in the spirit that sometimes no love nor hope nor faith can seem to outrace it. It was the feeling that blows would always fall, that the state of happiness was somehow unnatural and would, by necessity, be brief, perishing under the persistence by which Time arrives and passes. It was that they were fleeing, but Tom Blake did not know it. He imagined when he saw them get out of the car and cross the rain-swept deck to climb the iron steps and look out at the grey-green lump of Clare that they were estimating how long the crossing would take, and how long it would be before the enemy was after them. And there was something — in the way the long man leaned to the small woman, in the shape of her, was that a child she was carrying inside the raincoat? in the blown-about crazy scent of lilies that could not be lilies — that made him change his view and nod and decide that he hoped they made it.

When they drove off into County Clare, the light was still pale and the rain falling. Tom Blake waved them off. "Good luck now," he said, as if it were an innocent salute. They arrived up the sloped roadway at the café and souvenir shop, which was on the point of opening.

"Wait," said Gabriella. Stephen stopped the car short. "Tea," she said, "and a ring."

He looked at her.

"It does not mean I am marrying you," she said, raising an eyebrow and holding a half-smile, then turning away and looking at the rain that was not so heavy now, and waiting while the astonished man got out and crossed into the shop for the improbable purchase.

When he returned her heart lifted.

"Here," he said. "I do not take thee to be my wife," and placed it on her wedding finger. There was a moment, an instant in which she glanced at it and the awful resolve — her disbelief in her own ability to sustain love — might have eased, but the child moved inside her and she looked away.

"Here's your first cup of Clare tea," Stephen said.

And that was it, the smallest ceremony, the ordinary moment that memory would return to and crystallize and turn into the small preciousness that Stephen Griffin would carry everywhere. The ring on the road to Clare, the ring that was not for sacrament but for protection against the spite of others, but which from the moment Gabriella put it on became a kind of sacrament, nonetheless, and was a promise be-

411

yond their saying, a mute and fragile daring that perhaps something imperishable existed. They drove away. They travelled from Killimer along the apparent aimlessness of a quiet road that wound past the bird-heavy hedgerows of spring.

Gabriella watched everything. She had the sense of arriving in Stephen's landscape, and read its soft hills and white-thorn hedgerows like secret messages. This was not the lush and verdant paradise of Kenmare. This was nothing like that. What she saw was a desolate windburnt beauty, an endurance of the spirit in the face of hardship, a stone-walled resistance to the battering of the Atlantic air. A place where the trees stiffened in the long arthritis of brutal weathering and yet did not die, but grew sideways, like the severely backcombed heads of stern aunts who softened once a year and gave sweets in May like white blossoms. Gabriella saw it, and then saw the sea. She let out a little cry, and Stephen looked over at her.

"It's something, isn't it?" he said. But she did not reply. She was looking at the waves crashing in the mid-distance, the great shooting spume of white wind brushed into the air like a game for the gulls. She began to smile, smiling more and more as the car followed the sea road around by the beach at Spanish Point and the sandy field and the fallen-down house of Moses Mooney. Stephen slowed the car before the empty curve of sand.

"So this is your beach?" Gabriella said.

"This is it."

"Can we stop? It's so beautiful."

"We have nowhere else to go," Stephen said. "My house is over there."

And so they walked down onto the sand, and while the school buses were converging on the school, and cars and coaches and lorries were moving in the ordinariness of everyday, they instead felt the dimensions of freedom that blew in from the breaking waves of the sea. They walked across the wet sand of the foreshore with sunken steps and hopped from the waves in the place where Stephen had once almost drowned. Gabriella took his hand.

"If I died now I'd be happy," she said, but the wind took her words and he did not hear her.

15

They slept that night in Stephen's house by the sea. The wind made a creaking music in every window and door, and for hours Gabriella lay wide-eyed in a sleepless dream of happiness. The morning and afternoon had unpacked them into the house, and in the putting out of each thing — the herbal remedies of Nelly Grant, the music books from Venice — was another of the infinitesimal gestures of trust through which we make our covenant with the world. By six o'clock the rooms had begun to look like the rooms in Kenmare, and Gabriella became aware of how simply rooms could resemble a relationship. It was only the first of many such moments. She understood that in the afternoon's unpacking was a sense of more than mere geographical arrival. As each moment passed and she moved from one room to the next, she felt the physical ease of the child inside her. Stephen had set up the music player, and in the small island of the house his father's music sounded triumphant, heralding the heartsongs of ages while he came and went with the boxes.

All of this flew back through Gabriella's mind as she lay sleepless in bed. She fingered the ring and held it out in the starlight as if it belonged to another. Then suddenly she thought of Maria Feri, whose ringless hand in Venice she remembered when it touched the bars of the cage where the bird sang. She saw her cousin sitting in the evening that had just passed, she saw the stillness of the house and the courteous, diffident manner of the older woman who was more still than aged dust and more sorrowful than failed summer, and in that moment, lying on the bed beside Stephen in that first evening in west Clare, Gabriella saw the tragedy of wasted life and the uselessness of losing days in attending dreams. She heard the bird singing in the cage, and in the wind-creaking bedroom heard the singing as it grew louder and louder, until its notes transformed into another music and was the playing of violins, bowing a joy that made her smile in the darkness. It was imagined and not remembered music. It was the music she had dreamt of playing by the sea in Venice when she was a child, before she had ever mastered the violin. It was the perfect music that plays in visions and makes the world shake with possibilities when we are young and feel our souls limitless. It was the music of inspiration, the kind that plays in the heart and makes a child want to pick up an instrument for the first time. Gabriella heard it in the darkness and remembered. Then she turned and rocked Stephen's shoulder, and when he raised his head swiftly to ask her what was wrong, she told him, "Nothing is wrong."

Then she touched his face and said, "Stefano, I want to start a music school."

16

In the morning when Gabriella awoke, she had the luminous radiance of purpose. Where the idea of the music school came from was unclear, but did not matter. She did not quite compute the complex formula that music had been the saviour of her own childhood and relate that to the child she carried inside her. She thought only that it was right, and felt the zeal of those who discover in midlife the meaning of their lives. Over breakfast she looked out the window that gave onto the sea and began to plan with Stephen.

The extravagance of her idea, its wild improbability — a classical music school on the west coast of Clare, and beside a town with a legendary reputation for traditional players — did not disturb him in the slightest, and he sat opposite her at the table with that lit expression of love and belief that saw all things as possible. He did not think for a moment that this was her pregnancy speaking again, that it was the whimsical fantasy of a moment, or that in three days, maybe four, she would be returned to the lassitude of her bed. Instead, he sat and listened. He heard her tell him again with the visionary excitement of the night before how, on that desolately beautiful coastline where he had chosen to live, she could imagine a building where music played, where children came with their instruments and walked out afterwards into the big sky and crashing sea. Her cheeks were roses while she spoke, her eyes widened to see the wonder of the future, and her words tumbled like the streams of April. The quickened heartbeat of the season beat through her, and Stephen sat there that morning witnessing her rapture with passionate gratitude.

This, he thought, is my happiness, to be given this chance to make her happy.

While Gabriella elaborated on how the teachers were to be enlisted, where the pupils might come from, what instruments, Stephen had risen from the chair and paced about. Soon he was finishing the sentences she started. They were unable to speak quickly enough, telling of the different studios there could be, of the long panels of glass that would view the sea, of rooms, too, where parents could wait and listen to anything from a full library of discs, how there could be special morning classes for the retired or the unemployed, how the school itself could have guest rooms where visiting musicians might come and stay, and would, too, because there would be no charge but the sharing of their musicianship, and in that place where they made this building, somewhere right there by the sea, music would be celebrated and made alive and reach out into the lives of people. "And we," said Gabriella, "can make that . . ."

". . . happen," said Stephen. "Yes."

He stood in the kitchen with his hands prayerlike beneath his chin. "O God," he said, seeing the shape of his life and hers, and finding in that almost surreal vision the answers to many questions. It was a moment when he glimpsed where all the tortuous plotting of his days had been leading; it included the music of his father, the buying of the ticket to first hear Gabriella play, the journeys to find her, the money he was to inherit, and the flight out of Kerry to the cottage where, like some agonizingly slow healing of all the griefs from childhood to disappointed adulthood, Gabriella had dreamt the music school.

They drove into Miltown Malbay, unaware that a pale white scent was following them and spreading like a sweet contagion through the town the instant they arrived. Stephen went to the bank. Gabriella walked up the street to find rhubarb and honey, whose conflicting tastes are the antidotes to the sudden giddiness suffered by those who are airy with dreams.

She was crossing the street when Moira Fitzgibbon saw her. At first Moira did not believe it could be the same woman. She had fallen into a season of doubt and lost the conviction that had once seemed to visit her like an angel with a sword. Her hopes had been dulled; the death of Moses Mooney had taken her by surprise, and in its aftermath she had woken each morning with the sour berries of blame in her mouth. She could not spit them out, and for a time was a half sister of herself looking in at the empty tedium of a life drying out in the salt wind. She despised the hopes she had, and protected herself with a tone of mockery her teachers had taught her. She muttered names at herself alone at the sink and did not respond when the calendar reminded her she should make new appeals to raise funds for the Mooney Memorial Hall. Before the spring she let the days go by. She took her daughters to school, collected them, had their meals ready, made another for her husband, and lived on, letting yesterday's hopes slip like a bandaged corpse into the cold sea. Who did you think you were? her face said to her, and she could make no reply. Then she saw Gabriella Castoldi on the street in Miltown Malbay. When she saw her features she was startled — it was an apparition, a ghost rising out of her conscience, and she thought of what she had done to that poor man Griffin in giving him the false hope of her address. (Often since she had considered it, and on Friday nights, when the late TV movie had finished some time after the *Late Late Show* and Tom was snoring on the couch like a gored beast, Moira chided herself on holding even the thinnest illusion that such romance existed, that somehow the long teacher might have found her, and they might have been happy together. It belonged in girls' comics, she had told herself, and pushed Tom on the back to tell his startled, slack-jawed face it was time for bed.)

The apparition walked towards her, and Moira touched her fingers on the glass of Casey the auctioneer's window. Its cold reaffirmed her, and in those astonished moments in which a mind reverses itself and discovers that its lies were truths, Moira saw the shape of the child and dared to imagine it might be Stephen's.

She moved a step from the window. Her eyes were quicker than her mouth. In an instant, they had alighted on the ring and saw the happiness of the woman; the shock of new reality surged through Moira like a charge that explodes blossoms on the trees. She stepped forward and held out an uncertain hand.

"Excuse me," she said. "I'm sorry I . . ."

Gabriella was standing beside her. She smiled. "Yes?"

"Is it, are you? . . . I'm sorry, I'm a terrible fool, I never know what to, I just blurt. You won't remember me, but I . . . You are . . . ?"

"I remember you. Yes, I do. You are the woman here, in Ennis. The concert. Yes." Gabriella took her hand and held it. She did not know then that she was part of the fulfillment of Moira Fitzgibbon's hopes, that her arrival in Miltown Malbay was like the return of a long-sent messenger upon whose news a whole city of dreams had been waiting, and for whose return hope had finally been surrendered. She did not know when she held Moira's hand that she was holding the hand of the future manager of the music school, or that she could have met no one else in that town who would help her make it a reality. Gabriella knew only that it was a good sign and waited in that astonished moment for the shock to pass. It took Moira another minute before she could approach the question of who Gabriella's husband might be, and then she saw Stephen Griffin walking up the street and she laughed out loud.

Stephen wore his bashfulness like a confirmation suit, and stood next to the two smiling women. "It was Mrs. Fitzgibbon who sold me the ticket to come and hear you," he said, nodding the flashing pate of his head towards Moira.

"Otherwise you would not have come," Gabriella teased him, and turned to Moira. "So, you are Cupid."

"Well, I don't know."

"Yes, you are," Stephen said. And there was a brief moment of quiet acknowledgement in which Moira Fitzgibbon felt her spirits lift and fly about. They were still in the air when, like a tireless conjuror outdoing each extraordinary trick with another, Stephen announced: "We are going to build a music school. Here, out by the sea."

17

Within half an hour Moira Fitzgibbon was getting out of Stephen's car and leading the two of them up the grassy pathway to the ruined cottage of Moses Mooney. On the short journey from the town Moira had reminded Stephen and told Gabriella the story of the old man.

"I know it was mad, and it was, it was mad, mad altogether," she said, walking them to the door. "I mean, he had notions, wild mad notions, and to look at him you would think he was for the canaries, the big beard, the look he had when he went blind, like he was seeing something all the time somewhere else and, oh, I don't know, but there was something made me think of him, you know, that he had this one dream of the music, and well, he had no hope in the earthly world of making it happen, and maybe that was it, maybe that was what clicked with me. Anyway . . ."

She stopped and opened the front door.

They peered inside.

"He bought the field over," Moira said, "for his concert hall. It's mostly hares."

They looked in at the purple shadows of the old man's life, until at last the prompting of the sun on their backs turned them around and they saw the startling view of the sea. The light on the water made the sea seem like sky and the horizon infinitely in the distance.

"I think we should buy it," Stephen said. "Gabriella, it can be here."

She took his hand and held it, and was stilled with the knowledge of how much he wanted to give her. "I don't know. Do you think?"

"Yes," he said, and already it was decided. Already, within the space of less than twenty-four hours since their arrival in Clare, they had mapped out a life and found the place to begin building it. With the force of will and single-mindedness that sometimes belongs to those called simple, they saw the music school rise in the hillocky green field next to the house of Moses Mooney, they saw the money arriving from Dublin to Miltown Malbay and their hasty spending of it to secure first the field and then the planning permission and then the builders and then the students. Nothing that April day seemed beyond the capacity of their imagining, for the measure of love was to be not words or air but blocks and mortar and timber and glass, and in the bigness of their hearts that day they carried whole walls, windows, and doors with no effort at all.

They walked away from the cottage back to the car. Moira Fitzgibbon could scarcely believe what was happening, and said she needed the bracing exercise of a good walk back to the town to reassure herself that she had in fact got out of bed. "Go on," Moira said, shooing them off like hens, "you go away, I'll walk. I'll call up to the house tomorrow."

And it was only when they had driven away, and Moira had turned one last time to look back at the old man's cottage and whisper to him that maybe his dream was going to happen, that she saw three black cats coming from the cottage and tumbling on the wild long grass of the lawn.

18

The progress of dreams is in fits and starts. Time hastens and slows and makes of the clock of desire not minutes and hours but fevers, flushes, and languid long eternities. So in one day everything happened, and after it almost nothing at all.

Money does not travel quickly, and the more of it there is, the more leisurely its pace, Stephen learned. He imagined Moran, the assistant manager in Kenmare, reading with tight small eyes the request for the transfer of funds, and delaying it with a kind of exquisite spite that is the triumph of the small-minded. Nothing happened, no money arrived. Mr. MacNamara, a small man who came in a large exhausted car, told Stephen and Gabriella he was the auctioneer for the Mooney property. He laughed into his fist, as if holding a small microphone, and said yes yes yes in constant repetition, replying to some question no one could hear but himself. He looked at them and said yes yes yes; he looked at the window and did the same. When Stephen told him they were only waiting on the money to arrive, Mr. MacNamara gave his triple affirmative and added a wink, running his tongue about the inside of his mouth so it appeared he was chasing a lozenge and not a sale. He left abruptly after that, but returned the next day as if he had forgotten that he had ever been there. He stood in the doorway and said yes yes yes when Stephen told him he had no news. In the following two weeks he made six appearances, sometimes standing in the sitting room with his hands lost behind his back under the flaps of his jacket and looking about him for a clue as to his purpose.

While the plans for the building were in stasis, other aspects of the music school were not. Gabriella struck up a friendship with Moira Fitzgibbon, and in morning meetings over the strong tea which Stephen made in the kitchen they planned together how the word might be spread. Gabriella grew bigger almost by the moment. She sat at the table and bloomed, as if the hope in her spirit grew the child more quickly now and warmed the air in the room with incipient life. Moira Fitzgibbon gave her tips and counselled sea walks on the noon shore; she recounted the adventures of her own pregnancies, and through the simple means of her own personality gave Gabriella Castoldi the gift of being grounded. So while the talks began in air and music, they ended in the earthed practicalities of house heating, plumbing, and a place for the cot. After Moira's third visit, Gabriella had redrawn the inside of the cottage; as Stephen watched with a kind of fearful astonishment, she showed him where they should break out the roof and add skylights, where the extra bedroom needed to be made off their own, where the central heating pipes could run and the bathroom replace the hose-like shower that hung over a discoloured draining sink.

So, in those light blustery days at the end of April, when the sun appeared in the sky above the sea like a promise delivered, builders arrived at the cottage and broke holes in the slate for the skylights. Corry & Son & Nephew opened the roof like a great wound, pushing aside a thickly woven web of time and watching spiders fall down and scurry to new hiding across the floor below. Because Gabriella loved the idea of them so, Stephen doubled the order to four skylights and watched as the series of squares were cut away from the roof, making the house suddenly appear absurdly vulnerable and exciting at the same time, as if it were a giggling and intrepid centenarian going across the sunlit grass in the nude. Birds flew in and out of the house and bats arrived in the twilight, flickering across the starred heavens to alight inside the high ceilings in a sign Tom Clancy said guaranteed good fortune. For three days the house breathed through its top while Corry & Son & Nephew climbed the ladders and sat on the roof and smoked Woodbines, looking out at the fine view of the ocean; Corry said sometimes you wouldn't think it stretched all the way to America and watched the waves from that high position with a kind of grieven mesmerism that only Son knew betrayed he was thinking of Son Two, who was that noontime waking to work in Duggan's Bar in Brooklyn. The Corrys took their time; they threw down the old slates, which Son said were as crisp as cream crackers, and when Stephen at last broke through his diffidence and asked if the windows would be in soon because he feared a change in the weather, the father shouted down to him that he had it on several counts — the frog spawn, the movements of the heron, and the cloud formations reported over Mount Brandon — that the dry spell would continue for weeks. Nephew concurred. He had it from Sky News Long Range, he said, and looked up at the blue heavens as if towards a satellite God.

19

In a house of birds, bats, and spiders, then, Gabriella and Stephen lived within the breathing of the sea. Little by little word of their arrival had reached every house in the town and beyond. But there was something in that parish — perhaps it was the notion of its own broadmindedness, the influence of summer continentals, or the whole bizarre history of life which had finally exhausted the parish imagination and capacity for being surprised — that meant the news of Stephen and Gabriella did not raise an eyebrow, not even when the story of their proposed music school reached the bars at Considine's and Clancy's and circulated with the strange scent of apple blossom.

In the first days of May a letter came announcing that the money had arrived in Miltown Malbay.

There was £267,000.

That the figure was astonishingly high, and arrived now at the moment they needed it, did not strike Stephen as strongly as it might, for he believed that it came from his father, that it was evidence of his spirit watching over him and making easier the way ahead.

Mr. MacNamara was in the house on one of his visits when the news arrived, and saying yes yes yes to Corry & Son & Nephew, looking down through the skylights on the roof above him. When Stephen told him he was ready to pay for the Mooney land, Mr. MacNamara looked sincerely surprised, as if it was a remarkable coincidence that there might be some business to be done. "That's grand," he said, and scratched his left temple to recall who Mooney was. The following day Moira Fitzgibbon arrived in the olive-carpeted sitting room of Councillor O'Rourke and told him they would be seeking planning permission. She told him of the importance of the school, the need for the permission to be hurried, and knew enough to make the case seem impossible unless he was able to help them. She puffed a despairing sigh and watched it cross the room to arrive in the magnanimous heart of the councillor. He paused, and then like an emperor nodded a single nod.

Maytime blossomed. In the deep calm of

mid-morning Stephen and Gabriella took walks into the west Clare countryside. They did not go far. Ten minutes outside the town they walked along roads where the hedgerows of blackthorn were deeply tangled with wild blackberry. Birds flew before them and sang the songs of summer in the blue air. Dung flies buzzed where the cows had passed and formed into diamond-shaped gauzes as the walkers came upon them. The sound of tractors travelled everywhere, and was so steadily part of those walks that it became one with the landscape and was as if the throttling of those engines was the action of a supernatural sewing machine, going back and forth, stitching into being the patchwork of the fields. The noise itself was reassuring, and lent the walks the indolent pleasure of summer-afternoon sleeps while the lawn mower mows.

It was perfect. For Gabriella had arrived that May in a mood of quiet ease. The midwife had told her the pregnancy was going well, and by the time the first plans for the music school had been tacked up on the wall of the kitchen, she was feeling the absence of regret for the first time in her life. She sang notes in her bed in the morning while Stephen brought her herbal teas. She allowed her anxieties and the rigour of her self-criticism to slip gradually away, and instead adopted the new life in that cottage by the sea as if it were she and not the child that was being born.

In the afternoons she played the violin. When Stephen wanted to sit in the room listening, she told him it was not a public performance and laughed, saying, "Well, perhaps it is, for one member of the public." So he sat outside the door and listened; he heard her playing her way back into the first rooms of her childhood, heard the first music Scaramuzza had taught her returning now like a new season for the child she was carrying. She played the infant beginner's tunes with such feeling that even outside the door Stephen could imagine her weeping as she played. She played "Twinkle, Twinkle, Little Star" and then slid from the simple notes into a series of variations which grew ever more ornate and intricate, until they were the music of ineffable hope and longing, the music that contained the boundless dreams of mothers for their children's happiness. Gabriella played for an hour each afternoon, and Stephen did not disturb her. When she came out of the room she wore a rosy bloom and pretended she had not heard Stephen hurry away from the door.

"You have been doing great work out here," she said when she came across him in the kitchen.

"Oh yes." He turned to run a cloth across the sink. She stood beside him. "Feel," she said, and took his hand and put it on the place where the child was moving like a swimmer in a sea. "It's the music." They stood, innocent and hopeful, by the kitchen sink, and imagined the possibility that life could after all be that simple, that nothing would come and threaten that easeful and tender living by the sea, and that God was merciful and good and redeemed all grief in the end. They stood there, wordless, and felt the child. Looking on the slope of grass that ran down towards the fall to the sea, Gabriella said, "Could we have a garden?"

The following day Stephen bought a shovel and pitchfork. He returned from McInerney's in Miltown Malbay with the white wooden handles sticking out the car window and carried the tools onto the grassy space with the set jaw of a Wild West pioneer. He went to foot the shovel into the ground, but the old tufted grass resisted and the shovel made a slow fall to the side. Stephen was not to be outdone. He spat somewhat carefully on his hands and walked over

436

the ground where during the evening Gabriella had imagined out loud a perennial border. The grass was tall and wild and was like a long-enduring and hairy demon upon whom the shovel struck but made no impact. Stephen drove the blade again and again as a moon row of blisters opened in his palms. His long back curved into it. He had never dug a day in his life, and now in the breeze that came up from the sea he hacked and jabbed at the ground for the beginnings of a dream garden. His sweat fell in grey droplets. He watched the embrowned flaps of the blisters open and fingered them back into place like a child imagining damage repaired. The white handles of the shovel and fork grew smeared with the dull colour of labour.

That afternoon he worked on while the birds gathered. The following day and the next, though he woke with his body stiffly locked like a coffin, he did the same. He stretched his fingers and sat while Gabriella poured olive oil on them. He opened the ground for a vegetable garden, for a herbal border, and the curved shape where he imagined flowers would bloom for Gabriella and his child. He worked in silence to the whispering collapse of the sea, the crown of his head burning a red corona until

Tom Clancy, admiring the work from the stone wall that surrounded it, brought Stephen a straw hat that made him look like a gondolier.

20

The following day they bought the plants. Gabriella had a book with colour plates of poker-headed kniphofia, bright yellow achilleas, and crimson *rosa moyesii*, and with the childlike fantasy of a first gardener imagined them growing in the brown ground outside the window. In Miltown Malbay the selection of plants was too narrow for such dreams, and so they drove into north Clare to the hidden nursery of Mick Kinsella. He was a tall, ponytailed figure in jeans who had for fifteen years pretended to be an accountant in Dublin, until the morning he realized that he could not remember the smell of roses. Since then he had run the nursery in the hills of north Clare and with his wife, Maggie, reared three wild-looking girls among the tangle of flowers that were his garden. He sat inside the gateway in a small wooden hut, where he used his laptop computer to browse among the world's exotic plant catalogues. When Stephen and Gabriella arrived he told

them he had just found a new terrestrial or-
chid from New Zealand and ordered three
dozen of them. Then he walked them
through the heavily scented grass path into
the garden proper, pushing aside the
flowerheads.

"We have a garden dug out," Gabriella
told him.

Mick Kinsella looked at them. "It's your
first?" he said.

"Yes."

"Here, take a chair," he told Gabriella, and
sat her in the garden, where she could watch
while he and Stephen walked back and forth
picking out the plants that were not the ones
in the book but were the ones Mick Kinsella
said would grow. Stephen and Gabriella
brought them home, packed into the back of
the car like children going on summer holidays. That evening they placed them out in
the garden that faced the sea, and sat and
watched them until the light died away.

And so the summer rolled in. Somewhere
out in the Atlantic a dazzling blue formed
and stilled the winds and made the sea
warm and gentle and inviting, lapping all
the way to the shores of Clare. The sun
shone like Spain. Sombreros appeared like
strange blooms, and the smell of almond oil

hung in the air above the salmon-skinned and the freckled. Miltown Malbay sold out of electric fans. The evening the schoolchildren were released for the summer, the sea at Spanish Point was thronged with leaping white bodies, beating winglike arms against the waves that collapsed across their thighs. All through June the soft blue filled the sky. The tenderness of the days was a blessing which some called a curse and said the end of the world was beginning with a drought. But in the garden behind the house of Stephen and Gabriella the plants of Mick Kinsella grew. Stephen watered them three times a day. He fed them no fertilizer but, when Tom Clancy suggested it, he barrowed cow dung down the road and made a kind of manure dressing which stunk the air and kept the cats away for three days.

In the cool of the stone house Gabriella hid from the sun. The moment she appeared in the daylight, the sweat gathered beneath the heaviness of her breasts and ran cold rivers down her stomach. The heat made her heavier, and so instead, she sat in the lie-out chair-bed inside the house with the fan oscillating across her while she played the violin to the unborn. She wrote three short letters to Maria Feri, telling her in discreet language the progress of love, and then wrote another to Nelly Grant explaining the strange mixture of marvel and terror that was alternating through her spirit. No reply arrived from either woman.

Still, the days were delivered like polished gems. Gabriella said she woke and saw the sea and thought she was in Italy. Stephen opened all the skylights, and the house slept like that, with arched eyebrows, where the moon was reflected in quadruple. By the end of July Gabriella found it impossible to sleep during the nights. She lay on the bed beside the exhausted figure of Stephen and tapped his shoulder when his snoring sounded like pain. He woke with a suddenness, as if his world were a rolling glass globe, and shot out his hands to catch it in the dark. But she was all right. Sometimes she wanted to talk, sometimes she didn't. He brought her cocoa and herbal teas and water and chocolate. She told him he was too good for her, and sometimes the very act of him coming through the door with the mug made tears start in her eyes. "You are a saint," she said.

"No, I'm not."

"But I think you are. I am in bed with a saint." She said it and looked at him and smiled, and then she told the child and lay there in the grey starlight, where her face

442

was lost and none could read the gratitude and prayer in her eyes.

Often in those dead hours between the sunset and the four o'clock dawn they talked of the music school. It added another meaning to their days, though it still existed more solidly in words than in stone. They talked it into happening. They lay with their faces to the open skylight and told how it would be, as if telling the heavens to prepare the way. There was comfort in the company of that dream, and so almost like an incantation Stephen told Gabriella what it would be like, how the lessons would be, and the pupils, and the concerts they could have on the grass between the school and the sea. He told her until at last she asked him no more and he supposed she was sleeping. But she was not. She was closing her eyes and watching beneath her eyelids the extraordinary edifice of love built in solid air. And it was only in those moments, in that strange starry stillness when the world seemed to sleep without her, that she truly dared to believe it might happen.

21

Finally, the builders arrived in the hillocky field and began to dig out the foundations as the hares darted about into the dunes. To relieve herself of the overattentiveness of Stephen, Gabriella insisted he go each day to see what was happening and walk back along the seashore before coming to tell her. It gave her an hour on her own. For in the nearness of the birth she was revisited by visions of her mother's miscarriages, and although she was safely beyond miscarriage, she fretted about the possibility of an invisible curse moving in her bloodline. She sat in the deep armchair that looked out on the sea and tried to breathe with the focussed concentration she had when about to play extraordinary music.

Stephen stood, she sat in the chair.

"You'll stay there?" he said.

"Of course I will."

He put on a disc of Vivaldi's concertos. "I'll be back before it's over," he said.

"I know you will."

He went out the door. She stayed in the chair.

The music played.

Five minutes later she had risen with a sudden impatience. She saw the bitter face of her pregnant mother standing scouring the sink in the kitchen of their house in the Calle Visciga. She saw it. She saw the fist of steelwool circling, and she cried out. She stood up and crossed to turn the music up louder. She moved the volume until the notes were huge and full and pulsing through the cottage.

Then the pain lanced through her and she slid to the floor.

"O mio Dio."

She reached for the counter, but her fingers clenched in spasmic fists and hit against the wood. The sharpness of the pain was so severe that her back arched and her mouth opened wide with a soundless cry. She lay on the cold tiles and banged against them with the back of her head, sucking and blowing as if drowning in the tide of life. A minute seemed endless. The pain had a narrowness of point so exquisite that it seemed to find her deeply and then rip upwards. The floor pooled with a little blood and water. Gabriella screamed into the Vivaldi and banged her head again. She screamed

445

so loudly through the music that the black-birds rose off the roof and flew in the air about the house with the strange and morbid excitement of funeralgoers. They hung around. They mirrored her woe with a beakish crying that upset the cats who lay in the shadow of the plants in the garden and made them come to the windowsill, where the saucer was empty of milk. Time stopped. There was nothing but the waves of pain in the throbbing music, the urgent and relentless hurting that was the pain of sorrow and loss and doomed love and expectant tragedy, and was the pain of the beginning of life, too.

Oh God, Gabriella thought, we are going to die. Then the air seemed rung with muffled hornlike sounds and thickened with floating pinpricks of dusted light that were the onrush of a violent dizziness. And then, blackout.

22

Moira Fitzgibbon found her lying on the floor.

There had been no answer to the doorbell, and when Moira let herself in through the back door she caught at once the queer whiff of disaster. The atmosphere was weirdly aslant, like the grin on a misbehaved child when the crime is as monstrous as he imagines. The molecules themselves seemed disordered, as though the world had been bumped against and some secret and perfect order was discovered enormously flawed. Moira came in slowly, she called and heard no answer. The music player had stopped and was buzzing with the loud volume of emptiness.

Then Moira heard the breathing and, like a finger held upon a wound and now releasing, time rushed like blood. Gabriella was still alive, the child was not yet born. Moira Fitzgibbon made bloodprints with her feet and rang the mid-wife and the doctor and opened the door and called for Stephen in a voice the seawind whipped away. She hurried and ran water and got towels and lifted Gabriella's head and told her not to die, talked to her in a long and seamless stream of urgings that were the confession of her own longing for the child to be born and for the music lessons and the school and the dream of their life by the sea that she told Gabriella was proof of something, and which offered Moira, when she lay in the dark, the single best example of something good and true and beautiful.

23

On the beach Stephen walked beneath the crying of the seabirds. A breeze was gathering from somewhere out in mid-ocean, and the gulls came before it like grey prophecies across the cloudless sky. The wind was salted and dry. Stephen carried his shoes and walked in the wet sand, where the waves painted his turned-up trouser legs. He walked in the place where once he had thought his life was going to end. Now, on that afternoon beach, he walked to re-encounter that earlier self and renew his gratitude for so much that was given to him. The music school had been started, Gabriella was in their house where the garden was begun. He believed newly in God and felt the simplicity of grace.

He tried not to think that the music school might be a folly, that it might be built beside the sea and open and find no pupils. That within a year it might be an empty shell whistling the long, unhappy note of doomed dreams. That Gabriella might change her heart and want to leave. He did not want to think of such things and kept a waferlike belief in goodness balanced on his soul. He walked the long beach until he was past the cliffs and out almost to the broken rocks, where his figure was too small to be seen by those searching for him along the sand.

When he reached the remote end, he turned, tossed a stone in the water, and held back his head a moment until the brilliant light of the sky bathed his face.

He narrowed his eyes at the sun and did not hear the cries. The waves slapped. Gulls soared and screamed.

Then Stephen turned to see the three Coughlan children clambering over the rocks to tell him to come quickly, there was trouble.

His heart stopped. He imagined he was in a nightmare, for the journey back across the summer beach seemed to take place amidst the garish light and hollow cries of grim hallucination. Sunbathers sat up on their towels and watched him. He could not hurry quickly enough, and his long strides sank in the softened sand and gave him the jagged, uneven rhythm of a jogger suffering heart attack. His long neck angled forward, his arms pumped, and when his hat flew off he left it behind him on the water, running in a gasping horror, as if across his wide eyes there suddenly flashed the doomed future of all their loving, and upon his getting to the cottage depended one last chance for its rescue.

He came up the dunes on all fours. He saw the cars at the gateway to the cottage. Then he slowed down. His rib cage hurt, his arms were heavy. The blood in his legs felt like molten lead and swayed his walking, so that the Coughlans caught up with him and took his hands on either side, guiding him the last paces along the road to the cottage that he was now afraid to enter. He stopped at the gate. He stared at the house, and the children looked up at him. And for a moment he waited. His breath escaped in long sighs. And while he stood there, on that cusp of what he supposed to be unutterable loss, he begged God in a prayer for it not to be so.

Then he heard the baby cry.

24

Gabriella Castoldi did not die that afternoon in the hot July of the long summer but lived when her doctor said she should not have, and gave birth to a baby girl they called Alannah. A small, brown-eyed baby, she was born with a face that revealed neither her mother nor her father, though they each took turns to declare she was exactly like the other; as though they could not quite believe such tender beauty was their own.

For four days after Alannah was born, Gabriella did not move from her bed; she refused to travel to the hospital in Ennis and instead took the difficulties of the birth as a sign that within life was an inevitable force of goodness which flowed beyond our understanding. She relied upon the ancient knowledge of the mid-wife and summoned the healing energy of Nelly Grant to awaken within her. She wept and drowned the bed in water and milk, turning the bedroom air a pale creamy colour that was more filling than food and strangely without the scent of sourness. The near-tragedy brought company. When the word of what had happened reached the town, it had the double effect of raising anger by highlighting the absence of maternity facilities in Ennis and transforming Gabriella into a native of the parish. Visiting ladies brought Lucozade and chocolates and made soft noises above the baby. They relived the hard labour in vivid imaginations and revisited through the new mother their own birthings years earlier. Throughout the first week they came and went like swaddling maternal tides, sliding in around the sleeping mother and child to breathe the thick warm smell of the newborn like an aromatherapeutic remedy, and nodding themselves into dreamy naps that were filled with the downy comfort of first blankets. At once Stephen understood that the birth did not belong to Gabriella and him alone. So he made tea and brought it to the ladies and did not show surprise or resentment when he sometimes opened the bedroom door and saw a half-dozen women over sixty sitting around the bed.

It was in the evenings when the visitors left that he lay with Alannah on the bed. He could not look at her without seeing God. He did not deserve her, he thought, and then held the child in his arms in the tenderest embrace while the stars rose in the skylight overhead.

She became the clock of the cottage. Her wakes and sleeps dictated the rhythms of their days and nights. She was dark-haired and seemed in Stephen's arms the impossible lightness of air. He carried her around the house like the smallest parcel of hope, and though her eyes could not see that far, he pointed out the garden and the sea and then played softly the aching music of *Tosca* while she fell asleep on his shoulder.

When Moira Fitzgibbon called, he hugged her in the doorway with that combination of awkwardness and sincere deep feeling that was the badge of his character. He cut her flowers from the garden and doubled his own blushes when he saw how she almost wept to receive them. Then, for Alannah's first trip outside the cottage, he urged Moira to join them and drove in his father's car along the western edge of Clare, where the fine summer was just beginning to fade and the yellow stubble of the mown fields was giving way to the last soft green. On the quiet backroads between Miltown Malbay and the sea Stephen stopped the car time and again, and taking one of four dozen packets he had bought in the town, he got out and scattered wildflower seeds in the ditches and beneath the hedgerows.

"These are for you," he said. "These are for celebration." Gabriella held Alannah to the window to see, and even Moira became giddy with the notion of the secret sowings and came out from the car and threw fistfuls of poppy, rudbeckia, rose campion, dianthus, and feverfew into the gaiety of the wind.

On the Friday evening at the end of Alannah's first week, Gabriella wrote newly to Maria Feri and Nelly Grant. When she sat in the kitchen before the white pages, the enormity of what had happened to her life rose before her. It was the most ordinary event in the world, the love affair, the birth of the child, but somehow when she thought of it — that she was living now in the west of Ireland with a daughter a week old in the cradle beside her — it took on the dimensions of dreams. She hummed an air and wrote. To Maria Feri she told the news that she was an aunt, and how Alannah showed the time she had spent in Venice by the outrageous exuberance of her giggle, which, Gabriella wrote, was not in the least Irish. She sent her cousin wishes and thanks and lifted the pen from the white space where she glimpsed the evening sorrow of that small apartment above the canal. To Nelly Grant she wrote a shorter message: I have a baby girl. Please come visit.

But it was Maria and not Nelly who responded. In two weeks a piece of white lacework arrived from Venice with a note in the small careful hand of her cousin. It was written on handmade paper in violet ink and had the formal tone of old family property, offering congratulations in a manner that some might consider coldhearted. But Gabriella knew better, and read beyond the tone. She took the lacework in her hand and breathed its scent and caught at once the bittersweet melancholia of Venice; then she placed it in the case of her violin, as if for company.

From Nelly Grant there came no word, and by the time the first rains of autumn had begun to sweep in against the back of the cottage, Gabriella had written her three letters with no reply. Then, in the way a person can fall through the narrowest cracks of our lives, she wrote no more and put aside the little hurt of the silence by supposing that Nelly was simply a woman who disliked writing.

25

When the rain came it came in sheets. It was as if a great chest had been discovered in the heavens and an array of grey clothes were flung out of it into the skies. It streamed down. The light was washed out of the days, and the field where the music school was now almost complete was scored with streaks of an ochre mud. The building was a low glass pentagon with piers of Liscannor flagstone. The builders marvelled at it. Once they were inside it, finishing the timberwork and plastering, they felt something of the extraordinary nature of the thing they had created. It was a unique space, and felt as if it had fallen from the sky or risen from the ground. The golfers in the dunes nearby looked at it with the puzzled expressions of those who cannot imagine the reality of fantasy. But through the rainy days of September the men worked on inside it with a gathering good humour. There was something about the light, of how the rooms' long windows let in the sea views and blended them into the sky, of how strangely playful the space seemed, that made the carpenters whistle and the plasterers hum until the experience of each day inside that building took on the spirit-lifting quality of a concert in Verona. Men sang tunes they hardly knew. They teased each other and then responded to taunts by singing another, singing songs they sang only when drunk, and marvelling at how the sounds of their own voices rang in the high roof spaces.

Every day Stephen visited the building. The closer it came to being completed, the more uncertain he became that they would find the pupils to fill it. In the colder weather the population of the town shrunk. The whole landscape took on the air of a child crouching before a blow. And the rain swept on. Cold squalls blew in off the watery horizon, they lashed the coast of Clare, but according to the evening news on the television, seemed to have blown out and vanished long before they reached Dublin.

By the end of September Gabriella had returned to the violin with renewed energy. She played for Alannah, then played some more when the child was sleeping. Somewhere in the time she had spent away from it her style had changed. She had lost the sharp, edgy quality that was characteristic of her previous intensity. Now instead, she created a fuller and rounder sound and made a music that to Stephen seemed to echo his own feelings of grace. The two Fitzgibbon girls came for lessons. And one evening while Ciara, who was seven, was waiting in the sitting room, Stephen saw her looking at the chess set.

"Would you like to learn?" he asked her.

"Is it very hard?"

"Not for a girl who can play the violin."

And so they began. He taught her how to play while the rain whipped against the windows and her sister bowed "Song of the Wind" on the violin. He showed her the moves and watched her innocence and astonishment at the bizarre secrets of the game, how the knight could jump and the king castle, and as he lifted the pieces and spoke of them, he had to pause three times in mid-sentence, for in the timbre of his own voice he heard the unmistakable speech of Philip Griffin teaching him the same game so many years before. He moved the bishop and looked at his own hand holding it and, seeing the wrinkling he had not noticed before, realized how he had become his father.

On Saturday, the fifth of October, Stephen and Gabriella opened the music school in the pentagonal building of glass and stone in Mooney's field on the west coast of Clare. It was a day of wild weathers, and the beginning of that long season of flu, head colds, and chest coughs that were to mark that year's winter like overdue payment for a good summer. It was the predicted gloom that made happy the misfortunate. The wind came in broken, sudden breaths, as if the lungs of the year had collapsed inwards, and a momentary stillness was followed by forceful gasping. Rain was spat out and then vanished, then clattered again on the glass.

For a week the school had been advertised. Moira had made posters. She had spoken to the people at the *Clare Champion* and been promised an article, which did not appear. She had mentioned the virtuosity of Gabriella Castoldi, the great progress on the violin her own daughters were making, the opportunity of the school. She had even let slip the name of Moses Mooney and used it like a touchstone to remind those who did not wish to remember that he was a blind old man who had died disappointed. Moira had campaigned for the school tirelessly, but on the morning of the fifth of October she awoke with the terrible unease of those who are about to be ill. The weather was a bad omen. Perhaps no one will come, she thought. And for a final time in her life returned to the old doubt in herself: Perhaps behind my back they are laughing, thinking, Who does she think she is, she who failed more exams than anyone in the parish. Moira had stood at the rain window and cursed. Then said, God forgive me.

By ten o'clock she had arrived at the new building, where Stephen and Gabriella and the baby were waiting for her. The air in the school smelled of painted colours. Inside the front hall there was a music system softly playing Vivaldi's *Concerto in G major* for violoncello, strings, and basso continuo; there was a table with cheese and wine, and another with leaflets and admission forms overhung by the green and yellow paper ribbons that Moira had saved since the last World Cup. At half past ten Councillor O'Rourke arrived. He held his head at such a high angle that it was impossible to tell whether it was in disdain or approval (and in fact he himself was undecided and would wait for confirmation one way or the other when his constituents arrived); he studied the building carefully to avoid conversation and looked at his watch with the practised air of a man who must always seem to be urgently needed elsewhere.

Gabriella paced with the baby, and Stephen made small circles in the front hallway behind her. He was wearing the repaired suit made by his father. His eyes followed the floor. He walked and stopped abruptly, listening intently into the wind for the sound of cars and then hurrying on when there was none. Whenever he arrived close to Gabriella, he tried to tell her it would be all right. But by the fourth time he gave up and used only his eyes to give her the calm he did not possess.

It did not work. Gabriella glistened with perspiration. Alannah, picking up the high-frequency signal of her mother's fear, fretted and made a low moaning sound that wavered as Gabriella rocked her in her arms.

They walked around the hallway. They tried not to look out the long windows that showed the road where no cars were coming. The rain fell, and to protect the terrible vulnerability of their dream, Moira turned the music up loud, then took the councillor on a tour through the empty rooms.

It was eleven o'clock, half an hour past the advertised opening. At last, as if she had finally paced all the way to the far end of hope, Gabriella stopped in the middle of the hallway. She paused a moment for her spirit to break. Then Stephen told her, "There are two cars."

It was a moment typical of their life together, for within it was a kind of desperate yearning, an outrageous dreaming that belonged to a more innocent world than this, and which appeared to be always on the point of crashing headlong into the chill reality of failure, but then was rescued. As if God were juggling glass-ball moments with mischievous riskiness, letting them hurtle towards the ground and then defying the odds to pull off once more the little miracle of salvation.

There were two cars, the Kennys' and the O'Connells'. Then there were three more, The Mulvihills', Mangans', and Greenes'. They came in with the low-chinned circumspection of those who enter new rooms for the first time. They had come from the Lahiffe funeral, they explained over the Vivaldi, draining the councillor's face when he realized he had missed it. They smiled and shook hands and did not seem to resist the sudden switch from the mood of the graveside to the bright triumphant joy of the music. Others were coming along, Joe Kenny said. But the traffic was all caught up in Miltown Malbay. He took the wine Moira offered him and drank it back in a shot, then looked up at the bare walls as if at paintings.

Big Tom Lernihan came in the door. Then Josie Hassett, Nuala Normoyle, the three Looney girls, the Penders, the Reidys, the Mohallys, and six families of Ryans. Within half an hour the funeral had arrived at the music school. There were a hundred people in the hallway, and the mud of the graveyard slipped from their boots, and the heat of their bodies rose and filled the air with the smell of rain returning heavenward. The music played through the talking, the deep notes of the cello beating like rhythmic wings across the space above them all. Timmy Purtill said it was music like he'd never heard in his life and sat beside the speaker eating a cheese from Denmark. Mary Enright took the arm of Gabriella and told her she had a boy who wanted lessons. So did Maura Galvin. Then the barrel-chested Donie Cussen, who was called Casanova, smiled his full mouth of teeth at Gabriella and said, "Any chance of a tune for us?"

Then she was playing.

The disc was turned off, and while Stephen held the baby and the crowd hushed,

Gabriella Castoldi played Fibich's aching "Poeme." She played with slow and sweet melancholy, and stopped the hearts of those who heard her, so that their mouths opened and their spirits flowed out into that hallway to meet the soul of the woman with the violin. It was nothing less than that. For even from the first notes it was apparent to everyone that this was a woman communicating something rare and tender and profound, that the action of her bow on the strings was not simply the mechanics of music, but that between the instrument and her there was no distinction, and that the infinitesimal beauty of the high notes came like some ambrosial breath from within her. When Gabriella finished there was not a sound. There was only the astonished faces of those who had had no idea they could be so moved by such music. Casanova Cussen raised his big hands and crashed the air, but before the ovation could reach fullness Gabriella was playing again. "Party pieces," she said, and swept into Kreisler and then Dvořák. She played as if she were dancing. She played out of relief and gratitude, out of an understanding that she was not alone and that in the rain of west Clare that day in October, with Stephen Griffin holding their child, was as much happiness as she dared accept from the world. She played Brahms's "Hungarian Dance" and Dvořák's "Humoresque," and was pausing between pieces when she saw the tear-wet face of the woman who was Eileen Waters talking to Stephen and then taking his offered hand and slowly shaking it.

What happened after that occurred in the vague uncertain way that time has decided traditional *seisiúns* should begin; whether Francie Golden spoke first, told anyone, or simply carried his fiddle everywhere, whether there was an imperceptible signal, a nod or wink, or whether it was the moment the warming of the French wine in his blood reached the point of inspiring action, there was an instant when the crowd were clapping for Gabriella, and then it was Francie Golden who was playing "Upstairs in a Tent" and grinning sideways in the terrible pleasure of his own devilment. Like Gabriella he flowed one tune into the next, and for the first time in that building made the air dance to a jig. There was clapping along and toe-tapping and little waves of quick encouragements: "Good man, Francie," "That's it, boy," "Now ye're playin,'" and a few plain whoops of wordless gaiety.

The moment Francie finished, faces

turned to Gabriella, as if she might disapprove of that simple old jaunty music that was theirs. But at once she caught the violin under her chin and said, "Like this?" and played the same tune back to Francie Golden, who laughed and joined her, and led her on another tune in which she followed him and then another. Then Gabriella played Schubert, and Francie was urged to try his fist at it, and did; and the twin O'Gormans, who had been there and gone home for their instruments, arrived back and joined in on two flutes. And Moira Fitzgibbon called Frawley's from the car phone of the councillor and ordered all the hot food they had to be brought up to the school in Dempsey's van, and the four Keoghs went for stout and came back with it with Micky Killeen, the box player, and Johnsie Kelly, the pipe-playing tiler from Kilmurry. And though the rain beat on outside and the car park puddled deeply beneath the bruised sky, none in Miltown Malbay that day gave it a care, for the music was like a long and intricate spell, and transformed grief and worry to laughter and delight in the very same way it had done for centuries. The walls rang with it. Men took off their jackets and danced the Clare set with their wives. They battered with toes and heels on the carpeted floor, as if it were flagstone, and spun in giddying quick circles that returned them to the moments of their childhoods, when the magic of dancing first saw them leap and spin on kitchen floors. They danced and the music played on. More people arrived, and soon the crush of the crowd made some spin off down the corridors and dance in each of the rooms of that pentagonal building, dancing even beyond the hearing of the music, and making steps and keeping time to the music that was already inside them. Gabriella put down her violin and danced with Stephen and Alannah in a bumping, uneven jigtime. Stephen danced like a man who had been given wooden legs. They flew out in sharp angles and measured space like a pair of pincers. He kept his head bolt upright, where it perched above Gabriella's and caught the swirling perfume of lilies as it rose off her hair. He felt the smallness of her back beneath his hand and pressed there to draw her to him, so that she might feel his happiness and love and never leave that moment. And she was laughing while she danced. And while they flew through the other couples (passing the thrown-back head of Eileen Waters where she abandoned herself to the rhythm coming through the wine and danced Eamon with a particular and memorable vivacity), cars started to arrive from Mullagh and Quilty and Cree and Doonbeg, and the space inside those walls had to expand and defy laws of science to accommodate all the ghosts and musicians and dancers of those and other parishes, and that, although they did not know it, the music they were playing was already transforming, and becoming ever so slightly something new, something which absorbed, which was both of that place and others, and allowed the classical to speak to it and would become in time the music of the new millennium. It did not matter. They played and danced on and were like a sea, changing moods like tides, now bright and quick, now slow with airs of sorrow. And while the moon was lost beneath the coverings of thick cloud and the stars were put out in the western sky, the party continued. It continued all that starless, moonless night, while the rain fell and the wind blew and none cared, for it was as if in those moments of music and dance each man and woman was seized with the knowledge of the boundless hardship and injustice of life and knew that this night in the pentagonal building of the music school in Moses Mooney's field was one they would look back on from the edge of life and realize that yes, there they had come as close as they ever had to true happiness.

26

By All Souls' Day the school had thirty-five pupils. Gertie Morrisey taught piano, Martin Hosey the silver flute, and Seamus Cooney the traditional timber flute, while Gabriella and Sonny Mungovan divided the violin and fiddle. It was a school that broke all rules of musical education, that defied the strict classification of training practices and existed instead in a free-flowing river of styles and traditions, with the only aim being to foster the pleasure of playing. From the beginning Gabriella had decided that the school would enter no pupils for examinations, that those who wished could do so, but that no time or effort would be given towards the preparation of children to play for the judgement of others. In this Stephen was in complete accord and marvelled at how the very students who had trudged to school now came to the glass building with the enlivened air of children arriving at a swimming pool. His own function in the school was not clearly defined. Moira was its manager and showed a surprising capability for keeping timetables, organizing classes, and advertising. While Gabriella took classes in the five hours that followed schooltime, Stephen played with his daughter. He carried and wheeled her along the corridor that ran all the way around the pentagon, listening to the different musics escaping each room, telling Alannah what they were and watching how already she knew which playing was her mother's.

It was during those evenings while minding Alannah that he first brought the chess set there. While the baby slept he sat in a corner of the room and played against himself. Within two weeks he had a few regular opponents, the waiting parents of the children, and the chess and music became so entwined during that winter that sometimes Stephen stopped in mid-game and felt the spirit of Philip Griffin beside him.

Soon it was clear it was to be a wretched winter. The sea grew high and wild and angry. Morning evening and night the wind howled, until at last it was impossible to imagine a place far out in the Atlantic that was before the beginning of the wind. The new slates that Corry & Son & Nephew had put on came off and shattered on the road outside. The air was full of salt. Faces dried and cracked, and a general rheuminess ran through all the parishes of the western seaboard. In the garden that faced the sea the plants burned, and Stephen watched them from the kitchen window with a sudden chill in his heart. In the fierce winds of All Souls' Night whole shrubs were lifted out of the ground and tossed into Clancy's down the road. To Stephen it felt like a portent. For three days he went outside in the gusting seawinds and tried to secure the plants that remained. He dressed them in sacking and staked them and bound them with yellow baler twine, until they resembled weird effigies of the plants they had been in summer.

Despite the harshness of the season the music school prospered. Adults came for classes in the wild driven rain of the mornings, and sat on in the small coffee shop Moira ran, where they listened to music they had never heard before and which nourished them in their spirits and helped them endure the terrible vicissitudes of grief and loss that are the inheritance of all.

Gabriella was happy. She almost did not dare to admit it. When she held Alannah in her arms she felt the wonder of the child and wept often, alarming Stephen into offering all kinds of remedies, which she turned down, telling him he was such a great fool he did not know sorrow from joy. "This," she said, with lemon-scented tears flowing down her cheekbones, "is joy."

"Oh, right," he said, and stood there, hopeless and inadequate to understand what was flowing between the mother and the child.

And so, even in the battering and scouring of that winter, a kind of healing occurred for Stephen and Gabriella. It was the kind that comes when people are living side by side in a small house in a beautiful and desolate place, where little by little the past vanishes and the present moment seems large enough to contain a whole life. It was the kind of healing that is made of endless cups of tea, of changing nappies, of music playing, of books picked up and put down after three pages, of short naps and long dreams, and of the deeply comfortable silences that grow between a man and a woman who come to know each other so utterly that they breathe each other's breath and do not need many words. And in that winter, Stephen and Gabriella grew together, while the leafless plants in the garden were bound and motionless outside. They knew each other's rhythms like clocks in a jeweller's shop that chime at staggered midnights. Stephen began to learn Italian and walked through the cottage, at first saying phrases from *Frasi Utili e Idiomi,* and then progressing to short passages learned from Dante's *Purgatorio* and *Il Paradiso,* which had the double bonus of astonishing Alannah and making Gabriella laugh.

Gabriella knew how she could tease Stephen. She still loved to measure the sincerity of his feelings with countless tiny tests, requesting that he change his habit of leaving the tea caddy open, leave down the toilet seat, allow the bedroom window to be left open all night even in the fierce winds of November, let the cats sleep in the kitchen, wash his feet before bed. To all Stephen complied without hesitation. He saw them as a myriad of proofs of his own loving, and then recognized that each time Gabriella asked him something it was also to tell him that she was preparing to live with him forever.

At no time did Stephen ask Gabriella again to marry him. Sometimes, in a fit of gloom, Gabriella would feel the absence of space between them, the claustrophobia that weighs on lovers until they redefine each other's strangeness. Then she would look up from a book and think to throw it at him, to hit out at the suddenly infuriating omnipresence of his affection. She would make a demand: Did he not notice how the cooker was broken? how the gas kept shutting off and had to be fiddled to get right?

"Do you not notice things like that?"

"I will look at it now."

"No, it's too late. I don't mean you to do it now. It's just you don't . . ."

She would shake her head at herself and sit in the heavy silence, wondering why she felt the need to strike out at him. He had the dissatisfying reality of saints. He knew nothing of the real world. He would not know the names of three politicians, how to fill tax forms or fix the plumbing. But then, just as suddenly, the gloom would relent and she would look at him and be astonished that she was living with such an extraordinary man.

Then, on the last evening of that November, they returned home from the school and found a letter from Nelly Grant waiting. It was written in a rounded looping hand and told her own adventure, how she had shut the shop and left Kenmare two weeks after them to follow her imagination to Italy; how she had spent six months there, arriving in Venice in the rain and travelling the Adriatic coastline to Ravenna and

476

Rimini, where she had stayed, eating a diet of every kind of shellfish, until she said her dreams took on the warm and salty quality of that sea and left her experiencing the softness of life that we forget in building our shells. She had learned new cures, and discovered her age was imaginary, for when she returned to Kenmare she felt the bigness of the mountains like a child.

Stephen and Gabriella read the letter in turns, while the wind blew rain and sea foam against the windows and Alannah slept. And when Stephen was reading it Gabriella looked at him and saw the gladness moving across his face. The light from the tasselled lamp was beautiful upon him, and she understood with the sudden clarity of enlightenment that shows us the shape of the world. And it was his stillness and peace that she felt, the loving that was deeper and wider than she could encompass. And she whispered: "Stefano."

He was startled and looked up quickly from the page.

"You know I love you," she said.

He said nothing. The wind blew outside, the child slept.

"No matter how impossible I am."

The letter quivered in his hand.

"No matter what I say, I do," Gabriella

said. "Please don't ever leave me."

He had slipped across to her from his armchair and was crouched low beside her. Her hand touched his face.

"I won't," he said. "I couldn't live. I love the impossible."

27

They made love that night beneath the million drops of the rain running on the skylights above them like tears. They undressed each other by the turf fire, where the slowness of their movements was like the movements in a dance. There was no music playing, only the water falling out of the sky into the sea and the sea's slow churning in the ordinariness of time. With the small hollows of the palms of his hands Stephen pressed upon the warm skin of Gabriella and travelled the places of her body backward and forward in the endless sojourn of loving that finds no limit in the other's body but returns across the places caressed as if they were a New World discovered, warmed and scented like the tropics. They entwined each other, the small woman and the long man, sitting on the floor before the fire, where Gabriella held back her head so that he might kiss her neck and her breasts and so that she could hold his head against her in the dream of their being one.

The rain fell above them, and the sea sighed in thin chains of surf in the night outside. The cottage creaked like a ship, anchored at last in the known coordinates of Hope and Love, and secure in its own fastness. In the small hours Stephen and Gabriella lay by the low fire with a blanket pulled over them. They did not move. They slept like swimmers stilled in painted waters, one's arm around the other, leading towards the shore.

28

And there was a morning of brilliant light that came across the surface of the sea and arrived so brightly that at first it seemed the dazzlement of magic. The sky was cloudless and blue with the perfect weather of peaceful dreams. And into that morning Stephen dressed himself and was waking Gabriella and bringing her tea and carrying Alannah in his arms through the cottage to tell her mother how they could take the morning and drive into Ennis and buy a new cooker to replace the one that was broken. And he had to find the baby's cloth shoes and pack the bag with nappies and powder and cream and the bottle and the bibs, while Gabriella dressed in a burgundy dress and a black cardigan. And then they were driving into that brightness that was not the brightness of November. They were packed into the car, with Gabriella holding Alannah in her lap in the back seat and humming a tune for her and humming it over and over as the car drove on into Miltown Malbay and out the other side and on past all the watery fields where cattle watched across the strands of barbed wire for the coming of fodder and where none was coming, because there was nothing else on that road, no tractor or car, no man or woman, only the bright sunlight that was too bright and the polished surface of the puddles that looked like glassy tears or the fallen fragments of a cold heaven. And Stephen was driving and watching his hands turning the wheel and the road unspooling like a destiny before him as they sped onward, and he was able to look in the mirror at Gabriella and Alannah behind him and behind them the road they had come from and the fields flowing backward like a film blurring green and grey, and then there was suddenly the flooded bend by Inagh and the car flashing into it and across the water until it hit the stone wall and Stephen flew forward into the windscreen and felt the crash and the glass and the tremendous shattering and arrived in the terrible silence and the taste of blood and looked back and saw that Gabriella and Alannah were dead.

1

The enlightenment that comes from dreams is sometimes more potent than that which comes in the daylight. When Stephen lifted his head, Gabriella was lying in his arms on the rug on the floor before the fire. He was bathed in the sweat of his dream and drew back the blanket that covered them, to be reassured by the coolness of the morning. He turned towards Gabriella and watched the sleeping body of her and heard across the cottage the infant noises of Alannah sounding in her crib. There was a thin drizzle falling in the stillness outside.

It was some moments before the dream had left Stephen. He lay on the floor of the cottage, and Gabriella stirred beside him, and he leaned over and kissed the top of her head. Then he rose and walked out of the room and lifted Alannah and brought her back and placed her into the warmth of her mother. And he turned on Puccini's music and then lay down beneath the blanket once more.

The music rose. And for the first time Stephen heard not grief but an aching joy. He heard in that music the long-enduring love of his father, which had been undiminished by tragedy and had carried on like a difficult faith through all the lonely days of his living. He heard the victory of Love over Death. And while the music played on and washed over the three of them like grace, Stephen Griffin knew something of the puzzles of the world and understood that all love did not perish and could survive beyond pain and hardship and loneliness; and in that innocent vision with which he was gifted that morning he saw that the world fit together, each piece in its proper place, like the pieces on a chessboard, and that though the patterns that emerged were complex and difficult and grew more so all the time, there was a design nonetheless, for though we live in the impotency of our dreams to make better the world, the earth and its stars spin through the heavens at the rate of our loving and is made meaningful only in the way in which we give ourselves to each other.

Stephen saw. He saw and understood the way you do in the middle of a chess game when the openings have been played and the position takes on a beauty that belongs neither to one player nor to the other but is the perfect expression of both. He lay on the floor in the cottage and knew now that he would live with Gabriella without being afraid. That in the puzzle of love he was for her and Alannah, and they for him, and that what had happened so far was no more than the opening movement of the pieces.

He turned to Gabriella. The drizzle was falling. She reached and touched his face, then they moved closer together and held the child between them.

The employees of Thorndike Press hope you have enjoyed this Large Print book. All our Large Print titles are designed for easy reading, and all our books are made to last. Other Thorndike Press Large Print books are available at your library, through selected bookstores, or directly from us.

For information about titles, please call:

(800) 257-5157

To share your comments, please write:

Publisher
Thorndike Press
P.O. Box 159
Thorndike, Maine 04986